W9-ACC-177

Brunswick County Library
109 W. Moore Street
Southport NC 28461

WITHDRAWN

MISSING

Center Point
Large Print

Also by Lisa Harris and available from
Center Point Large Print:

Dangerous Passage
Hidden Agenda
Taken
Vendetta
Deadly Safari

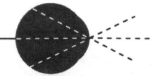

**This Large Print Book carries the
Seal of Approval of N.A.V.H.**

Hickmans

The Nikki Boyd Files, #2

MISSING

Lisa Harris

Brunswick County Library
109 W. Moore Street
Southport NC 28461

CENTER POINT LARGE PRINT
THORNDIKE, MAINE

This Center Point Large Print edition is published in the year 2016 by arrangement with Revell, a division of Baker Publishing Group.

Copyright © 2016 by Lisa Harris.

All rights reserved.

Scripture quotations are from the Holy Bible, New International Version®. NIV®. Copyright © 1973, 1978, 1984, 2011 by Biblica, Inc.™ Used by permission of Zondervan. All rights reserved worldwide. www.zondervan.com

This book is a work of fiction. Names, characters, places, and incidents are the product of the author's imagination or are used fictitiously. Any resemblance to actual events, locales, or persons, living or dead, is coincidental.

The text of this Large Print edition is unabridged. In other aspects, this book may vary from the original edition. Printed in the United States of America on permanent paper. Set in 16-point Times New Roman type.

ISBN: 978-1-68324-069-3

Library of Congress Cataloging-in-Publication Data

Names: Harris, Lisa, 1969– author.
Title: Missing : the Nikki Boyd files / Lisa Harris.
Description: Center Point Large Print edition. | Thorndike, Maine : Center Point Large Print, 2016.
Identifiers: LCCN 2016018586 | ISBN 9781683240693 (hardcover : alk. paper)
Subjects: LCSH: Women detectives—Fiction. | Missing persons—Investigation—Fiction. | Murder—Investigation—Fiction. | Large type books. | GSAFD: Christian fiction. | Mystery fiction. | Suspense fiction.
Classification: LCC PS3608.A78315 M57 2016b | DDC 813/.6—dc23
LC record available at https://lccn.loc.gov/2016018586

MISSING

1

8:25 a.m., Thursday
Nashville suburb

Nikki Boyd slid out of her white Mini Cooper as two bagged bodies were being wheeled from the one-story house nestled in one of Nashville's nicer suburbs. Her stomach clenched. Even after eight years on the force, the emotional challenges of the job had yet to make her completely calloused. It was impossible not to personalize some of what she saw. The cases she couldn't solve. The brokenness she couldn't fix.

But neither could she let her cases become personal.

She started down the walk where half a dozen police cars and the local medical examiner had parked in front of the taped-off crime scene, allowing both uniformed and plain-clothed officers to take over the sleepy, tree-lined street. One of her teammates, Jack Spencer, stood waiting for her on the curb dressed in one of his suit jackets and white dress shirt paired with a typical blue-and-orange paisley tie.

"Morning," she said, holding up a takeaway box from her parents' barbeque restaurant. "I was having breakfast with my mom and Jamie when the call came in. Thought you might like a couple of my mom's homemade cinnamon rolls to celebrate your first day back to work."

Five weeks ago, he'd gotten shot in the middle of a hostage situation that had almost gotten both of them killed.

"You can't imagine how happy I am to be back in the field," Jack said. "Though next time, I'd appreciate it if you'd remind me to duck when someone starts shooting at me." He laughed, then took the offered takeaway box and dropped it into the backseat of his car. He slammed the door shut. "I love your mom's cinnamon rolls."

"I know."

"How's that little niece of yours?" he asked.

Nikki smiled at the question. "Five weeks old tomorrow and a perfect little angel."

She started for the house with him, then stopped, noticing the red marks around his wrist and the fact that his face looked a bit . . . chalky. She pulled up the sleeve of his jacket a couple inches, revealing a line of ugly splotches. "What in the world happened to you?"

He frowned, then moved his arm away in order to pull down the jacket sleeve. "It's nothing."

"Nothing? Are you kidding me?" she asked. "That looks horrible."

"I was in the middle of a session with my allergist when we got the call to come in."

8

Nikki pressed her lips together to keep from smiling. It hadn't taken long for her to discover that not only was Jack a magnet to anything that stung, bit, or floated in the air, he was also a bit of a hypochondriac.

"It's not funny," he said, heading toward the crime scene.

"I didn't say it was funny. I'm just curious about why you got retested. I thought you went through that a few months ago."

"The previous tests were . . . inconclusive."

Nikki matched his stride as they walked down the sidewalk toward the house, waiting for him to elaborate. When he didn't, she decided to change the subject. "Any clue about why we're getting involved in a double homicide?"

Homicide detectives handled homicide cases. The Missing Persons Special Task Force typically did not.

"You know as much as I do at this point," he said as his phone went off. He pulled it out of his pocket. Checked the caller ID, then put it back in his pocket without answering.

"What about Gwen?" she asked.

"Boss asked her to go to the precinct. We'll meet her there when we're done here." Jack flashed his badge at one of the officers. "We're here to see Sergeant Dillard."

The officer nodded. "He's expecting you. He's there at the front door talking with the ME."

9

Jack nodded. "Thanks."

Sergeant Dillard stepped away from the medical examiner as they walked up the sidewalk. The older man stood a couple inches shorter than Jack's six foot two, with a slight pudge around the middle.

He shot them both a friendly smile before shaking their hands. "You two are with the missing persons task force?"

"Yes. We were told to report to you, but . . ." Nikki caught the flashing lights of the vehicle as the ME finished loading the bodies into the back of the van. "I'm still not sure why we're here."

"I opted to call your team in because I've got two dead bodies *and* two missing persons. This house belongs to Mac and Lucy Hudson, but those two men in body bags aren't the home owners."

Jack's brows furrowed. "Then who are they?"

"Haven't been able to ID the bodies yet, so at this point, your guess is as good as mine. We've been here over two hours processing the scene, and my team's still trying to come up with a timeline of what happened. If you want to come inside with me, you can see for yourselves."

Nikki slipped on a pair of latex gloves and booties, then stepped into the ransacked living room behind Jack. She sucked in her breath at the scene surrounding her. The scent of death permeated the space. Dozens of yellow markers had been set up in the aftermath of whatever had

10

happened in the house. Bullet fragments, shell casings, and fluid samples were being recorded by CSU. Blood pooled on the hardwood flooring and seeped onto a rug in the center of the room. A couple of slugs had hit the far wall and splattered blood against its creamy beige finish.

A shiver shot through Nikki. Things like this weren't supposed to happen on a quiet street in the suburbs.

But they did.

"As you might have guessed," the sergeant said, "both men presumably died from gunshot wounds."

Nikki scanned the rest of the room. It had been completely trashed. "Do you have any idea when the shootings took place?"

"Rigor mortis was completely set in on the two bodies we just took out," the sergeant said. "The ME said we're probably looking at some time yesterday evening, though we'll have to wait to hear back from him after the autopsies."

"Yesterday?" Nikki glanced at Jack and then back at the sergeant. "At least half a dozen shots are fired in a sleepy suburb and the authorities are just showing up now? You can't tell me no one heard a disturbance."

"That's exactly what I'm saying. Our initial findings show there were at least three weapons involved, including that of the home owner, Mac Hudson."

"So Mr. Hudson was defending himself?" Jack said.

"That's my best guess. According to the records we pulled, he owned two handguns, and one of the neighbors said he spends a lot of his free time down at a local shooting range."

"So what are you thinking?" Jack asked. "The home owner shoots the intruders, killing them, and then what? Panics and runs?"

"That's one of the theories we're looking at," the sergeant said. "But here's why we brought you in. A call came through to 911 last night, and we've finally been able to identify the caller as Mac Hudson."

"Why did IDing the call take so long?" Nikki asked.

"It came through on a prepaid cell phone," the sergeant said. "He must have been indoors, since the operator wasn't able to get a location."

He pulled out his smartphone and played the file.

911. What is your emergency?

I need help. They're going to kill me.

What is your location, sir? . . . Sir, I need you to tell me your location so I can send someone to help you.

My wife . . . Lucy . . . Please . . . you have to help her . . .

His voice sounded panicked. Someone scuffled in the background. Then nothing.

"So the wife was kidnapped?" Nikki asked.

"Implying there was a third intruder," Jack added.

"Agreed, but this is all we've got," the sergeant said. "That and the fact he was using a prepaid cell instead of his regular phone when he called 911, which is also odd."

Nikki looked again at the mess around them. "Is the rest of the house trashed like the living room?"

Dillard nodded. "Most of it. Yes."

"A typical burglar uses a search pattern—master bedroom, bathroom, living room—a quick sweep for electronics and valuables," Jack said. "No more than a minute to break in, and out in under ten. But in this case, the entire place is trashed, and they certainly didn't try to cover their tracks."

"Because they were looking for something specific," Nikki said.

She worked through the limited information the sergeant had just given them. What had been worth searching for that had ended up costing the two men their lives?

"But something still seems off," she continued. "Going with the theory that the home owner killed a couple intruders and ran, my question is, why run? If Mr. Hudson owned two guns, legally, he should have known that when facing imminent danger of death, he's allowed to use deadly force. If this was a burglary, he had every right to defend his property."

"And if he did run, where is he now?" Jack asked. "And what did he mean, 'You have to help her'?"

"Those are the questions I'm hoping the two of you will help us answer," Sergeant Dillard said.

"What do you know about the Hudsons?" Nikki asked.

"I've got officers canvassing the neighborhood now. From the limited information we've been able to gather so far, we know a couple things. Lucy's boss told us she didn't show up for work this morning, which apparently isn't like her. Same is true for her husband. He never showed up at work today."

"What else do you know about them?" Nikki asked. With every missing person case, time was of the essence. They needed to get through the basic facts as quickly as possible.

The sergeant flipped open his notebook. "The profile I have so far is sketchy. No children. No family in the area. They were friendly to their neighbors, though kept to themselves. According to the next-door neighbor, Mac Hudson is a research scientist who works for Byrne Laboratories. Lucy's a kindergarten teacher who works a couple miles down the road where she's been teaching the past five or six years."

"And beyond this 911 call, no one heard anything?" Nikki asked.

"At least two of the neighbors are retired and on vacation. The weather's been pretty warm the past few days, which means people have their windows shut and their air conditioners on."

Nikki picked up an eight-by-ten framed photo of the couple on their wedding day. They looked happy. Content. Lucy smiled up at the camera beside her husband, a radiant bride with her ebony skin, long, straight hair, and a stunning white dress.

Nikki set the photo back down and glanced around the living room. The neutral-colored throw pillows on the gray suede couch had been ripped open. Accent pieces from the coffee table had been knocked to the floor, and an embroidered wall hanging that said Happily Ever After had fallen to the ground, its glass cover shattered.

Something had gone terribly wrong in their fairy-tale world.

"What about their cars?" Jack asked.

"Mac's car is still in the garage. Lucy's is gone."

"And who initially made the 911 call this morning?" Nikki asked.

"A neighbor found their two dogs wandering around her yard and realized no one was home. She went into the backyard, planning to lock them up in the house with the spare key the Hudsons had given her, and discovered the dead bodies inside."

"I'd like to see the rest of the house," Nikki said. "Then we can talk to the neighbor."

They started in the back of the house in the master bedroom. Once again, the room had been ransacked, but makeup, toothbrushes, and a contact lens case were still sitting on the bathroom sink. If either of them had run, they hadn't taken the time to grab anything personal.

The second bedroom had been set up as an office and looked even more disheveled than the master bedroom. Files were scattered across the floor alongside books and reference materials. A broken laptop lay on top of the pile.

"The last room is an unfinished nursery," the sergeant said as they moved on. "Doesn't look like it was touched."

The room was empty except for a pile of baby clothes, a bassinet covered with white lace, and a few baby blankets.

"Is Lucy pregnant?" Nikki asked.

"If she is, no one has mentioned it," the sergeant said. "Our crime scene unit will finish going through the house, then we'll pass on whatever we find."

"Great," Nikki said. "What's the name of the neighbor who called 911?"

The sergeant glanced at his notepad. "Colleen Jeffers. She lives in the house next door. She's pretty shaken—she was the one who discovered the bodies. According to her, she and Mrs.

Hudson are good friends. Last time I saw her, she was standing on her front porch."

"Sergeant Dillard?" Someone from the other room called the officer.

"I need to go," he said. "We'll keep you in the loop."

Jack glanced at his phone as they headed for the front door, then shoved it into his back pocket.

"If you need to take a call . . . ," Nikki said.

"It's nothing."

"Am I missing something here?" Nikki stopped beside him on the porch, pulled off her gloves and booties, and handed them to one of the officers. "Your phone's been going off every five minutes."

"It's nobody," he said.

"You met someone?" she asked.

Jack frowned. "I didn't say anything about meeting someone."

"You didn't have to. I can see it in your eyes." Nikki grinned at him as they headed for the neighbor's house. At nine o'clock, the temperature was already rising. It was going to be another hot, humid day.

"Fine. I went to see a different allergist a couple of weeks ago," Jack said, matching her pace. "We hit it off and have gone out a couple times. End of story."

"And the real reason you went to be retested. Hmm . . ." She glanced at his profile. "Though I sense a 'but' coming."

"I don't know yet. She's beautiful. Stunning, actually. But she might be a bit needy. She won't stop calling me." Jack tugged on the end of his tie. "Back to our case, what do you think?"

"You're changing the subject," Nikki said.

"You bet I am."

Nikki's phone rang. Gwen was on the line. She answered the call and put it on speakerphone.

"Carter caught me up on what's going on from this end. I've been trying to trace the Hudsons' phones and finally got a hit on the husband's," Gwen said.

"Where is it?" Jack asked.

"At a marina about fifteen minutes from where you are. The Royal Harbor Marina. I'm sending you the address now."

"That's okay," Nikki said. "I know the place."

Seventeen minutes later, Jack pulled into the marina parking lot while Nikki got Gwen back on the phone.

"Tell me what we're looking for, Gwen. There are hundreds of boats, a restaurant—"

"Give me a second . . . Take the left pier and head toward the end of the dock. I'll get you as close as I can."

Nikki hurried in the direction Gwen gave them, with Jack right behind her. The full-service marina would be crowded and noisy on the weekend, especially in the summer, but it was the middle of the week and fairly quiet. Dozens of boats filled the slips, primarily small sailboats and a few larger yachts. She stopped and told Gwen where they were.

"Another fifty feet or so," Gwen said. "End of the pier."

Nikki continued down the pier, then stopped in front of a forty-foot boat. "Wait a minute. Are you sure? This can't be the boat."

"What do you mean?" Jack asked. "You recognize it?"

"Yeah." Nikki felt an odd sense of dread sweep over her. "It's the *Isabella*."

"That's got to be it," Gwen said. "Looks like it's registered to . . . Tyler Grant."

Nikki's mind whirled with confusion. "Yes."

Jack's initial look of surprise turned to one of concern.

"Tyler's been planning to sell the boat," Nikki said, "but as far as I know, he's not even been back since Katie died. We're here now. I'll call you back in a minute."

She squeezed her eyes shut and breathed in the damp, sweet smell of the lake. Tyler had inherited the boat from his father. Before Katie had died, she and Tyler spent every free day they could out on the water, often inviting Nikki to come with them. Cutting ties with someone you cared about, even though they were gone, wasn't easy. Which was why selling the boat was another piece of closure Tyler had yet to conquer.

The three of them—Tyler, Katie, and their son, Liam—had gone sailing last spring. Everything had seemed perfect. Tyler was home from the Middle East and promised Katie he wasn't going on another tour. They were awaiting their second child, and Liam was over the moon with the news of a baby sibling. They hadn't decided on a name yet. At three months along in the pregnancy, there was plenty of time to choose one.

Or so they'd thought.

Katie had been feeling tired that week. Tired of feeling nauseated. Tired of feeling tired. Tyler thought a day on the water would make her feel better. His guilt over that decision had yet to completely fade. He'd told Nikki that it was his job to protect Katie, and yet he hadn't been able to stop her from dying. She'd slipped, hit her head, and fallen out of the boat. By the time Tyler managed to pull her back in, it was already too late.

"Nikki?" Jack's voice pulled her back to the present. "What's the connection between Tyler and our missing couple?"

She opened her eyes and shook her head. "None that I know of."

Which was why it didn't make sense. Why would Mac and Lucy Hudson's disappearance lead them to Tyler's boat? Shoving the question aside for the moment, she stepped onto the boat ahead of Jack.

She climbed down into the cabin, taking in the details of the familiar room. Michael Grant had spared no expense when he bought the boat over a decade ago, eventually willing it to his son. Cherry cabinetry, leather seating, and an updated drop-down flat-screen TV . . . But none of those things had her attention. For the second time today, the scent of death filled her nostrils. Her mind tried to process the scene in front of her. Blood pooled on the carpeted floor. And Tyler Grant hovered over a man's lifeless body.

2

9:12 a.m.
Royal Harbor Marina outside Nashville

Nikki's mind fought to process the scene in front of her. She recognized the man lying on the cabin floor from the crime scene photos.

Mac Hudson.

And then there was Tyler.

"What are you doing here?" she asked.

Tyler looked at Nikki. "I came down to the marina to make one final run in the boat before selling it. When I got here, I spent a few minutes checking out the engines, then this is what I found. I just got off the phone with 911."

Jack had pulled out his weapon from his stance on the staircase behind her and was aiming at Tyler's chest. Blood was smeared across the bottom of his sleeve.

She held up her hand. "It's okay."

"Nikki—"

Tyler took a step back while she moved close enough to the body to check the man's pulse.

Nothing.

"He's dead." She looked up at Tyler again and caught his gaze.

"There's blood on your shirt," Jack said.

"It was kind of hard to avoid," Tyler said. "I wanted to see if the man was alive. Looks like someone shot him in the stomach."

She turned to Jack. "It's Mac Hudson."

"You know him?" Tyler asked.

"We're looking for him."

Now they needed to figure out why Mac Hudson was dead on the *Isabella* and where Lucy was.

"Was he dead when you found him?" she asked.

"Yes. I checked his pulse. Tried to see if there was anything I could do, but it was too late. That's all I know, Nikki. I don't know who he is or what he's doing on my boat."

She motioned to Jack. "Notify the park rangers, then get CSU down here to have every inch of this boat searched. Tyler and I need to talk for a couple minutes up on the deck."

Jack hesitated, then headed out of the cabin.

Tyler followed Nikki up the narrow staircase to the deck of the boat. Beyond them, sunlight danced off the blue waters. Jack was already on his phone, calling the crime scene unit, but all she could think about were the dozens of memories flooding through her of all the times the three of them had gone out in this boat. Katie had always been trying to set her up with someone, inviting her for a day out on the *Isabella* with her and Tyler, while she tried to find a way to avoid her friend's attempts to give her matrimonial bliss, preferring a day out on the water without the pressure of dealing with a first date.

Nikki forced her thoughts back to the situation below deck. "You said you don't know who he is?"

"Should I?" he asked.

"I don't know."

She took a step toward him and felt her stomach quiver at his dark, military-style haircut. That touch of shadow across his jawline. And those familiar brown eyes that always managed to pull her heart to a stop. She hadn't meant to fall in love with her best friend's husband. But somehow she had. And he didn't have a clue.

"You called 911?"

"Of course. I found a man dead on my boat, but I didn't kill him, Nikki. Surely you don't think—"

"No . . . of course not. But someone killed him."

She caught the sadness in his eyes and felt a shiver seep through her, despite the warm sunshine. They both knew Mac Hudson wasn't the only person who'd died on this boat. This was where he'd lost Katie, and today had just become another reminder of how quickly death could grab its victims.

"Was anyone else on the boat when you got here?" she asked.

"No . . . Just him. I got here . . . I don't know, ten . . . fifteen minutes ago. I spent a few minutes tinkering with the engine before going downstairs. I've had someone look after her for me this past year, but I wanted to make sure she would still run. When I went downstairs, I found the body. Checked to see if he was alive, then called 911. I tried not to touch anything except to check his pulse. That's when you showed up."

"I'm sorry," she said.

"Don't be. You're just doing your job."

"Maybe, but it's not just that. I'm sorry that you came to say goodbye and now have to deal with this."

He shot her a weary smile. "If there's anything I've learned over the past few months, it's that you never know what you're going to have to deal with. Life isn't exactly straightforward."

Her heart ached for him. Tyler was strong both mentally and emotionally. He'd experienced things overseas he'd never be able to tell anyone. Yet somehow he'd survived. He'd also been strong enough to survive the loss of his wife and adjust to his newly found role as a single dad. But no matter how strong he was emotionally, he couldn't escape the process of grief, along with the vulnerability the healing process brought with it.

She drew in a slow, steady breath. "You said you came today because you're planning to sell the boat?"

He nodded. "I thought I'd take one last trip out on the water. Then, yeah . . . I planned to sell. I'm ready for closure. I need closure in order to move forward."

It was what he'd been searching for the last thirteen months. She'd stood beside him in the emergency room when the doctor told him Katie was gone. Spent the one-year anniversary of Katie's death with him in the middle of the Smoky Mountains. Always as friends. Nothing more.

He was the husband of her best friend. A grieving father and husband. Which was why after Katie's death, she'd done everything she could to help him and Liam cope. Taking them Chinese takeout, watching movies, and playing on the Wii with Liam had come naturally.

Until the dynamics of their relationship had shifted. At least for her. Falling for him had been completely unexpected. And something she'd never meant to happen. Which was why she had no idea what to do with those feelings other than stuff them back into the secret crevices of her heart where no one could discover them.

She looked up at him, wishing it were possible to simply turn off her feelings like one turned off a faucet. She wasn't waiting for him, nor did she have any expectations. But she also didn't know how to ignore her heart when he caught her gaze. Or the rush of her breath when he touched the back of her hand. They'd been friends for years, but now . . . Somehow she'd allowed everything to change.

"You should have called me," she said, giving up on trying to keep this from being personal. "I could have taken time off and come here with you."

His gaze searched hers. "I knew you would've come if I asked. But this time—it was something I needed to do on my own."

She nodded. Tyler didn't owe her anything. He didn't reciprocate the feelings she had toward him, and she had no intention of letting him know how she felt. Too much stood between them.

Katie.

The past.

"But I admit I didn't know how hard it was going to be," he said. "Coming back to the last place I saw her alive. When I stepped into the cabin . . . he was there, staring up at me with those vacant eyes. For a moment it was Katie looking up at me all over again."

Familiar memories swirled between them. Dark. Haunting.

"It's funny how life works," he continued. "Sometimes I feel like I'm living again. Like I can go on and make a real life again with Liam. But I'm still working through the guilt of what happened that day."

She reached up and ran her thumb down his cheek, longing to make everything okay again. "Her death wasn't your fault. You know that, Tyler."

"I've told you this before. It was my job to protect her, and I wasn't there. I couldn't stop her from dying. I didn't stop her from dying."

"I know."

"It just all feels so real again, standing here." He stared out at the water. Jaw tense, his gaze lost in the hurts of the past. "I served in the Middle East for three tours and somehow managed to cheat death while good men died around me. They gave me a Purple Heart for being wounded in the line of duty to my country, and yet I let Katie and our baby die. And after all those arguments we had over my leaving the military . . . suddenly none of that matters anymore."

"You didn't let them die, Tyler."

Nikki couldn't fight the emotions anymore. Her eyes burned with tears, but her heart hurt even worse. It had been an accident. No one—not even the police—had blamed him after the initial investigation was completed. It had simply been one of those freak accidents no one had control over. But that didn't erase the guilt. Something she knew all too well.

Her hand went automatically to the heart necklace where she kept her sister's photo, wondering for the millionth time what she'd look like today if she walked through the door. Ten years, and she'd yet to give up hope that Sarah was still alive. Never yet completely let go of the fact that her sister's disappearance was her fault. She'd watched her parents over the years as they struggled after Sarah's abduction to put the shattered pieces of their lives back together—if that were even possible. Not with the gaping hole Sarah had left. Because it wasn't over yet. And Nikki wasn't sure it would ever be over.

Maybe that's how it was with grief. The years eased the heartache, smoothed out the edges a bit, but it never went away. And sometimes, when it hovered all around you, there was no escape.

"Her death was an accident, Tyler. Not your fault."

"I know. Deep down I know that, but some-times . . . I just can't stop thinking, if I could go back and change that day. If I'd been with her at that moment instead of below deck . . . I thought coming back here was going to be a step forward, but instead I was forced to realize that I don't know how to do this."

But neither of them could go back and change the past. She looked up at him and caught the deep sadness in his gaze. Just like her, he was going to carry this guilt with him the rest of his life if he didn't learn to let it go.

"We should go." Her voice was barely above a whisper. "You'll need to come down to the station and answer some questions."

"Okay. I'm still feeling a bit numb." He nodded toward the cabin below. "I'm just glad I decided not to bring Liam. If he'd been here with me . . ."

It would have been like the day Katie had died. Both of them shared vivid memories of that afternoon. Nikki had met the ambulance at the hospital, but by the time they rolled her into the ER, Katie was already gone.

She studied Tyler's expression and resisted the urge to step into his arms. To make him understand that she'd always be here for him, even if they never shared the same feelings. And in the meantime, she needed to find a way to tame her own feelings that had morphed into something over the past few weeks she could hardly recognize.

"It shouldn't take long," she said, starting for the dock.

"It's fine, Nikki. I can handle it, but first . . ."

She stopped and turned back to him.

"I know this isn't the place or the time, but I haven't seen you in over a month. You've been . . . distant. If I did something—"

"No . . . It's not you. Work's just been busy."

It was an excuse, and he knew it. She could see it in his eyes. But neither could she simply tell him the truth.

I realized I'm in love with you and have been too afraid to ask if you feel the same way . . .

"Liam misses you," Tyler said. "He asked me just last night when you were coming over to hang out."

And you? Have you missed me?

She wanted him to tell her that as well. Tell her that he missed her. But he wasn't going to. And she didn't know how to keep things as a simple friendship when her heart wanted more. And that was the reason she'd stayed away.

What was she supposed to tell him now?

That she hadn't been returning his phone calls because she was in love with him. That Katie might be dead, but the guilt hadn't been enough to stop her from feeling the way she did. But Tyler wasn't ready to move on with his life. Not yet. And he certainly wasn't looking for romance. If she told him how she felt now, things might never be the same between them again. That wasn't a risk she was willing to take.

She stepped onto the dock with him, then made her way toward Jack, who was still talking on his cell. This would all be over soon. Forensics would sweep in and prove that Tyler's story was true. And hopefully find out the truth behind the murder of Mac Hudson.

"Nikki!" Jack shouted at her from the end of the floating dock, then started running toward her. "The boat!"

Nikki and Tyler spun around as a silhouetted figure powered up the *Isabella*'s engines and sped away from the dock.

3

9:26 a.m.

Nikki sprinted toward the *Isabella*, but it was too late to jump on board. The boat was already speeding away from the marina. She hesitated on the floating dock, furious she'd let her emotions get in the way of doing her job. This never should have happened. She should have secured the boat before having a personal discussion with Tyler.

Weighing her options, she ran toward the next slip. A man was waxing the surface of his express cruiser next to where the *Isabella* had been parked only seconds before. She glanced out across the blue water again. The *Isabella* was leaving the marina with a dead body and possible murderer on board. And every second that ticked by meant whoever was on it was getting farther away. Along with their chances of finding Lucy. There were no other options.

She held up her badge and stepped aboard the cruiser. "Sir, I need to commandeer your boat."

"You need to do what?" The man held up his hands at the sight of her badge.

Jack joined her on the boat. "You heard her. We need your boat. Now."

"Wait a minute." He adjusted his ball cap. "Can you do that? Just . . . take my boat?"

"Looks to me like we are doing it," Jack said, heading for the helm.

"We're after a murder suspect," Nikki said, starting to untie the docking lines with Tyler's help. "So unless you want to be charged with obstruction—"

"Murder? No way . . . I don't want anything to do with that." The man looked startled, but quickly jumped onto the dock. "But I do want my boat back in one piece."

"You'll get your boat back," she said.

"Find out who's behind this," Tyler said, handing her the last docking line.

She nodded, then stepped back onto the boat. It was all the motivation she needed. She was convinced that finding Mac's killer would lead them to Lucy.

"You know how to pilot a boat?" She shouted at Jack above the sound of the motor as he adjusted the tiller in an attempt not to crash the stern into the dock. "We can't lose him."

"Have a little confidence in your partner." Jack

eased the boat out from the dock. "My father owned one of these when I was in high school. I ended up spending more than my fair share of time out on the water. Piloting the boat was a lot more fun than swimming in some germ-infested lake."

Water sprayed across the bow as Jack moved the throttle forward, increasing speed as they headed toward the open water of the large lake that was sprinkled with small islands and forested inlets. A sense of urgency swept through her. Three men were dead, and they still had no idea who was behind it or who was in the other boat.

"I'm calling Gwen to have her call in a helicopter to assist," Nikki said, grabbing on to a metal rail for balance. "We need to get this guy."

Her heart pounded as she waited for Gwen to pick up, while Jack maneuvered the craft across the water. A chilly breeze whipped around them, splattering droplets of water across the windshield. Jack increased his speed. The boat rocked as they hit a series of waves on the otherwise quiet lake, but they were slowly gaining on the other boat.

Gwen finally answered on the fourth ring.

"Gwen . . . ," Nikki said.

"Where are you? I can barely hear you."

"After a suspect on a commandeered boat in the middle of Percy Priest Lake," Nikki said, raising her voice.

"I really hope you're kidding me," Gwen said. "I just sent CSU to your location. Jack told me you found Mac Hudson's body."

"We did, but there was someone else on board. How soon can you get us aerial backup?"

"Give me a second . . ."

Nikki held on tighter to the handrails while she waited for Gwen's response. Jack worked beside her to keep the boat steady while managing to bridge the gap between them and the *Isabella*, but it wasn't enough. And the other boat showed no signs of slowing down.

"Looks like Metro Police have one up in the air right now," Gwen said. "And they're not far from your location. I'll also inform the park rangers of what is happening and get a patrol boat out there."

A moment later Nikki hung up the call. Wind blew through her hair, whipping it around her face as she scanned the horizon. She felt her jaw tense. Ahead of them, to the left, another boat was leaving the shore and moving in their direction.

The *Isabella* kept to her course and speed.

"Jack . . . He's going to hit that other boat if one of them doesn't turn."

"I see it, but there's nothing I can do."

At the last second the other pilot veered to the right, barely missing the *Isabella*. Nikki gnawed on her lip, her irritation growing. Jack pressed the throttle farther, still trying to bridge the gap between them, as their boat bounced along the surface of the water.

"He's still going too fast."

"Just hang on," Jack said. "How long before backup gets here?"

"I don't know. A minute . . . maybe two at the most."

Forty-five seconds later, the buzz of the Metro Police helicopter swirled above them. Nikki looked up as the blue bird swept past them toward the other boat.

The helo's loudspeaker boomed above them. "This is the Metro Police's aviation unit. Stop your boat and turn off the engine."

The *Isabella* didn't even slow down.

"Does he really think he's going to get away with this?" Nikki asked.

She watched as the helicopter edged past the other boat, waiting for them to cut their engines. Seconds later, the helo fired warning shots across the bow of the *Isabella*. The boat veered to the right, then reduced its speed.

Jack pulled back on the throttle. The whine of the engine dropped as the boat slowed down.

"Shut down your engine." The loudspeaker boomed again. "Then step onto the bow with your hands in the air."

Nikki dropped two of their fenders onto the boat's starboard side to protect the craft's hull, while Jack maneuvered next to the *Isabella*, ready to tether the two boats.

Using one of the lines, Nikki tied the two crafts together, then, careful not to lose her balance, she jumped onto the other boat, weapon raised. The boat bobbed beneath her. "We're with the Tennessee Bureau of Investigation. I want you on the bow now, with your hands in the air."

A man started toward the bow, his hands in the air. Midfifties, paunch around the middle . . . balding . . .

Nikki recognized him immediately. "George?"

"Please." Panic engulfed his expression. "Don't shoot. I can explain."

Nikki grabbed her handcuffs and started toward him, trying to put the pieces together.

George Brennan was Tyler's father-in-law. But what in the world was he doing on Tyler's boat?

Another swell hit the boats, jarring them both forward. George grabbed on to the handrail while Nikki struggled to keep her balance.

"Nikki!" Jack shouted from the other boat where he'd been trying to grab another line.

She turned just in time to see the swells rock the boat again and Jack plunge overboard.

Nikki quickly handcuffed George to the railing, praying Jack knew how to swim. "Don't go anywhere. I'll be back."

The police helicopter hovered above her as she

jumped onto the cruiser. Adrenaline continued to pump through her as she located Jack treading water on the port side. Grabbing the lifebuoy with the attached line, she threw it into the water, then helped him hoist himself up onto the swim platform.

"You okay?" she asked once he'd managed to catch his breath.

"Yes, but I just had to be the one who got knocked into the water, didn't I?" He combed his fingers through his wet hair while she searched for a blanket in one of the deck storage lockers. "Promise you won't say a word of this to anyone." He pulled off his soaked jacket and rolled up the sleeves of his dress shirt before taking the blanket she handed him.

"It might be too late," Nikki said, nodding at the ranger's patrol boat that was arriving at the scene.

"Great," he said. "Why do I have the feeling I'm never going to live this down?"

"You will . . ." Nikki shot him a smile, simply relieved he was okay. "Eventually."

"Thanks."

One of the park rangers hollered at them from their boat. "Heard you might need some help?"

"We've just secured a murder suspect in the other boat," Nikki said.

"We'll be happy to take this boat back to the marina," the ranger offered.

"That would be great," Nikki said, giving him the slip number. "Thank you."

"Need anything else?"

"I think we're good."

Nikki quickly helped Jack untether the two boats, then gave Gwen a call while one of the rangers boarded the cruiser.

"We've got him," she said. "You can let the tactical flight officer know we're good to go."

"Roger that," Gwen said. "We'll see you back at the precinct."

Nikki waved at the chopper as it hovered for a few seconds longer, then flew toward the shoreline.

"I know our suspect," Nikki said as they stepped onto the *Isabella.*

"Really? You know this guy?" Jack asked as they headed toward the helm.

Nikki nodded. Whatever happened was going to take a lot of explaining. On both George's and Tyler's parts. "It's George Brennan. Tyler's father-in-law."

"His father-in-law? You've got to be kidding me."

She shook her head, but there was no time to consider what it could mean. Not now. All she knew was that Tyler couldn't be involved in a murder. And he wouldn't have lied to her. They knew each other too well for that. But both he and George were on the boat where a man had been murdered.

She stepped back onto the bow, then shifted her weight as Jack started the engines.

"Nikki?" George asked.

"It's Special Agent Boyd to you," she said. "I'm going to uncuff you, then you're going to come with me, sit down, and not move."

"Fine, but I need to tell you something first," George said as she uncuffed him. Sweat was beaded across his forehead. "I didn't kill that man."

She led him back to the open cockpit seating. As soon as she'd handcuffed him again and they were settled, Jack turned the boat around and headed back toward the marina.

"Then what were you doing on your son-in-law's boat?" she asked him. "And why in the world did you try to flee?"

"I . . . panicked. It was stupid, I know, but I swear I didn't kill anyone. Please. You've got to believe that."

"So you did notice the dead body inside the cabin?"

"Yes, but . . ." He shook his head, his eyes pleading with her to believe him. "I know you probably don't think the best of me, but you have to believe that I'd never kill anyone. Never."

Nikki pressed her lips together. There were so many things she wanted to say to him if the circumstances were different. That he'd never really been a father to Katie. That his actions made it almost impossible for her to believe anything that came out of his mouth. And they had cost him his daughter and his wife . . .

But being judge and jury at this point wasn't her place.

"Don't worry. You'll have plenty of time to tell your side of the story."

She stared out across the rippling water to the shoreline. Nothing made sense. Tyler and his father-in-law had both been on this boat. There was no way she was going to believe Tyler had been involved in murder. But neither could she allow her personal feelings to influence her reasoning. Carter would pull her off the case before she had time to blink.

CSU was already at the marina when Jack maneuvered the boat back into the slip. Tyler stood on the dock as well, waiting for them.

"George?" Confusion marked Tyler's face as Nikki led his father-in-law off the boat. "What were you doing on my boat?"

George turned to his son-in-law and shook his head. "You wouldn't believe me if I told you."

"Try me," Tyler said.

"Not now," Nikki said. She looked at Tyler and caught his gaze. "We're going to have to take both of you in for questioning while CSU goes over this scene. Because in case either of you forgot, there's still a dead body on the boat. And you're both our primary suspects."

4

Nikki stared through the one-way mirror to where Tyler sat in the small interrogation room, hands folded in front of him, brow furrowed in frustration. Her heart broke. How had a day meant to close a page of his past spiral into a situation that left Tyler sitting in a police station, waiting to be interrogated in connection to a murder investigation?

She knew he wasn't guilty. She knew him too well to believe he'd had anything to do with Mac Hudson's murder. And yet they needed answers. To Mac Hudson's death, and now even more urgently, to Lucy's disappearance.

"Homicide wants to talk to him," Jack said, stepping up beside her. "They're on their way now."

"They can wait their turn." She wasn't going to budge on this one. Not this time. There would be plenty of time to find answers to the homicide case after they found out what they needed. "We've got a missing woman and right now Tyler and his father-in-law are the best leads we have."

41

"You're right, but you're not going in there today."

Nikki turned around at her boss's voice. Tom Carter ran the team both efficiently and fairly, which was why she rarely questioned his judgment. But this time he was wrong.

"You're too close to this one, and you know it," he said.

She matched his determined gaze with her own. She wasn't ready to step away. Not yet. "I can handle this objectively. You know that."

He let out a short huff of air. "Here's the thing. I'm heading to the airport in less than an hour to catch a plane to Maine with my wife and three boys to spend the entire weekend with my in-laws for Susan's little sister's wedding. I need to know that this case is progressing better than a weekend spent in a rented tux and a bunch of small talk."

Nikki shook her head. "Right now my job is to find Lucy Hudson, and in order to do that, we need to find out what Tyler and George Brennan know. And out of any of us, I have the best chance at getting the truth out of them."

He stood beside her, hands on his waist as he considered his decision. "There's something else you need to know, and you're not going to like it."

The tension gathered in knots, spreading across her shoulders and up her neck. She was being ambushed again. She could see it in his eyes. "What?"

"We just got a call from the crime scene unit that's working on the boat right now."

"And?"

"They're not done with their search, but they found a stash of cocaine on the boat."

"Cocaine? Wait a minute!" Nikki shook her head. "You've worked with Tyler before. You and I both know there's no way that he's involved in drugs, just like he's not involved in murder."

Carter and Tyler had worked together on a joint military training exercise that had been designed to increase the military's ability to function in an urban setting. At the time, Tyler had made a definite impact on Carter with his skills and instincts, but at the moment, her boss looked anything but impressed.

"This is exactly what I mean. You're reacting from emotion instead of from facts. Drugs were found on his boat. Along with a dead body in the cabin. I can't just sweep all this aside because you know him. Granted, none of it proves Tyler's involved, but it does raise some questions about what he was doing on his boat. It's a bit of a coincidence that he decides to show up the same day a man is murdered."

Nikki searched for a response. It was all circumstantial evidence. "He called 911. He hasn't been on that boat for months. I need to talk to him."

"Nikki—"

"Please."

Carter hesitated again. "Fine, but I'll be standing on this side of the mirror. And if I decide to pull you out, then this is over."

Nikki nodded her thanks, then walked into the interrogation room behind Jack. There had to be a logical explanation for what CSU had found. Hadn't three tours fighting for his country proved Tyler's loyalty and his integrity? Maybe she was biased, but Tyler was a man of honor who would never get involved with the schemes of a lowlife like George Brennan. Even if the man was "family."

"We need you to tell us exactly what happened on that boat today." Jack started the interview before Nikki had a chance to say anything.

Tyler turned to Nikki. "They think I'm involved with that man's death."

Nikki studied the bloodstains on his sleeve. "I can't make this personal, Tyler. You know that."

"I don't know what else to say other than what I've already said. I don't know anything about the man who was on the boat. I took the morning off to go sailing one last time before selling the boat. He was already dead when I found him. I called 911, you showed up. I had no idea that my father-in-law was on board, let alone a dead body."

"Do you have any idea why George was on your boat?"

"No. All I know is that Katie didn't trust him, and neither do I."

"Why didn't she trust him?" Jack asked.

"George was an alcoholic who let his addictions get in the way of everything. His family, his work . . . He used to be a police detective and he was a good one, but he ended up losing his career, along with two wives and his daughter."

Jack scribbled something on a notepad in front of him. "What kind of role did he play in your lives?"

Tyler shook his head. "To be honest, he wasn't a part of our lives. At least not for the past few years."

"When's the last time you saw him?"

Tyler clasped his hands together in front of him. "Katie's funeral. He showed up drunk. A couple guys had to escort him out. Thankfully, Liam didn't see him."

Nikki remembered that day as if were yesterday. George had shown up at the graveside service, wearing a suit and clearly drunk. His theatrics had been like pouring salt on fresh wounds. On the day meant to remember Katie, he was carrying a bottle of whiskey, screaming about how he'd been betrayed by his daughter.

"And you haven't seen George since," Jack said.

"No. Though he did call me a few months back. Asked me to forgive him. He needed money and a place to stay. Told me he was finally going straight, but he needed some help to get back on his feet. Also told me he wanted to get to know his grandson. But it was the same story he'd used on Katie a hundred times. I could forgive him, but that didn't mean I was going to allow him back into our lives. It was too late for that. Besides, I'd heard all of his promises and resolutions in the past, so I told him no. There was no way I wanted him in Liam's life. Cold as it sounds, I know Katie would have wanted it that way as well. The man can't be trusted."

"So you never met with him in person or spoke to him since that one phone call and seeing him last year at the funeral."

"No."

"You mentioned his addictions," Jack continued. "Did he have any besides alcohol?"

Tyler shrugged. "Not that I know of. Why?"

"We found a stash of cocaine on your boat."

"On my boat . . . You've got to be kidding me."

"Unfortunately, I'm not."

Tyler turned to Nikki. "You know this is all crazy. Drugs . . . murder . . ."

"And there's one other thing." Jack slid another batch of papers in front of Tyler. "We found a bank account in your name with deposits—and withdrawals—totaling over fifty grand over the past fifteen months. The mailing address is in Antioch."

46

Nikki felt as if the ground were crumbling beneath her. "What are you talking about?"

Jack ignored her question. "Do you know about this account?"

"Are you kidding me? Fifty thousand dollars? I certainly don't have that kind of money sitting around." Tyler leaned forward and caught Jack's gaze. "I don't know what's going on, but I'm telling the truth. I don't know anything about the bank account or the cocaine, and I certainly don't know anything about Mr. Hudson's death."

Nikki glanced at the one-way mirror, then back to Jack, angry that she'd been blindsided. Angry that they hadn't trusted her enough to give her all the details.

She pushed her chair back and stood up. "Jack, I need a word with you outside."

With Jack behind her, Nikki stepped into the room where Carter was watching the interview and took a deep breath. "You both just blindsided me."

"We needed to see his reaction and not give you the chance to lead up to it. Besides, we just got the information right before you walked in there."

Nikki fought to push aside her growing frustration. Sarah's disappearance made every case she worked on personal, but she'd always managed to find ways to keep her private life separate from her work. And this case was no different. "Any-thing else you need to tell me before we go back in there?"

"I've got something." Gwen stepped into the room with them. "Information is still trickling in, but his story seems to check out. I found him on the marina video surveillance cameras. He arrived just before nine, alone. Twelve minutes later, his call came through to 911."

"Just like he told us," Nikki said.

Gwen nodded. "I'm still trying to find out when George arrived, but I believe Tyler's telling the truth. At least about when he showed up at the *Isabella*."

"What about the bank account?" Carter asked.

"That's proving harder to verify. If Tyler's telling the truth, it's very possible that someone stole his identity and set it up. All it would have taken, really, is access to a key piece of personal information, like his Social Security number, for example. I also discovered a number of credit cards opened up under Tyler's name, using the same address in Antioch. I'm tracking down the address now. It was probably just a matter of time before Tyler found out what was going on. Typically, bills don't get paid and the creditors come after you, forcing you to clean up the mess and clear your credit report."

"George could be behind this," Nikki said. "There have been numerous occasions in the past when he had access to Tyler's personal information."

"It's possible," Carter said, but he didn't look convinced. "The only thing we know for sure, though, is that George was on Tyler's boat. Beyond that, your guess is nothing more than speculation. Get in there and see if you can tie up the loose ends. Then George Brennan is next."

Nikki slipped back into the room with Jack, a part of her thankful Katie wasn't here to see what was going on. She'd spent most of her life at odds with her father, but she'd still loved him.

"According to some of the records we've been able to dig up, we believe it's possible that someone stole your identity," Jack said as they reentered the room.

"You're kidding me." Tyler shook his head. "This whole situation just keeps getting weirder and weirder."

"Is it possible George had access to some of your personal records in the past couple of years?" Nikki asked, taking the seat across from Tyler. "Possibly even before Katie's death."

"I don't know . . . maybe." Tyler rubbed his temples. "A few months before Katie died, he showed up on our doorstep. As usual, he claimed he'd changed. For some reason Katie believed him. And I felt like I should support her. He needed a place to stay for a few days while he sorted out money someone owed him. I guess

49

he could have accessed my personal files while he was with us. I keep everything password protected, but he's been a detective most of his life, so I suppose it wouldn't have been that difficult for him to figure it out."

Nikki searched for the memory. Tyler had been home, going to physical therapy three times a week for the damage the bullet had done to his leg. Katie had come over one afternoon worried about how to tell Tyler about her father. She'd ended up convincing him to let her father stay with them, promising him it was just temporary.

"And Katie?" Jack continued his questioning. "What was her reaction at the time?"

"She was leery, but hopeful. He ended up living with us for several weeks. She wanted so badly to get back the father she remembered from when she was young. But unfortunately, like every other time, we discovered that man was gone."

Normally Katie was open about anything bothering her, but whenever the subject of her father came up, she simply dismissed it. This time had been no different.

"Did you and Katie ever fight about him?" Jack asked.

Tyler let out a nervous chuckle. "Are you kidding me? Of course. The man was impossible. But I really did try to be patient. I mean, he was her father. But then after about five or six weeks of him living in our guest room, I came home from work one afternoon and George was gone. Katie told me he wouldn't be coming back."

Jack took a step forward and grasped the back of the chair. "Do you know why he left?"

Tyler shook his head. "I know there'd been a fight between the two of them, but Katie just told me to let it go, and that he wasn't going to be a part of our lives anymore. I knew what it was like to be without a father, but I decided she was right."

"Okay . . . I think that's all for now," Jack said. "Just don't plan on leaving town until all of this is sorted out."

"Of course."

Jack headed toward the door, but Nikki hesitated.

"I'll be out in a minute," she said.

"You think they believe me?" Tyler said after the door shut.

She nodded. "So far everything you've told us has held up. Not that there still aren't a few unanswered questions."

"Like a dead body on my boat and a secret bank account?" Tyler shook his head. "All I know is that I went on the *Isabella* today to say goodbye to Katie, and I haven't seen George in over a year. I haven't even been on the boat in over a year."

"Your story checks out so far, but if you do

think of anything else, promise you'll call me."

"I will. Though I don't exactly see George as a murderer either. At least I hope not. Katie would never have been able to live with that." He looked up and caught her gaze. "Today—being on the boat—brought everything back. It didn't exactly turn out the way I wanted. Every time I try to let go, something happens to bring everything back."

The silence hovered between them for a few seconds.

"You know he blames me for Katie's death," Tyler said.

"George?"

"Yeah." Tyler's expression darkened. "I never told you this, but on the day of Katie's funeral, I went to see him. I was so furious at how he'd shown up drunk. He didn't deserve to claim her as his daughter."

"What happened?" Nikki asked.

"He was drunk. Said a lot of crazy things."

"Like . . ."

"It was my fault that his baby girl was dead. My fault I'd ruined her life. I shouldn't have left her alone all those months while I was off trying to save the world. Shouldn't have gone below deck the day she died." Tyler caught her gaze, giving her a peek past the steady strength she was used to seeing, to his vulnerability. "Because of my choices, she became a single mom struggling to raise Liam on her own."

Nikki shook her head. "But they weren't just your choices. They were both of yours. And while the life you chose might have been hard on Katie, she never looked at things that way."

"Maybe not, but that doesn't justify what I did. Maybe I should have quit the military, knowing she was struggling with my being gone, but I thought we could make it. She always supported me, at least from the outside, but lately . . . lately I can't help but wonder if there were signs I missed. Things she didn't tell me. Like she was resentful that I was gone so much. Makes me wonder what would have happened between us if she were still alive."

"Don't even go there." Nikki fingered the file Jack had left in the room. "You left the military because of her, Tyler."

"I know. I also know that all of this would have hurt her. Do you really think George is somehow involved in Mac Hudson's death and his wife's disappearance?"

"I'm not sure at this point," she said. "What do you think?"

He shook his head. "I don't know about his involvement with the Hudsons or even what happened on the boat today, but I do know this. George is smarter than you think, but he's also both impulsive and manipulative. Just promise me you'll be careful."

5

11:46 a.m.

Nikki stepped into the interrogation room in front of Jack for the second time in the past hour. George Brennan—Tyler's father-in-law—sat on the far side of the table, wearing a plaid suit jacket that looked to be at least a decade old. A bruise had formed just under his left eye—a bruise he'd told one of the officers he'd gotten at some point on the *Isabella*. He stared at an invisible spot on the table, head bowed, hands clasped together tightly in front of him. If she hadn't known why he was here, she might actually feel sorry for her best friend's father. But from everything she knew so far, George Brennan had brought this on himself.

She'd met him for the first time a few years ago when the older man had more hair and far less of a gut. Drinking and whatever else he was into had aged him faster than it should have. He'd moved from one wife to the next, but in the end had still ended up alone.

Which was one reason she found it sad that his relationship with his daughter had soured over the years. Katie might not have spoken much about her father, except that she missed the man he'd been when she was a child, when he used to take her to the park on the weekends and the circus whenever it came to town. Missed the relationship she knew they'd never be able to have again because of his drinking. Katie's death might have been a wake-up call, reminding him of what he'd missed, but clearly even that hadn't been enough for him to get his life back on track.

But despite George's bad habits and even worse decisions, Katie had loved him. Nikki knew that. Unfortunately, her patience and love weren't enough to help George find a way to get past his bad habits and make a decent life for himself. And now those bad choices had him facing prison time.

Nikki dropped the case file onto the table, then slid into the empty seat across from the older man, knowing it didn't matter at this moment who George was. They might still not know everything that was going on, but right now he was their only link to not only what had happened to Mac but to finding Lucy. And if Lucy was still out there alive, they needed to do everything in their power to find her.

"It's been a long time, George," she said.

"Thirteen months since Katie's funeral." A flicker of pain flashed in his eyes. "I always appreciated the friend you were to Katie. She told me more than once that the two of you were like sisters."

"I miss her too, but right now I have a few questions for you before homicide takes over."

George shot her a half smile. "I didn't know you'd become a detective. Congratulations."

Nikki ignored the compliment. "I'm working on the missing persons task force. Which is why we're here."

"Missing persons?"

"Mac Hudson, the dead man on the boat . . . his wife is missing."

Nikki watched his expression. He blinked rapidly. The same tic she'd noticed when he used to try to convince Katie he was going to change.

"We need to know what you were doing on Tyler's boat with Mac Hudson, and where his wife, Lucy, is," Jack said.

"I swear I didn't have anything to do with his death. And I don't know anything about his wife." George leaned forward, his hands trembling on the table in front of him. "You know me, Nikki. I wasn't always the best father to Katie. Shoot, I've never been good at most anything. Keeping a job . . . keeping a wife. But not murder. I could never kill anyone, and I didn't kill that man."

"Then would you care to explain why we found you on the boat with his dead body?" Jack said.

George's gaze shifted to the wall, then dropped to the table. Guilt, or simply nerves at play from being interrogated? Either way, she intended to find out.

"You have to understand, first of all, that the past few months—the past year, really—have been tough. Not only did I lose Katie, but my marriage recently fell apart. Which means I'm fifty-five years old and have nothing to show for my life. And I'm still trying to get over Katie's death." He wiped at his mouth with the back of his hand. "You of all people, Nikki, have to understand at least some of what I've been going through. Maybe it sounds . . . creepy, but sometimes, when I miss her the most, I hang out on the boat. It's the last place she was alive, and a place I felt like I could connect with her."

He was pleading with her to understand. She could hear the appeal in the tone of his voice and see it in his body language. But George had always been one for a good embellished story with that extra tug of emotion. And while George might seemingly be a failure at a lot of things, Tyler had definitely been right about one thing. The man wasn't stupid. He'd practiced his manipulations on Katie many times. She'd finally seen through his constant attempts to prey on her emotions and, even worse, her guilt. And today he was attempting it again, by reminding Nikki of her own grief and how much they had in common over losing Katie.

"Did Tyler know you were hanging around the boat?" she asked.

"No." George held up his hand. "Though I

admit—especially in retrospect—I should have spoken to Tyler, but I didn't think he'd mind. And it was just a couple of times."

"A couple times?" Nikki frowned, not willing to blindly believe anything he said. "We just received a preliminary report from CSU. They found your fingerprints all over the boat, along with a suitcase full of clothes, a cupboard full of food, and a number of personal items. That doesn't look like someone who was there just a couple of times. And on top of that, you ran. An innocent man wouldn't have run. You knew Mac was on that boat."

George combed his fingers through his thinning hair. "I was scared. I knew how it looked. Because yes, I have been living on the boat—temporarily —but I swear I didn't kill him."

"Then why were you living on the *Isabella*?" Nikki said. "Because regardless of whether or not you killed Mac Hudson, his wife is missing, and we believe her life could be in danger."

George shifted in his seat before answering. "I've been living there, but like I said, it's only been temporarily. Only for the past couple weeks. I've had a bit of a financial setback. A couple clients refused to pay me for my services, I got behind on my rent and was evicted . . . but it was nothing serious or long term. I just needed a temporary place to stay."

"Any reason why you didn't go to Tyler and ask him for help?"

George shrugged. "You know Tyler. We haven't exactly been on speaking terms since my little girl's funeral. Since before that, actually. Though I suppose I can't blame him."

"I know. I was there. You came drunk to the funeral and caused a scene."

"And I didn't exactly want to tell him the truth," George said. "I might not be the most upright citizen, but I really am trying to get my life together. After my Katie died . . . it shook me up. I started going to my AA meetings. Staying out of the bars . . . If Tyler knew I'd been evicted again, it would be one more reason he'd have for me to stay away from Liam."

"Along with the fact you'd opened up a bank account and several credit cards in Tyler's name?" Nikki asked, hoping he'd give them the answer they needed.

"Of course not. Why would I do that?" George asked.

"Because you needed money. You were living on his boat because you couldn't even afford a place to stay."

"No—"

Nikki leaned forward. "Don't lie to me."

George pressed his fingers against his temples and shook his head. "Fine. I had some debts that needed to be paid off, and couldn't get any credit. I used Tyler's name, transferred the money into an account—"

Nikki glanced at Jack. "*Stole* his name. That's what it's really called."

"Which makes me wonder what really happened on that boat," Jack said. "We know you had to have seen something."

George shook his head. "I . . . I panicked. I knew my fingerprints were going to be found. Knew I'd look guilty, but I didn't see anything. I swear. I was in the head when a couple guys came on board. I didn't see them, but I heard them talking."

"And you didn't come out and try to do anything?"

"Are you kidding me? There were gunshots. I didn't want to be next."

"So you just stayed hidden," Jack said.

He nodded.

"And you didn't think to call 911?" Nikki asked.

"I didn't have my phone with me. Then they left and someone else showed up. I had no idea it was Tyler."

"Here's the problem. There are a dozen holes in your story." Jack pulled out a photo of Mac Hudson from the file and shoved it in front of George. "Have you seen this man before today on the boat?"

George shook his head.

"Another hole in your story, George. Mac wasn't shot on the boat. Surely you knew we'd figure that out."

Nikki caught and held George's gaze. "And there was something else found on the boat. A kilo of cocaine."

"Whoa . . . wait a minute." Genuine surprise flashed across his face. "I don't do drugs. Whatever you found isn't mine."

"Really?" Jack asked. "Then whose is it? Been entertaining some of your old friends while you were living on your son-in-law's boat?"

George turned to Nikki. "You were Katie's best friend—"

"Stop," she said. "This isn't about Katie or me right now. In fact, it's not even about you. Tell us the truth about Mac Hudson."

"Fine." Defeat settled across George's expression. "Mac was a client."

"A client?" Nikki asked.

"I'd been working for him the past two weeks. Mainly surveillance, but a job's a job."

"You know the requirements for a PI in Tennessee," Nikki said.

"I have a license."

"Be of good moral character and not addicted to narcotics."

"I'm not a user. Those weren't my drugs."

"We'll discuss the drug charges later," Jack said, "but for now I want to know your connection to the Hudsons. What did he hire you to do? Spy on his wife?"

George shrugged. "It isn't the first time a man's

tried to find out what his wife's up to when he's working late."

Nikki frowned. "You're telling me she was having an affair?"

"That's what he thought. Turns out she wasn't."

If George actually was telling the truth, whether she was having an affair or not, there was apparently trouble in paradise.

"Where did you meet Mac?" Jack asked.

"I knew Mac's father from way back. We were buddies in the military when we were in our twenties. He passed away a few years ago, but I heard from Mac every now and then. He called me about three weeks ago, asked me to look into a delicate matter."

"He believed his wife was having an affair," Nikki said.

George nodded.

"When's the last time you spoke with him?"

"Two . . . maybe three days ago."

"Tell us why you were on the boat with Mac. Because eventually we're going to find out exactly what happened, and it's only going to get far worse for you if you don't tell us the truth."

George looked down at the table, fidgeting in his chair. Sweat beaded on his forehead, the conflict clear in his eyes.

"George . . ."

"He called me yesterday around five from his house. Mac was . . . in a panic."

Nikki watched his body language and waited for him to continue.

"I could tell something bad had happened, told him to call 911, and I'd be there as soon as I could. When I got there, two men had already broken into the house, and Mac had been shot. They must not have known Mac was a crack shot. They\ were both lying on the living room floor. Dead."

"What happened next?"

"He told me he needed a place to hide. That someone was trying to kill him."

"Where was Lucy?"

"I don't know. I didn't see her there."

"Do you think she was behind the hits?"

He paused, then shook his head. "No. I don't think so. He was worried about her. I tried to call her, but she never answered."

"Why didn't you simply call 911?"

"Mac was really shaken up and afraid that whoever had come after him would try again. Said he didn't want to get the police involved and refused to go to a hospital. He thought he would be okay, but by the time we made it to the boat, he was too far gone. I did everything I could to help him, but he died right there on the boat. I was getting ready to call the police when Tyler showed up. Of course, I didn't know it was Tyler."

"Why didn't you tell us this from the beginning?" Nikki asked.

"Because I was found on a boat with a dead

man. And then I panicked and ran. I know what this looks like."

"What about his wife?" Jack asked.

"I called her a dozen times over the course of the night and this morning. I never got ahold of her. Mac was terrified something had happened to her."

Nikki looked up as a man in his early thirties wearing a gray suit with a white collared shirt and a blue silk tie walked into the room. "Mr. Brennan, don't say anything else. Your bail's been posted and you're free to leave."

"Excuse me?" Nikki stood, almost knocking over her chair behind her. "What do you mean, he's free to leave?"

"I didn't hire a lawyer." George looked just as surprised as she was.

"Unless you want to be charged on drug possession and murder charges, I suggest you be quiet and do what I say."

"George, wait a minute," Nikki said. "There's a woman's life at stake here. I need your help to find her."

"I can't help you, Nikki. I'm sorry."

Nikki rushed out into the crowded bullpen where Gwen stood talking on the phone. "What's going on?"

"I'm trying to find out now, but everything seems legit." Gwen hung up the call. "I'm sorry. Either George decides to talk, or for now we'll have to get our information elsewhere."

Nikki shook her head. "He's our only lead. We can't just let him walk away."

"We don't have a choice. He has rights. His bail's been paid."

"He has answers. I know he does."

"I'm sorry, Nikki, but our hands are tied. Someone managed to pull some heavy strings."

"Let him go for now, Nikki," Jack said. "We're going to find her. Just not this way."

Nikki shook her head. "I need some air."

George strode out of the station ahead of her beside his lawyer. Nikki felt her gut clench. Something wasn't right. If George couldn't afford a place to stay, how in the world could he afford to hire his own lawyer? But someone had put down the cash for his bail.

"George . . ." Nikki stepped out of the brick precinct and ran to catch up with him. "Just tell me what you know about Lucy. Where is she, George? If we don't find her—"

"I said I don't know where she is."

"And I thought I made myself clear that my client has nothing else to say." The lawyer ushered George toward the east parking lot, empty except for a few cars.

She rushed after them. "George, please. We need to find her."

Shots rang out. Someone screamed.

Nikki stumbled backward as George dropped to the pavement, a red stain seeping across his chest.

6

Nikki ducked behind the wheel of one of the parked cars and shouted at George's lawyer to get down. Instead he stood frozen over George's body.

She grabbed the hem of his suit jacket, anticipating another shot. "Get. Down. Now."

He crouched down beside her, his breaths coming in rapid succession. "I'm sorry, I just . . ."

She frowned. At least she had his attention. "Stay with him and call 911. You can use your jacket to try and stop the bleeding." Nikki called dispatch. "I've got an active shooter in the east parking lot of the precinct and a man down. A possible long-range sniper. I need backup immediately."

She pulled out her duty pistol, then headed in the direction of the shots, taking cover behind a row of cars as she ran, more for concealment than protection from another shot. Vehicles might not be the best cover, but they were better than nothing. And as long as he didn't know where she was, the odds shifted in her favor. Besides, she

66

had no idea how many shooters were involved or if George was their only target. She waited for another shot, but all she could hear was her heart pounding in her chest.

Nikki's breaths came in rapid bursts as she searched the edges of the parking lot. Adrenaline raced through her. She'd been trained to deal with an active shooter incident, but preparation didn't take away the apprehension of dealing with the situation on her own. Most of the time, an active shooter hadn't been trained in combat, which gave her the advantage. Though this situation felt different. The shot had to have come from a distance. Whoever was on the other side of that gun knew what they were doing.

But waiting for backup would come with a price. First responders in a crisis often became the difference between life and death. Nikki hesitated another second, then decided to move. Most active shooters had only one thing in mind. They were driven toward their prey. And without knowing if George was their only intended target, there was no way to know when or how this was going to end.

She glanced toward the adjoining property where there was a slight rise in the terrain at the edge of the parking lot. The two-story roof of the neighboring warehouse would give a sniper the best access. She scanned the property, needing to identify the location of the sniper before he shot again. That had to be where he was perched.

Nikki searched the horizon, including the top of the warehouse, for any signs of movement. Five seconds later, she spotted him.

Bingo.

A man was running across the roof toward the side of the building, wearing a dark hat and a black sweatshirt, and carrying a rifle. She sprinted across the parking lot toward his position, still careful to use cover as much as possible in order to avoid becoming another target. Before she could reach the building, the shooter began climbing down the side.

Glancing behind her, she caught sight of half a dozen uniformed officers making their way to her, but there was no time to wait. The man jumped onto the ground, then turned back toward the parking lot, spotting her in the process. She crouched behind the engine block of one of the cars as a bullet whizzed past her ear.

She kept her cover for a few seconds, then glanced out from behind the car. He was running toward a blue sedan that had just pulled into an empty drive in front of the warehouse. She was closing in on the shooter, but she had to get to him first and stop him. She started again toward the suspect, still careful to use cover as she moved, chest heaving, heart racing, as she weighed her options. Shooting at the tires of the car he was getting into risked a bullet hitting a passing car on the road that ran along the front of the precinct.

Nikki swung around at the sound of another vehicle, its tires crunching against the gravel.

Jack.

She let out a sigh of relief as she slid into the car. "Suspect just got into that sedan up ahead. Hurry."

She fastened her seatbelt as Jack pulled onto the main road that ran in front of the precinct, then sped away, weaving through traffic, his siren blazing.

"He shot George," she said, breaking the silence between them as Jack flew down the street through a red light.

"I heard. How bad is it?"

"I don't know. I left him with his lawyer."

"There'll be other officers at the scene by now. Hopefully he'll be okay."

But his reassurance wasn't enough to take away the anxiety. She'd seen the shot and the amount of blood he'd lost, and she wasn't sure he was going to make it. "He needs to be okay, because we need answers."

Mac was dead. George had just been hit, and Lucy was out there somewhere. But why? What had Mac—and George—known that could end up costing both their lives?

Jack kept up with the suspects while Nikki called for backup. She grasped the armrest as they headed toward a railroad crossing. The red lights were flashing and the crossing-barricade arm was lowering.

But the car in front of them wasn't slowing down.

"Jack . . ." Nikki leaned forward and caught sight of the train coming down the tracks to the right. "He's going to try to get through."

And he wasn't going to make it.

Jack slammed on his brakes and turned the steering wheel as they skidded to a stop in front of the tracks. The sniper's car kept going.

The train hit the car at full force. The crunch of metal was followed by the shrill grinding of brakes piercing the air. In an instant, the car was gone, dragged down the tracks until the train finally screeched to a stop.

Nikki jumped out of the car and started running alongside the tracks toward the accident, her shoes crunching against the gravel. There had to be a connection. Between George . . . Mac . . . and Lucy. The sniper had either been hired or was doing his own dirty work, but either way he knew something.

Her breath caught at the sight of the mangled vehicle lying on the track. Orange flames shot out of the back of the car, now surrounded by heavy gray smoke.

The engineer was already running along the track with a fire extinguisher while another crewman tugged on the passenger door. "I called 911, but we've got to get them out."

Nikki felt the heat from the flames as she moved in beside Jack, who was attempting to open the driver-side door. Smoke filled her lungs. The fire was blazing hotter now. Orange sparks filled the air. While the chance of the gas tank exploding was slim, there was still the smoke and noxious gases and the chance of the tires blowing out.

The two men managed to pull the first victim out of the passenger seat and drag him away from the wreck. Nikki recognized the shooter from the roof. Same dark blue ball cap. Same jacket . . .

"Is he alive?" she shouted.

The crewman shook his head. "He's dead."

Flames continued to spread, engulfing the car as they dragged the driver out next.

Nikki knelt down beside him, then pressed her fingers against the man's neck, searching for a pulse. There were burn marks across his face and right arm, and his leg was twisted at an odd angle.

His eyes opened.

"What's your name?"

He struggled to turn his head. "Cameron . . . Is he . . . alive?"

She looked over at where the sniper lay, guessing he must be Cameron. "He's gone. What's your name?"

"Tell him it wasn't worth it. None of this was worth it."

"What are you talking about?" Nikki pressed.

"We should have gotten out while we could. It wasn't supposed to end this way."

"Tell who?" Nikki said. "Who sent you to kill George?"

His eyes fluttered shut. They were losing him.

"No . . . no . . . no . . . You can't die on me. Not now."

Nikki shook his shoulder, but he wasn't responding. She knelt beside him, laced her fingers together, and started doing CPR compressions in the center of the man's chest. She needed information. And she needed him to live. There had been too many deaths today already.

She started counting. Twenty . . . forty . . . sixty . . .

He still wasn't breathing.

Another minute passed. She could feel the tension in her arms and wrists. But there was still no response.

"Nikki."

She looked up at Jack. Sirens blared beside them. Lights flashed from the ambulance.

"He's not going to make it," she said, sitting up as paramedics took over the scene.

"I know."

She searched his pockets for his ID, then moved out of the way. Micky Reed. Twenty-six years old. Five foot eight. Brown eyes . . .

Jack reached for her hand and pulled her back.

"We'll let uniforms take over the scene. There's nothing else we can do here."

She let out a breath of frustration. "I'll call Gwen and have her get whatever information she can on this guy. And they were working with someone. This is all related somehow."

"I know, but they're not going to give you answers now. Besides, more than likely they were hired guns. We'll ID them and go from there."

"And Lucy?" she asked.

"We'll find her."

And this had all happened for what reason? To silence George?

Worry nudged itself back to the forefront. This was far bigger than a simple missing person or domestic violence case. People didn't hire hitmen or snipers unless they wanted someone silenced.

She headed toward the car. "We need to go back to the precinct and see if we can talk with George."

But her gut told her he wasn't alive either.

An ambulance was pulling out of the precinct parking lot as Jack parked in an empty space in the front lot. Sergeant Dillard, who had taken the lead on this morning's two homicides, was walking toward the front entrance.

"Sergeant?" Nikki hurried to catch up. "Do you know anything about the man who was shot in the parking lot a few minutes ago? George Brennan."

"They're taking him to the hospital now, but from what I saw, it doesn't look good. Since he's connected to my homicide case, I've given orders to be notified if he is able to talk."

"Good. What have you got from the scene?"

"Not much. Three shell casings on the roof of the building on the adjoining property. That's it." The detective pulled off his sunglasses. "I heard the two of you chased down the sniper."

Jack nodded. "But he and his driver are dead. Gwen's running down their IDs right now."

"What about Brennan's lawyer?" Nikki asked.

"He's waiting in interrogation room 3. I'm going in now to see what he knows."

The three of them headed through the glass door of the precinct entrance.

"Has he said anything?" Jack asked Gwen once they were inside.

"Not yet. He seems pretty scared."

"We want to talk to him first," Nikki said.

Detective Dillard turned around to face her. "I'm not looking to make this into a turf war, but this is a murder investigation, and the body count is growing by the hour."

"I understand, and you can have him as soon as we're finished with him. But we've got a missing woman somewhere out there, and I think we can all agree her life's in danger and the clock's running out. Give us five minutes, and he's all yours."

The detective hesitated. "Fine. Five minutes."

Inside the interrogation room, Nikki slammed her palms against the metal table. "What's your name?"

"Tanner Chapman." He pushed up his glasses, fingers shaking. "I guess you figured out I'm not a lawyer."

"Then who are you? The man you just escorted out of here probably won't live the rest of the day."

"This is all a huge mistake. You have to believe me. I had nothing to do with that. I'm just an actor, and I had no idea that was going to happen." His voice cracked. So much for the tough lawyer persona. "I didn't know they were going to shoot someone. Please. You've got to believe me."

He pulled his wallet from his back pocket, fingers still shaking as he grabbed a business card and slid it across the table.

"Tanner Chapman?" Jack read the card and frowned. "I'm going to guess that this isn't your real name?"

"No, it's . . . Alfred Winston the Third. Named after my grandfather. But most people in the biz call me Tanner. Well . . . those I work with. Alfred doesn't exactly fit the image I'm going for."

Great. A wannabe actor.

"Okay, Tanner." Jack sat on the edge of the table. "Here's the thing. I have the feeling another lawyer isn't going to come walking through that door to rescue you like you tried to do for George Brennan. So we need some answers. Now. How did you know George?"

"I didn't know him at all."

"What?" Nikki said.

"You don't understand." He combed his fingers through his hair, then laced his fingers behind his neck. "This can't be happening. The worst trouble I've been in with the law was a speeding ticket when I was eighteen."

Jack shook his head. "I think you're the one who doesn't get it. A man is dying. Five other men are dead, and I need to know who hired you."

Tanner tapped his fingers on the table in front of him and pressed his lips together before responding. "I don't know."

"What do you mean you don't know?" Nikki asked. "You didn't know George or you don't know who hired you?"

"Both."

"You're going to have to do a whole lot better than that."

He let out a sharp breath. "I work for a small acting agency. Some guy called me a couple hours ago and promised me five thousand dollars. Half up front. The rest of the money if I completed my job successfully. All I had to do was play the role of a hard-hitting lawyer and walk Mr. Brennan out of the police station."

Nikki shook her head. "And you didn't see a

problem with your posing as a lawyer even though I'm going to assume you've never stepped foot in law school?"

"I didn't know it was against the law. I was just acting."

"Seriously?" Nikki frowned. "Who's the guy who hired you?"

"I don't have a name. He sent the first half of the payment to my agency. Cash."

"And you didn't think this whole setup sounded a bit fishy?" Jack asked.

"I just thought it sounded like an easy way to make money." Tanner's face paled. "I guess I won't be getting the rest of the money."

"You're kidding, right?" Jack asked.

Tanner shrugged. "Sorry, but do you know how long it would take me to make that kind of money? And his bail really was paid. How was I supposed to know they wanted him dead? I figured it was some sort of gag."

"You didn't think there might be issues with your impersonating a lawyer in a police station?"

Tanner gave Nikki a blank look. "All I know is that I didn't have anything to do with him being shot. Do you actually think I would have agreed to help if I knew the dude was going to get blown away right beside me? And on top of that, do you know how close they came to shooting *me?* Another inch or two and I'd be the one lying on the pavement, or at least next to him—"

"Sounds like you're having a bad day." Jack stood up and headed toward the door. "Lost out on half a payment, almost got shot . . ."

"And in the meantime we've got a stack of dead bodies and a missing woman," Nikki said.

She and Jack stepped outside the interrogation room where Gwen and Carter were waiting for them.

"This isn't going anywhere," Jack said.

"So you think this was a plan to stop George from talking?" Gwen asked.

"Pretty risky, taking out a suspect in front of a police station," Carter said.

"Well, unfortunately for us, their plan worked," Gwen said. "The hospital just called. George is dead. I'm sorry."

Nikki might not have liked the man, but that didn't mean he deserved to die. Not this way.

"We need to know why Mac was afraid and what George was looking for," Jack said. "He must have had files he kept on the case. What was found on the boat?"

"We should have something soon. CSU is finishing up an inventory now," Gwen said.

"Do you know where Tyler is?" Nikki asked.

"When he found out his father-in-law had been shot, he left for the hospital," Carter said.

Nikki hesitated. She needed to go see if he was okay.

"Gwen and Jack, keep digging into the

backgrounds of George and our victims," Carter said. "Nikki, go find out how Tyler is. I've got to leave, but hopefully by the time you get back, we'll have something solid from CSU."

7

1:23 p.m.
Hospital emergency room

Nikki found Tyler sitting along the back wall of the lobby in the emergency room where medics had rushed George after the shooting. Rows of blue cushioned chairs and cream-colored walls surrounded her, while physicians, nurses, and technicians did their jobs.

She handed Tyler the coffee she'd picked up for him—two sugars, one cream, just the way he liked it. Funny how many little things she'd learned about him over the last year. How he had a penchant for grilled peanut butter sandwiches. How he loved ketchup, but hated tomatoes. Loved eighties rock bands and anything Sherlock Holmes or sci-fi. And how he always laughed at her jokes, even when they weren't funny, and how he had no idea that he made her feel like she was the only one in the room.

"Hey." She sat down beside him and took a sip

of her own coffee, burning the tip of her tongue in the process. Tyler and George might not have been close, but she knew the news of the older man's death would still sting. George was Katie's father, and Liam had always adored the older man who had a knack for spoiling him.

Tyler let out a huff of air. "The doctors did everything they could, but he didn't make it."

"I just heard the news."

"It's crazy. I never thought his death would affect me, but it does." He looked up at her, hands wrapped around his coffee, his eyes searching hers. "Did you find out why he was shot?"

"All I can do right now is speculate that someone wanted to silence him. But we've got the best homicide team working the case. And they will find the answers."

Tyler glanced down at his coffee cup. "I guess I knew this day would come eventually. George was bound to get himself into trouble. He always managed to get involved with the wrong people."

Nikki sat quietly beside him, waiting for him to continue at his own pace.

"I might not have liked the man, but he was family, and I know that in spite of everything he did to Katie, she still loved him. And never gave up on the possibility that he might one day be the father she knew he could be. The father he used to be. I just don't understand how this happened."

"I'm sorry," she said.

"Me too."

Nikki studied his expression, knowing there was nothing she could say to fix things. No words to take away the grief and frustration he was feeling at this moment. Because this wasn't just about George. His death had managed to dredge up a flood of memories. And like with Katie's death, all she really knew how to do was simply be there for Tyler. And hope that was enough.

Tyler took a long drink of coffee, his gaze resting somewhere on the other side of the half-full room. "If it wasn't so serious, I'd be tempted to laugh. George always told Katie he planned to go out with a bang. Running from the cops in a stolen boat, then shot down by a sniper while being escorted out of the police station. I'm sorry. It sounds like some crazy episode of *NCIS*."

He shifted his gaze to a dark stain on the carpet, then turned back to Nikki. "And you know what's not so funny? How every time I try to put things behind me and move on, the past manages to rear its ugly head and latch on to me. I don't know how to get away from it."

She could hear the hurt in his voice. The raw notes of emotion in his words. But sometimes life didn't play fair.

He shook his head. "I can't get away from it, Nikki. From Katie's death. The feelings of loss. From Liam's questions. I feel like I'm supposed to be the strong one, and yet some days—like today—I wonder how long I can keep going through the motions. It's like every time I take a step forward, something drags me back and I have to suck it up and start over. And I'm just . . . I'm tired. Bone-weary tired of trying to keep everything together. And now I have to tell Liam that his grandfather—like his mother—is dead. After him coming so far these past few weeks."

"I know and I'm so sorry." She struggled to find the right words. "Remember when you talked to me about complicated grief? You told me how Sarah's disappearance has had no resolution because the story hasn't ended yet. And that not knowing has been what's brought my family the greatest hurt. But your grief really isn't that different, because your story hasn't ended yet either. The bottom line is—and you know this—but there is no checklist of getting through grief. You can't run away from it. And neither can Liam."

She grasped her necklace, a gesture that brought with it her own thoughts and grief. Ten years hadn't begun to diminish the loss that had settled in her gut. If anything, every year that passed made her even more determined to find out what had happened to Sarah.

"Maybe this is simply life." Nikki shrugged, talking to herself as much as to Tyler. "It's made up of all kinds of memories and events. Some are good. Others not so good. But in the end, they manage to make you who you are. Both the good and the bad. And more often than not, those memories end up popping up at the wrong time."

Sarah's disappearance had changed the direction of her life, shifting her focus from teaching to joining the academy. And had brought her to this moment, ten years later, working on a missing persons task force. She might not have found her sister yet, but at least she was where she needed to be for people like Lucy.

EMTs pushed a gurney through the set of swinging doors at the entrance of the ER, followed by two police officers. Another moment that had potentially just changed someone's world forever. Life was like that. Unpredictable. Uncertain. They couldn't know what was around the next corner, but that shouldn't stop them from living.

"Sometimes I wish I was the one who'd drowned the day Katie died," Tyler said, pulling her out of her thoughts.

Nikki pressed her lips together and forced herself to just listen. She'd felt the same way about Sarah as she'd dealt with both the loss and the guilt.

"Liam still talks about his mother and how much he misses her," he continued. "Reminders are everywhere. And every time I try to let go . . . Every time I try to take the next step, I feel like something's holding me back. And then there are days like today . . . a day when I planned to move a step closer to healing, and look where I am now."

"It's just been a little over a year, Tyler. You need to give yourself time."

"Maybe." He reached out and wrapped his fingers around hers.

Someone spoke over the loud speaker. A TV blared in the corner of the room. A man stepped through the entrance, carrying a sick child. But all Nikki could see was Tyler.

"You know this," she said, "but everything you're going through is normal. There isn't an easy way through."

"I know." He squeezed her hand, then pulled her closer until their foreheads barely touched. "Thank you. Just for being here."

She closed her eyes, her breath quickening at the intimate gesture. And at the depth of emotion hovering between them. Because no matter how hard she tried to fight what she felt, she'd given her heart to the man beside her. Except this wasn't about her or her feelings toward him. This was about Tyler. About grief. And finding ways to push through that grief. Not avoid it.

He pulled back and caught her gaze.

The room disappeared around her. Time suspended as she caught the hint of desire in his eyes. He was so close to her. Close enough that she could feel his breath against her face.

There had never been any expectations between them. Tyler had been nothing more than the husband of her best friend. But no matter how hard she tried to bury those feelings, they managed to find a way to the surface and, if anything, grow stronger.

He let go of her hand and the moment quickly faded into the realization that she'd only imagined the desire.

"You're a good friend, Nikki." His words confirmed the realization. "You always have been. To Katie, and also to me. I hope you know that and how much I appreciate everything you've done for Liam and me."

Nikki swallowed hard. Emotionally, she needed to go back to the place she'd been before Katie's death. Where her feelings toward Tyler were nothing more than friendship. Because she couldn't keep doing this. She needed to walk away from these feelings and find someone else before she was swept away so far she wasn't able to return.

Please, God . . . help me to stop loving him.

He ran his fingers down her arms, then laced their fingers together, completely unaware of what his touch did to her. "Thank you . . . again . . . I don't know how you do it, but you've always been here for me. With the right words. Willing to listen. Anticipating what I need. Like when to show up with Chinese takeout."

Nikki swallowed hard at his smile. They were friends. Nothing more. And she'd been wrong, imagining what she'd seen just moments before in his eyes. There had been no intimate gesture. No subtle declaration of his feelings. But the desire to cross the line, to tell him how she felt and move their relationship to a different level, had only deepened inside her. It was a place she knew she couldn't go. Not now. Not while he was still grieving for Katie. Not until he was able to find out who he was without Katie.

"You okay?" he asked.

"Yeah. Of course. I just . . . I need to get back to work. There's a connection between George and Lucy and I need to find it."

"Of course. I'm sorry—"

"No. It's fine." She let out a slow breath. "Are you going to be okay?"

He nodded. "Yeah. I'll be fine. My mom already planned to keep Liam for the day, so I think I'll still take the day off and try to get my bearings."

"If you need anything—"

"I need you to find out what my father-in-law was involved in and to find Lucy Hudson."

She nodded and pulled out her cell phone. "I'll call Gwen and see where they are."

Gwen answered with an update. "CSU didn't find any of George's files or work-related items on the boat. But I did speak briefly to Lucy's principal. He was in meetings all morning with the school superintendent but is finally free. Jack's planning to head there now and see what he can find out."

Nikki glanced at Tyler. "Tell him I'll meet him there."

8

2:14 p.m.
Glendale Elementary

Glendale Elementary sat at the edge of a quiet suburban neighborhood less than two miles from the Hudsons' home. Nikki found Jack waiting for her on the sidewalk at the end of the half-empty school parking lot. An eerie shiver slid down her spine as she hurried to meet him. She scanned the perimeter of the property, then shook off the uneasy feeling. There were no snipers hiding in the distance. No hired hitmen waiting to gun her down.

"Looks like I'm just in time," she said, nodding as an older-model Buick pulled into the parking space marked PRINCIPAL.

"And as long as this doesn't involve another chase of any kind, I'll be fine," Jack said.

"Principal Perez?" Nikki held up her badge as an older Hispanic man slid out of the driver's seat, carrying a thick briefcase. "We're with TBI."

"You're here about Lucy." He locked his car and pocketed his keys. "Please tell me you found her."

"Unfortunately, we haven't," Jack said, "but we do need to ask you a few questions."

"Of course, though I'm not sure I'm going to be any help." Perez nodded toward the school's main office. "Do you mind walking with me? I need to get back to my office before school lets out for the day. Rumors have been spreading like wildfire over Lucy's disappearance, and my secretary's having to field calls. Needless to say, it's been a difficult day."

"I understand you called 911 this morning," Nikki said, matching his stride across the quiet campus.

"It was one of my other teachers, actually. She came to see me sometime after eight. Lucy wasn't the type of person to just not show up for work, which is why we called the authorities when we couldn't get ahold of either her or her husband."

"What can you tell me about her?" Jack asked.

Perez shook his head. "Truth is, she's the last person I can imagine being involved in some sort of drama that ends up on the nightly news."

"Why do you say that?" Nikki asked.

"I've worked in education for thirty years, and as a principal the past eight. Lucy's the kind of employee I'm always looking for. She doesn't complain, works hard, kids love her, and she rarely misses a day. And I'm pretty sure if you were to ask the other teachers she works with, they'd say the same thing."

"So you wouldn't know if there was someone who might have some sort of grudge against her or her husband?"

"A grudge?" Perez stopped and shook his head. "That's hard to imagine, though Lucy was a very private person. If there was drama at home or in her life outside school, she didn't bring it to work."

"What about her husband?" Jack asked. "Did you ever meet him?"

Perez started walking again. "I spoke with him a handful of times at various school events. I think he worked for a drug company."

"He was a scientist," Nikki said.

"He always made a good impression, and I never heard of any problems between the two of them, but like I said, Lucy was a private person, so even if there were problems, I don't think I would have heard about it."

"What about family?" Nikki asked. "We're having a hard time tracking anyone down."

They stopped again at the front entrance of the school. "I do know that Lucy was raised in a foster home, but beyond that . . . I don't know. I wish I could help, but like everyone else, I'm having a hard time believing something could have happened to her."

Nikki pressed her lips together. She'd heard those words so many times before.

"And the teacher who called 911 this morning," she said, pushing the past aside where it belonged for the moment. "Where can we find her?"

"Rachel Adams." Perez glanced at his watch. "She teaches kindergarten like Lucy and should be at the playground right now."

The bell rang, and students began filing out of their classrooms into the long hallway of the main building, but Perez didn't move from the front steps. "I've heard rumors that her husband's dead. I was hoping . . ."

Nikki shook her head. "I'm sorry, but Mac Hudson was found dead this morning from a gunshot wound."

They found Rachel Adams on the playground behind the kindergarten wing with twenty or so energetic five-year-olds who were running around the rubber mulch flooring.

"Miss Adams?" Nikki said.

The thirtysomething-year-old with short, bottle-red hair stepped away from the swing set. "Yes . . . Can I help you?"

"We're with the Tennessee Bureau of Investigation," Nikki said, quickly introducing themselves. "Principal Perez told us you were the one who called the police this morning regarding Lucy Hudson."

"Yes, I . . . Just a second." She turned to two of the children who'd started fighting over an empty swing. "Lily . . . Elijah. Go find another place to play, and no more fighting."

The two ran off in separate directions.

"Sorry," she said, turning back to them.

"It's no problem." Nikki grinned. "You have your hands full, Miss Adams."

"Please, call me Rachel, and yes, every day's a bit chaotic, though today . . . Have you found her yet?"

Nikki shook her head. "No. I'm sorry."

Rachel shoved a lock of hair behind her ear and frowned. "I honestly thought I was just overreacting when I called, but Lucy never misses work, and on the off chance she does have to miss school, she always calls in. So when I couldn't get ahold of her or her husband this morning, I knew something was wrong."

"We understand the two of you are friends," Nikki said.

"Yeah. We eat lunch together most days. She's quiet, but a wonderful teacher. You can ask any of her students or their parents. Everyone adored her. If anything's happened to her . . ." She pulled a tissue out of her pocket and blew her nose. "I'm sorry. I've barely made it through the day, worrying about her. I've left a couple dozen messages on her phone, hoping she'll call me back, but so far she hasn't responded."

"How was she the past week or so?" Jack asked.

"She hasn't been herself, which is one of the reasons I've been worried."

"What do you mean?"

"Normally, Lucy was laid back and relaxed. She teaches kindergarten like I do, and we have to be flexible and have an enormous amount of patience. But over the past couple of weeks . . . I'm not sure what happened, but something changed. She was scared about something. It was like she was always looking over her shoulder, afraid someone was after her, which didn't make sense. I mean . . . we're schoolteachers. We're not exactly in a high-risk business."

"Did you ask her what was wrong?"

"Not at first, because honestly, I thought I was imagining things. You know, maybe it was just because I was reading too many mystery novels late at night. But then she said something to me a couple days ago." She turned back to the kids and told one of the boys to sit down on the slide. "Sorry. Anyway, we were having lunch, and she was . . . I don't know . . . *jumpy* is the only word I can think of to describe her."

"Did you ask her what was wrong?" Nikki asked.

"Not at first. I knew that she was trying to get pregnant. She'd gone to several fertility specialists, and she'd told me that the hormones she was taking to get pregnant were messing with her emotions and had her jumping at every shadow."

She fiddled with the thick leather belt around her waist. "My sister-in-law did the whole fertility thing, so I know there are definite mood swings involved with some of the medicines they give you. But this seemed like . . . I don't know. Something else. She wasn't just sad or moody, she seemed paranoid. Like she was truly afraid someone was after her. I asked her about it again later that day."

"And?" Nikki pressed.

"It was weird. She told me if anything should happen to her, I should get in contact with this reporter she knew because it wouldn't be an accident." Rachel frowned. "But then she just laughed and said my love for murder mysteries must be rubbing off on her. Said the book I'd given her had totally creeped her out. She told me to forget what she'd said, and that she was fine."

"But you didn't believe her?"

"All I know is that something had her scared. So when she didn't show up for work today, I started to get really worried."

"Do you remember the name of the reporter?"

"Yeah, it was Mallory Philips. I actually left a message with her today, but I haven't heard back from her yet. She'll probably think I'm a crazy stalker or something when she listens to me rambling."

"We'll track her down and see if there's anything to it," Nikki said, hoping they'd finally found a lead they could run with. "One last thing . . . What about family? Did she ever talk about her parents? Maybe a brother or sister?"

Rachel shook her head. "Sorry. If she had any family, I always assumed they were estranged, because she never talked about them."

Nikki thanked her, then handed her a card with her number. "If Lucy happens to call you, would you please let me know? We need to find her."

"Of course," Rachel said, putting the card into her pocket. "I just hope she's okay."

Nikki punched Gwen's speed-dial number as she and Jack headed back toward their cars. "Gwen, we're at Lucy's school. I need you to see if you can get ahold of a reporter named Mallory Philips. We need to speak with her as soon as possible."

"Think she's knows where our girl is?"

"I'm not sure what the connection is at this point, but get back to me as soon as you get ahold of her."

"You got it."

"What are you thinking?" Jack asked as she hung up the call.

She knew he was asking her what she thought about the case, but so much had happened today it was hard not to look back.

Six weeks before Sarah disappeared, she had called Nikki in a panic. Nikki remembered the phone call like it was yesterday. At half past eight, it was already dark outside. She'd been grading history papers while munching on stale popcorn and wishing it was the weekend.

"Nikki . . . It's Sarah."

Her sister was crying and struggling to catch her breath. Nikki dropped her red pen onto the table and pressed the cordless phone against her ear. A dozen scenarios raced through her mind while she tried to get Sarah to calm down.

"Sarah, take a deep breath and tell me what happened."

"There . . . there was an accident."

Nikki felt her heart race. "Are you hurt?"

"I don't know . . . I don't think so, but Cassie's hurt. It's bad, Nikki. There's blood everywhere and I'm scared."

By the time Nikki arrived at the scene, it was already filled with police cars and several ambulances. She'd made her way through the crowd of spectators, the fear in her gut mounting as she searched for Sarah.

The car—or what was left of the car—lay in a mangled heap of metal against a tree. Paramedics were putting someone into an ambulance. Onlookers hovered around the edges of the scene.

Oh God . . . there's no way anyone could have survived that wreck.

Nikki struggled to control the fear. She knew Sarah was alive. She'd spoken to her just minutes ago. After the accident. Which meant at least she was alive. But what had happened? The last Nikki had heard, Sarah had planned to spend the evening with a friend at the library. The library was eight blocks in the other direction.

She drew in a deep breath, but as hard as she tried, she couldn't control the panic building. She found a police officer who looked like he was in charge. "I'm looking for my sister. She's here somewhere. I think she was in the car. She's got long blond hair."

"Try checking the other side of the ambulances."

She found Sarah sitting on the curb a few yards away from the accident scene with one of the officers who was trying to calm her down.

"Sarah?" Nikki knelt down beside her, then turned to the officer. "I'm her sister."

The officer nodded, then took a step back, looking relieved. "I'll give you a minute, but she needs to go to the hospital to get checked out."

Nikki sat down beside Sarah and put her arm around her sister's shoulders. "It's going to be okay."

"Nikki . . . I'm so . . . so sorry. I never should have got in that car, but . . . I don't know. I wasn't thinking."

"Forget about all of that right now, sweetie." Nikki brushed a strand of hair out of Sarah's face and discovered a bruise developing. "All I want you to do is take a deep breath and try to calm down."

Sarah leaned forward. "They're taking the others to the hospital. I saw Ricky. He wasn't moving. I don't know if he's alive, Nikki. And Cassie . . . They had a hard time getting her out of the car. If anything happens to them . . ."

"Slow down. Why don't you start from the beginning and tell me what happened?"

Sarah was hiccuping now. "I told Mom and Dad that Cassie and I were going to study. And we were. But then Ricky and Hayden called. We were just going out for ice cream. I didn't think it was a big deal. And I promise we weren't drinking. But Ricky was driving too fast. I told him to slow down, but the guys just laughed at us . . . showing off . . .

"After that . . . I don't know what happened. I remember headlights coming at us. Cassie screamed and Ricky swerved. Everything went black. When I woke up, Cassie was crying and someone was trying to pull us out. Everything smelled like gas. Oh, Nikki . . . I've never been so scared. I called 911, but my seatbelt was jammed, and I couldn't get out."

"Did you call Mom and Dad?" Nikki asked.

"Not yet." She was crying again. "They're going to kill me."

"No, they're not. Trust me. They're going to be grateful you're okay."

"Ma'am." The officer was back. "We need to take her to the hospital and have her checked out. I'll find out where they're planning to take her and you can meet her there."

Nikki squeezed Sarah's hand. "I'll call Mom and Dad, and we'll meet you at the hospital."

Tears streamed down her sister's face. "They're going to be so mad at me."

"Yes, but they love you, Sarah. They're just going to be happy you're okay. It's going to be all right. Everything's going to be all right."

And it had been. For a while.

Cassie and the boys had made a full recovery, but the incident had sobered both girls. And reminded Nikki of how fragile life really was. Because at that moment, Nikki had no idea that in a few short weeks, Sarah would vanish. Sometimes life was messy. And sometimes, things didn't end up all right.

"Nikki . . . You okay?"

She turned to Jack as they stopped in front of her car. "Yeah. I'm fine."

They'd lost Sarah. Maybe forever. But they still had a chance of finding Lucy.

9

Nikki strode into the precinct behind Jack, who was carrying the Thai takeaway they'd picked up on the way back from the elementary school. When the governor had established the new task force, they'd been given space in the back of one of the precincts. The cramped quarters wasn't much more than four desks, but it was enough. Gwen sat at her uncluttered desktop beside the team's whiteboard that displayed a current photo of Lucy, photos from the crime scene, and an incomplete timeline of Lucy's last twenty-four hours.

Nikki stopped in front of Lucy's photo, a reminder of all the holes that still needed to be filled in. Who killed the men in her living room . . . who killed Mac . . . who killed George . . . and at what point had Lucy vanished into thin air.

"Looks like you've been busy?" Jack said. He set the three boxes on the edge of Gwen's desk, then scratched at his swollen wrist.

"Jack was in the mood for Thai," Nikki said,

99

handing out the boxes before sitting down on the edge of Gwen's desk and taking a bite of her noodles.

"Perfect. You guys are a lifesaver." Gwen grabbed one of the plastic forks in the sack. "I'm not sure how it got to be so late, but I'm starving."

"Good, because I got you that pork salad you liked last time."

"Perfect."

"Were you able to track down the reporter?" Nikki dug out a piece of chicken from her pad Thai noodles.

"Not yet." Gwen pulled off her trendy, black glasses and set them down on the desk in front of her. "Still waiting for her to return my call, but in the meantime, I've been digging into both Mac's and Lucy's backgrounds."

"Anything worth following up on?"

"To be honest, there isn't a lot. Besides a couple speeding tickets over the past decade, Mac's record is clean. He graduated top of his class from the University of Tennessee in Memphis with a double degree in chemistry and started working right away as a pharmaceutical scientist. A few years later, he got a master of science. There's been regular job promotions ever since, and even a handful of awards over the years. So far, there's no indication that I can find anywhere that he might have been involved in anything illegal."

"What about Lucy?" Jack asked.

"Her background isn't quite so cut-and-dried." Gwen leaned back in her chair. "I was able to verify she was raised in the foster care system and spent most of her time bouncing from one place to another. Apparently she never formed ties with most of the people she stayed with and, in the process, ended up with the wrong crowd. At seventeen, she ran away from her foster home at the time and moved in with a guy. She ended up with two misdemeanors on her record for cases of minor burglary."

"The records must have been sealed for her to get a job as a teacher," Nikki said.

"They were. Homicide was able to get a court order to have them opened. But since then, it looks as if she got her life together and became a model citizen."

"Any contact with old friends? Maybe someone who might have it out for her from her past?" Nikki asked.

"I was able to track down the juvenile court counselor who handled her case for the court system." Gwen nodded at her notes. "Two of Lucy's old friends are dead and a third one is currently in prison for armed robbery. So far I can't tie them together. At least nothing recently."

"Sounds like it was a good move to leave her past behind," Jack said.

"But that was a decade ago." Nikki looked back

at the board. "Not that this can't be related to her past, but she's a schoolteacher who spends her days with five-year-olds."

And so far the only thing they really knew about the Lucy of today was that she was both a model employee and friend, with a stable marriage. Something wasn't adding up. None of those things pointed to the reason her husband had just been murdered or why they'd found two dead men in her living room.

"Theories at this point?" Nikki threw out.

"We'll see if forensics backs any of this up, but my gut tells me that Lucy Hudson isn't as innocent as everyone says she was," Jack said. "Mac hires a private detective—George— because he thinks she's having an affair. She finds out and hires a couple thugs to take him out, but things go terribly wrong."

"What about the 911 call?" Nikki said. "Mac didn't sound like a man who was running from his wife. He was worried about her."

"Let's stick to what we do know for now." Gwen set her salad down and flipped through her notes. "There is one woman . . . a Flo Lerner, who's stayed in touch with Lucy over the years. And according to Lucy's phone records, she calls Flo every few weeks, including last week."

Nikki glanced at Jack. "We could go talk to her. See if she knows something."

Gwen nodded. "I agree. In the meantime, I'll

keep trying to get ahold of that reporter and Mac's boss. Apparently everyone's in meetings today."

Gwen's phone rang. She held up her finger and mouthed, *Hold on*.

"That was the ME's office," she said a few moments later. "They've just identified our two dead bodies from the house."

"Who are they?" Jack asked.

"A couple of local thugs. They've both got arrest records a mile long."

"Which fits into my theory that she hired them to knock off her husband," Jack said.

"The two of you go track down Flo Lerner. I'm going to try and track down the dead men's parole officers and see what I can find out. If we can discover who hired them, it will help us find Lucy."

Twenty minutes later Jack pulled into the parking lot of the Meadow Hills apartment complex. Past the swimming pool and tennis courts and manicured lawns of the apartment complex to number 75, which had a homemade wreath of yellow forsythia branches and white daisies.

A woman in her midsixties with silver hair and a lilac polka-dot dress answered the door.

"Mrs. Lerner?"

"Yes." A small dog started yapping beside her. She reached down and picked up the perfectly groomed Maltese. "I'm sorry. Sugar normally doesn't mind guests, but she's feeling out of sorts today."

"My name's Special Agent Nikki Boyd, and this is my partner, Jack Spencer. We'd like to talk to you for a few minutes about Lucy Hudson."

"Lucy?" The woman's gaze narrowed. "Is something wrong?"

Nikki hesitated. "May we come in?"

"Yes, of course."

They stepped into the outdated but cozy living room with a floral sofa and rose-colored carpet. A hutch in the corner was crammed full of Precious Moments collectibles and glass figurines.

Mrs. Lerner set the dog inside a rattan pet cage before turning back to them. "Please. Sit down. Can I get you anything? I have some sun tea I just brought in."

"Thank you, Mrs. Lerner, but I'm fine," Nikki said, sitting on the couch.

"Me too," said Jack.

"Has something happened to Lucy? I just spoke to her a few days ago, but . . ." Mrs. Lerner's voice trailed off as she sat down across from them on a matching recliner.

"How was she when you spoke with her?" Jack asked.

"She seemed . . . tired, though she kept assuring me everything was fine. You have to understand that Lucy's like a daughter to me. My Robert and I never had children of our own. So Lucy—and the others we took in through foster care—they were like family. Some I've lost track of over the years, but not Lucy. She was so good at keeping in touch. She's okay, isn't she? If anything happened to her . . ."

"That's why we're here, ma'am." Nikki bit her lip before continuing. It didn't matter how many times she'd sat in front of someone and told them the gut-wrenching reality that someone they loved might not be coming home. She never got used to it.

Because she'd been there.

She'd waited in her parents' living room while the police spoke to each one of them, then scoured the neighborhood and spoke to potential witnesses. She'd waited on the front porch for the detectives to return, saying they'd found her sister and it had just been a mistake. But that had never happened. And ten years later she was still waiting.

"Lucy didn't show up for work this morning," Nikki said finally. "We're doing everything we can to find her, but we need more information. That's why we're here."

Mrs. Lerner pressed her hand against her mouth and shook her head.

"Mrs. Lerner," Nikki said, "are you going to be okay?"

The older woman nodded, but her eyes filled

with tears. "I'm sorry, it's just that I've known Lucy since she was in high school. Poor girl had a tough start in life, but today . . . I couldn't be prouder of the way she turned her life around." She grabbed a tissue from the floral box beside her and dabbed at her eyes. "What about Mac? If something happened to her, he would have called me."

Nikki drew in a deep breath. "I'm sorry to have to be the one to tell you this, but Mac was found dead this morning."

"Dead?" The older woman's face paled. "That's not possible. I saw him . . . just two weeks ago. He stopped by to fix my vacuum cleaner. He was good about that. Fixing things around the house for me. Never complained about catering to an old lady's needs. Lucy . . ." Mrs. Lerner's voice cracked. "Please don't tell me she might be dead as well."

"We have no evidence that points to that right now, ma'am," Jack said. "This is why we wanted to talk with you. We understand you had regular contact with her."

"I spoke with her just last week." Mrs. Lerner shifted in her chair. "At first it was just a normal conversation. Lucy was so good about calling me every week or two, and visiting when she could. And when she comes she always brings me a grilled cheese sandwich from one of those food trucks—cheddar blend on sourdough—or some spicy hot chicken."

"And this call?" Nikki pressed. "Was there anything different about your conversation with her?"

"At first I thought she just wanted to talk. I get a bit lonely with Robert gone, and she knows that."

"How did she sound? Scared or anxious?"

"No. At least not at first." Mrs. Lerner's expression darkened. "We talked about how school was about out, our dogs, and their decision to try in vitro one more time. But after a while, the conversation shifted. She told me that something had come up—that she was going away for a while—and that she wouldn't be able to come by."

Nikki glanced at Jack. Had Lucy known something was going to happen in advance? Had she been the one behind Mac's death, or was someone after both of them?

"Mrs. Lerner," Nikki said. "This is really important. I need to know exactly what Lucy said."

The older woman shook her head. "She just said she couldn't give me any details yet, but that she'd be in contact as soon as she could, and that I shouldn't worry. Which, of course, is impossible. There has to be a connection with what she said and her disappearance, doesn't there?"

"It would make sense," Nikki said. "Did she say anything else?"

"No. I just don't understand. Lucy was special."

Mrs. Lerner walked across the living room to the fireplace, picked up an eight-by-ten silver-framed photo, and handed it to Nikki. "This is one of the few pictures I have of the two of us back then, and one of my favorites."

"She was beautiful," Nikki said.

"She came to live with us when she was fifteen. By then, I was the fifth or sixth home she'd been placed in, and I know there were at least two more after me. She was serious and quiet, but there was always something special about that girl."

Nikki stared at the photo of fifteen-year-old Lucy standing next to Mrs. Lerner. Dark curly hair, big brown eyes, and a lost look hiding behind a smile.

"Why did she leave your home?" Jack asked.

"Like most teenagers, Lucy struggled to find acceptance, but with her background, it was particularly tough for her. About a year after she came to us, she decided she wanted to find her birth mother. We were supportive of her, and she even tried living with her—her name was Jane —for a few months, but it didn't work out."

"Do you know where Jane is now?"

"She died of an overdose soon after. It was such a tragedy. After that, Lucy started running with the wrong crowd, and things started spiraling out of hand. I wanted her back, but at that time

108

we had a full household again, and she was placed somewhere else."

"Did you stay in touch back then?"

"Not like we do now. But I did hear from her every few months. I was always just grateful she was still alive."

Nikki handed the photo back to her. "What about her birth family? Besides her mother, does she have contact with any of them?"

Mrs. Lerner shrugged. "She has a half sister, but beyond that, no. And her birth father was never in the picture. As far as I know—and I think she would have told me—she never found him. Never wanted to, really."

"What about Mac? Where did she meet him?"

The older woman sat back down in her chair. "They met at a political fundraiser. It was sweet, really. She's always said that Mac was the man who saved her. For her it was love at first sight. He's a few years older than she is, but that's what she needed. They hit it off immediately. She told him about her past, but he didn't care. Six months later, he asked her to marry him. You can't imagine how happy I was when she told me she'd found someone like him. Mac was perfect for her. She'd come so close to losing everything. In trouble with the law and hanging out with the wrong friends. Mac, on the other hand, was stable and good for her. Now that he's gone, I don't know how she's going to handle things on her own."

Nikki leaned forward. "I know these questions are difficult, but we need to know about Lucy's relationship with her husband. Do you think it's possible she was planning on leaving him?"

"Leave Mac? Never. She loved him, and he was so good to her."

"So you don't believe there were problems in their marriage? Something she might have hidden from you?"

"They argued from time to time, but what couple doesn't? But to walk away from their marriage? No. I don't believe that for a moment."

"We understand they were having problems having children. That can put a lot of strain on a marriage."

"Are you thinking Lucy was involved in Mac's death?"

"From everything we've heard so far, I don't think so," Nikki said, "but we have to look into all the possibilities."

"There is no way she killed Mac. They'd been married almost seven years now, and he's always been good to her. Even with all the struggles she'd had getting pregnant. It was an emotional roller coaster, but he . . . he kept her grounded. Without him . . . No . . . there's no way she killed him."

"What about the fertility problems? Do you think that could have affected her?"

"Affect her, yes. But not to hurt Mac or run

away. She told me one day that even if she was never able to get pregnant, she still had Mac and her kids at school."

"What about her friends from her past?" Jack asked. "Did she have any contact with them?"

"She doesn't really talk about her past—not anymore. But I'm pretty sure she doesn't have contact with any of them. She's really done everything she can to make a fresh start, and from what I know, that included severing ties with that crowd."

"Is it possible that one of them had a grudge against her?"

Mrs. Lerner pressed her lips together, then shrugged. "It's possible, I suppose, but it's been years. I can't imagine someone holding a grudge that long."

"Then what about today? Is there anyone you know of who might want to hurt her?"

"Like who? She's a kindergarten teacher. Her students love her, and I know why. She's fantastic with them."

Nikki frowned as she stood up to leave, feeling they were still missing something. If Lucy was on the run, why?

"Are you going to be all right?" Nikki asked, hesitant to leave. "Can I call someone for you?"

Mrs. Lerner shook her head. "I'll be fine. My sister lives nearby. If I need someone, I'll call and ask her to come by."

Nikki pulled out a card with her number. "If you hear from Lucy, please give me a call."

The older woman's hands shook as she took the card. "Yes, of course. Just please . . . please find her."

"We're missing something," Nikki said as she and Jack walked back to the car.

"I agree," he said. "Too much isn't adding up. Perfect marriage. Perfect job. No one's life is perfect. Especially when there are two hit men in the scenario. Someone's hiding something."

"You don't really think she had her husband murdered?" Nikki asked.

"I'm definitely not ready to rule it out."

"I guess I'm not either." Nikki's phone rang and she grabbed it from her back pocket and put it on speakerphone. "What have you got, Gwen?"

"I think I've just found Lucy's car."

"Where?" Nikki asked.

"In a parking garage about ten minutes away from her house. I tracked it down using video footage, and the timeframe matches. She arrived last night just after seven."

Nikki stopped beside Jack's car. "Where did she go after that?"

"That's the strange thing. I've watched the video a dozen times. There's a time-stamped photo of her arriving, but there is no sign of her leaving the garage."

Nikki waited for Jack to unlock the car, then slipped into the passenger seat. "We're on our way there now. Keep checking all the cameras in the surrounding area. We need to find out where Lucy went."

10

4:26 p.m.
Parking garage, downtown Nashville

As Jack drove up the ramps toward the third floor of the parking garage, questions raced through Nikki's mind. The woman had been in this parking garage less than twenty-four hours ago, making it another point of reference to add to the timeline on the marker board. But would finding Lucy's car be enough to find Lucy?

And then there was the question of Lucy's involvement in her husband's death. Had she hired the men to have her husband killed, like Jack believed? Or had she shown up, found two dead bodies in her house, and then bolted? But if that was true, why not simply call 911 instead of running? And why park here, ten minutes from her house, in a parking garage?

Nothing was adding up.

"Looks like a red Honda Civic up ahead on our right," Jack said.

She checked the license plate as they passed. "769 . . . That's it."

Jack drove another dozen yards ahead until he found an empty spot and parked the car. They headed back toward the Honda.

Movement to the left caught Nikki's eye. Two men wearing ski masks crouched beside Lucy's car.

"Police!" Nikki pulled out her weapon as she approached the vehicle. "Come out with your hands up."

One of the men drew a weapon and fired it. The bullet embedded itself in the side of a van beside Nikki. Adrenaline rushed through her as she slid behind a cement pillar for cover. A second shot ricocheted off the pillar, inches from her head.

Nikki called Gwen on speed dial.

"We need backup," she said as soon as Gwen answered. "We've got an active shooter on the third level of the parking garage."

"They're on the run," Jack yelled.

Nikki dropped her phone back into her pocket, stepped slowly out into the open, then broke into a sprint behind the men. This was no coincidence. There was no way these were just a couple of random guys breaking into cars. If they worked for the same people who'd killed Mac—which she was going to assume they did— they weren't going to want to take a chance of blowing it again.

And she already knew they were willing to kill.

Her shoes pounded on the cement. A car alarm sounded. Bits of sunlight streamed through the sides of the darkened garage, creating shadows as the men ran between the cars. One of them shouted something before they split up.

"Take the one heading down," Jack yelled from right behind her. "I've got the other one."

She cut through the row of cars toward the ramp leading to level 2, sprinting after the one who'd shot at her. He swerved to the left, forcing her to skid over the hood of a vehicle in order to keep up. Her heart raced, lungs pumping frantically in order to keep up with the demand for air. He was tall, over six feet, with broad shoulders, but she was faster. And the gap between them was narrowing.

Movement to the right caught her eye. A woman was heading for her car with a young boy of seven or eight. Dressed in a gray Titans T-shirt, the boy tugged on his ball cap while the mom clicked on her key fob, ready to get into their car. Nikki shouted at them to move back as she ran through her options. She couldn't fire her weapon and take the chance of hitting an innocent bystander. But neither could she let this turn into a hostage situation.

In a split second the decision was out of her hands.

The man grabbed the woman from behind and

started dragging her toward the exit. The woman screamed as the boy disappeared behind the line of cars.

Nikki felt her heart plummet. The situation had just morphed into the worst possible scenario.

God, I need a way out of this one . . .

The man stopped, pressed the gun against the woman's temple, and held her in front of him. "Get. Back. Now."

Nikki took a step back but kept her weapon level in front of her. The woman was whimpering, and Nikki had no idea where the boy had gone. And while she knew the basic rules of negotiating, she also knew that, as with a missing person, if she failed, a life could be lost.

She sucked in a steadying breath. The guy had on a ski mask, so there was no way to try to read his expression beyond his eyes. But at the moment she didn't need to see any more of his face. He'd made his intentions perfectly clear. Whatever they were after was worth taking, no matter the cost.

Even the cost of someone's life.

Nikki caught the man's gaze. "I need you to let her go."

"Please do what she says," the woman pleaded.

He laughed. "I don't think so. And I won't hesitate to kill her if you try to stop me from getting out of here."

"This doesn't have to end with someone dying,"

Nikki said. "All you have to do is let her walk away."

"And then what? You just let me go? Like I said. Not happening."

"What's your name?" she asked the woman.

"You don't need to be talking to her," he said.

"Mindy." Her voice cracked.

"Good. Mindy, I want you to stay there and do what he says for right now." If she couldn't get him to let Mindy go, maybe she could get some answers from him. "Who hired you to find Lucy's car?"

"That doesn't concern you."

"Maybe not me, but it should concern you."

He hesitated. "Why?"

"Because you say you don't care if someone dies. Well, neither does your boss. Four of his men are dead right now."

"I don't believe you."

She could see the surprise in his eyes. At least he was listening to her.

"We found two men dead this morning," she said. "Both of them shot at close range. Another two were killed while trying to escape from the authorities."

He glanced at the ramp as if he were waiting for someone. They had to have a getaway vehicle. Or was there another person involved?

"Even if that's true," he said, "none of it matters right now."

A black van came speeding up behind him from the ramp below. Someone fired another shot. Nikki dove between two cars, her palms grinding into the rough cement.

She breathed in the smell of fuel, then pushed herself up. The van's brakes squeaked to a stop. The masked man threw the woman onto the pavement and jumped into the vehicle.

Sirens blared in the distance, but it was too late. She needed to find Jack. Needed to find the little boy. She pulled out her phone, called for an ambulance, then knelt down beside the woman.

"My son . . . You've got to find him. His name is Toby."

"I will. But first—are you okay?"

"I think I might have sprained my ankle when he pushed me down, but please." She started tugging off her shoe. "You've got to find Toby."

"I will, but I want you to wait here. I've already called for an ambulance."

"If they come back?"

She squeezed Mindy's hand. "They won't come back."

Two police cars pulled up, and the officers exited their vehicles. Nikki held up her badge and quickly explained the situation. They needed to block off the area and search Lucy's car, but even more urgently, they needed to find the boy. She hurried back toward where she'd watched him disappear while one of the officers went to stay with his mother.

She ran back down the line of cars where she'd last seen the boy. The contents of Mindy's purse were flung out across the cement. Lipstick, car keys, a wallet, a small container of breath mints . . .

She left the purse. Toby could be anywhere by now. There were dozens of cars. Dozens of places to hide. He could have run to another level or even made his way into one of the nearby stores. He had to be terrified.

Twenty feet ahead was the entrance to a stairwell. She ran to it and shoved open the heavy door. There he was, hovering on the landing.

A whoosh of air escaped her lungs.

"I've got him," she yelled back at the other officers, then crouched down beside him. "Hey . . . my name's Nikki. I'm a detective. This has been a scary day, hasn't it?"

Toby stared at the floor and nodded.

"Your mom's okay," Nikki said. "The bad guys are gone."

She touched his shoulder, but he jerked away, so instead, she held out her badge and let him touch it. "You're Toby, right?"

He nodded. "You're a detective?"

"I am. My job is to find people who are missing."

"Those men . . . they were trying to hurt my mom." He held his hands over his ears and started rocking. "They were shooting at her."

"Toby . . . I need you to listen to me. I just spoke to your mom. She twisted her ankle, but she's going to be fine. I promise."

A tear streaked down his cheek. "I saw their gun. I thought they were going to kill her."

"They can't hurt her. Not anymore." Nikki tugged on the bill of his ball cap. "Can I take you to your mom? She's worried about you too."

He looked up at her and nodded.

"She'll probably have to go to the hospital in an ambulance to make sure her ankle's okay. But there's nothing you need to worry about."

"Can I ride with her?" he asked.

Nikki grinned. "I'm pretty sure we can arrange that."

She stood up, opened the door leading back into the parking garage, and waited for him to follow.

"Did you catch them?" he asked. "The men who were shooting at us?"

Nikki reached out and took his hand. "Not yet, but we're going to."

Five minutes later, she watched the paramedics load Toby and his mother into the back of the ambulance as Jack escorted the second suspect in handcuffs into one of the police vehicles.

"You got him?" Nikki asked.

"Looks like it ended with a bit less drama than with your guy. Maybe you need to take up Taekwondo with me."

Nikki groaned. "Funny. Is he saying anything?"

"Not yet. I figure we can do a quick sweep of the car, then go down to the station and see what we can get out of him." They started toward Lucy's car. "I also called CSU. They should be here soon to go over the car."

Glass crunched beneath Nikki's shoes as she walked up beside the car. "What I want to know is, how did they find her car before we did? Does that mean she told them where it was?"

"They were clearly looking for something."

"Or maybe they're looking for Lucy," Nikki said as she started digging through the glove compartment.

Inside were all the typical items—proof of car insurance, city maps, a flashlight, and a first-aid kit.

What were those guys looking for?

Jack moved to the rear of the car to the open trunk. "So you're not buying my theory that she hired a couple of thugs to knock off her husband."

"Definitely not now. These guys have to somehow be connected. The two dead men at the Hudson home. The two men killed in the train accident, and now the men who broke into her car . . . If she wanted to have Mac killed, it's done. What's the rest of this for?"

"I agree there has to be a connection, but whether it's gang related or they were hired—"

"That's what we need to find out."

Jack stepped back from the trunk. "It doesn't look as if she took anything when she left."

"Even spare change and shopping bags," Nikki said. "So where has she been the past twenty-four hours?"

"Either someone took her, or this was a part of some plan."

"You're right." Nikki looked up at Jack. "She told Mrs. Lerner she was going away. She had a plan."

"To kill her husband and run," Jack said.

Nikki shook her head in bewilderment. "She parks the car here, then walks away and leaves it."

"But why here?"

Nikki tried to sort through the most obvious answers to his question. "Maybe there was another car."

"Another car? You mean someone picked her up? Now you're strengthening my theory. She kills her husband, then goes to meet her lover."

"In a parking garage?" Nikki asked.

"Why not?"

Nikki picked up her phone, dialed Gwen, and waited for her to answer, still not wanting to accept Jack's theory. "Gwen, we're on our way back to the precinct now, but I need you to recheck every bit of video footage around the same timeframe you had Lucy arriving at the parking garage. We need to find out where she went from this point. We'll be there in twenty minutes."

"You were right," Gwen said as Nikki and Jack walked up to her desk. "I missed it earlier, but there she is." She pointed to the computer screen at the car exiting the parking garage. "It's an older-model sedan that left the garage about ten minutes after Lucy arrived. I'm running the plates now."

"She's alone," Jack said. "And she looks scared."

Nikki studied Lucy's expression on the grainy screen. He was right. She was looking over her shoulder, as if she was worried someone was after her. But they still had no idea why she was running.

"They're still out there looking for her."

"And if they find her before we do?"

The knot in Nikki's stomach tightened. There was no doubt anymore that they were after Lucy now. And they were looking for something. Something worth killing her husband for. Something worth tracking her down for.

What secret are you hiding, Lucy?

If only there was a way they could communicate with her. Let her know they could keep her safe from whoever was after her.

But Nikki couldn't promise her that.

The thought tried to drag her back to a dark place. Because there were some promises you simply couldn't keep.

11

7:53 p.m.
Precinct

Nikki stood in front of the whiteboard in the middle of the squad room and felt the familiar frustration pulse through her. The few notations it held were a reminder of how little they knew. Setbacks always came with the territory, as most cases ended up being the proverbial one step forward, three steps back. And of course, there were the dozens of dead ends, eating up their very little precious time.

She set her coffee on her desk, then reached up to work out a knot in her shoulder. She and Jack had started interrogating Charles Bak, the man Jack had arrested, but he'd played the game before and lawyered up before they were able to get any information. On top of that, they'd spent the past few hours chasing down leads, but they were no closer to finding Lucy than they had been when they left the parking garage. No sign of the black van or the car Lucy had been photographed in. If Lucy really was on the run, she could easily be in another state by now.

Unless whoever was after her had already found her.

"Nikki . . . Jack . . . I think I might have something."

Nikki took a step away from the whiteboard and gave Gwen her full attention.

"I've been going through Lucy's credit card bills. There's one purchase that fits our timeframe. Wednesday night, she was at a pharmacy three miles from her house, less than five minutes before the 911 call."

"So she definitely wasn't at the house during the attack."

Gwen shook her head. "No, and I was able to check the cameras outside the store. It was Lucy."

"That's it, then," Nikki said, turning back to the board. "The point where she vanished."

"Yeah, but there are still a few interesting things," Gwen continued. "There hasn't been any activity on her credit cards since that purchase at the pharmacy, and no cash withdrawals."

"Maybe she went to a friend's house," Jack threw out.

"That's possible," Gwen said. "But over the past few months, Mac has been drawing cash out of their account on a fairly regular basis."

"How much?" Nikki asked.

"Roughly fifteen hundred a month for the past six months."

"That's quite a nest egg," Jack said.

Nikki stared at the board as the pieces of the puzzle started to come together. The second car . . . hoarding cash . . .

"They knew something like this was going to happen," she said. "And this isn't just a couple prepping for the end of the world. They knew these guys were going to come after them, and they had a plan."

Gwen picked up her ringing phone.

"If there was a plan, then they would have had an arranged meeting place," Jack said.

Gwen hung up a minute later. "We might have just found it," she said. "That was the missing persons hotline. We've got a possible sighting of Lucy at a hotel north of downtown."

"Who called in the tip?" Nikki asked.

"It was anonymous."

"An anonymous tip?" Nikki frowned. "Always love those. What are the chances there's any validity to the information?"

"Enough that I think it's worth the trip. The caller had information about what Lucy was wearing that wasn't included in the news broad-cast."

"Then we'll hope this isn't another wild-goose chase."

Twenty-five minutes later, Nikki and Jack pulled into the parking lot of a hotel that looked as if it hadn't been updated for years. The outside desperately needed a fresh coat of paint and a professional landscaper.

"I don't get it." Jack pulled off his seatbelt and reached for the door handle. "Lucy comes from a decent, middle-class neighborhood, with two cars, a mortgage, and a drawer full of nice jewelry, and she decides to crash here?"

"I was just thinking the same thing." Nikki got out of the car and started toward the front office beside him. "But maybe that's just it. The last place anyone would look for her."

The inside of the hotel was no better than the outside. At the front desk they were gruffly greeted by a man in his midfifties with graying hair and a well-endowed beer belly, who seemed as if he'd rather be watching the television at the end of the counter than dealing with customers. A glance around the dimly lit lobby showed no signs of security cameras.

Jack definitely had a valid point. What in the world was Lucy doing at a place like this?

Nikki flashed her badge, then quickly intro-duced herself and Jack before sliding a photo of Lucy across the counter. "Do you recognize this woman?"

The manager glanced at the photo, then turned back to the television. "No, sorry."

Jack grabbed the remote sitting beside him and flicked off the television. "My partner asked you a question. And in case you didn't understand the directions, in order to know if you recognize someone, you have to actually look at their photo."

The man wiped his hands across the front of his T-shirt, then shifted his gaze back to the photo. "Never seen her. Are you happy?"

"Are you sure?" Jack asked.

"I said I've never seen her."

"So you're not the one who called in with a tip?"

"Nope."

"We believe her life could be in danger," Nikki said. "If she was here, we need to know about it."

The manager glanced at the blank television screen. "I have people coming in and out of this place all hours of the day and night. There's no way I can remember every person who walks through those doors."

Nikki let out an irritated sigh. "I'm assuming you have some kind of guest registry?"

He grabbed an oversized book from beneath the counter and set it in front of her.

She skimmed through the list of names. "John Smith . . . Clark Kent . . . Are you kidding me?"

"It's not exactly against the law to use an assumed name. So long as they pay cash up front, I don't ask questions."

"Well, maybe you should." Jack looked at Nikki. "Because I'm not sure what my partner here is thinking, but I can see at least half a dozen violations, just from here, in this lobby. It wouldn't take long to get someone here from the Division of Environmental Health."

"Wait a minute—"

"I was thinking the same thing, actually." Nikki folded her arms across her chest and caught the man's gaze. "Fire extinguisher is out of date, there are obvious repair issues, and we haven't even taken a look at the place beyond the lobby."

"And here's another thing," Jack continued before the man had a chance to respond. "You see, I have these allergy issues that drive me crazy in certain situations." He started scratching his wrist again. "Now normally, they only bother me when I'm outdoors. Like hiking. But sometimes, especially when it comes to things like mold, I start sneezing and my eyes start watering, and then my chest starts tightening up. You might call it my own spidey sense. And guess what. My spidey sense is off the charts right now."

Nikki took a step back from the counter. "And I'm pretty sure I saw a couple roaches scurrying across the floor just now."

"Whoa . . . you don't have to go there. I might be behind on a few repairs, but you try getting decent help. It's not exactly easy." The man blew out a sharp huff. "Show me the photo again. I'll take another look."

Jack held up the photo.

"Maybe I've seen her."

"She would have checked in today or possibly

last night," Nikki said. "Does your memory go back that far?"

"She . . . yeah . . . she looks vaguely familiar."

"So she did stay here?" Jack asked.

"Yeah, I think so. She checked in last night. Paid for two nights up front."

Jack looked at Nikki. "Suddenly he remembers."

"So she's still here?" she asked.

The man glanced at the registry. "She's in room 117, though I can't tell you for sure if she's in there right now. Looks like she checked in as . . . Lucinda Roe."

"Care to show us the way?" Jack asked.

The manager heaved a sigh and slowly came around the counter. He led them down the narrow hall toward room 117. "So what did she do?" the manager asked. "Knock someone off?"

"She's missing."

"Oh . . . I'm sorry."

Nikki's brow rose at the hint of humanity, then she stepped inside a room that matched the rest of the hotel's seedy décor. The smell of stale cigarette smoke greeted her, along with out-of-date floral carpeting, gaudy bedspreads, and a water stain on the wall. It looked as if no one had cleaned the room for days.

Nikki turned back to the manager. "What do you remember about her?"

The manager shrugged. "Not much. She came in alone, carrying a small bag, and paid cash for the room. Seemed . . . nervous, I guess. Kept looking over her shoulder like she thought someone might be following her."

Nikki's frown deepened. For someone who didn't remember seeing her in the first place, he sure was coming up with a lot of details.

"Did she say anything about meeting someone?" she asked.

"No."

"Give any indication as to how long she was going to stay?" Jack asked.

"Like I said, she paid for two nights up front the night she arrived. Beyond taking her money, I didn't talk with her."

Nikki checked the closet. There was no suitcase. No clothes. No sign at all that Lucy had ever been here.

"Assuming she was here," Jack said. "She's gone."

The knot in Nikki's stomach grew. There had been no sign of the car Lucy'd been driving in the parking lot. If she'd planned to stay for an extra night, something must have spooked her.

"It doesn't look as if she plans to return." Nikki turned to the manager, who was still standing in the doorway. "What about security tapes?"

He furrowed his brow. "Most of our clientele prefer—how shall I put it—anonymity."

Maybe their initial thoughts had been right. Maybe Lucy thought no one would find her here. But if she'd run—again—then what had spooked her? Or had she been taken against her will? Had they killed her like they'd killed her hus-band?

Nikki moved into the rectangular-shaped bathroom and frowned at the moldy spots on the tile. What if Lucy had chosen to leave on her own? There were dozens of reasons why an adult might choose to disappear. But Mac's death pointed elsewhere. She still didn't buy the theory that Lucy had killed her husband, leaving behind everything she knew to start a new life. Then why? Why this hotel? Was she running from something or to something?

Witnesses claimed their marriage had been solid. That Mac adored her. Their one struggle had been trying to have a baby. Nikki had seen with her brother and sister-in-law how infertility could take a toll on a marriage, but had that been enough to motivate Lucy to murder?

After her sister's disappearance ten years ago, she'd researched every serial killer and kidnapping case across the state over the past twenty years, noting and memorizing every detail. And it was that knowledge that had landed her a position on the governor's Missing Persons Task Force. But so far, this didn't look like the work of a serial killer.

Lucy was running. They needed to find out from whom.

"Nikki?" Jack called to her from the bedroom. "Find anything?"

She stared at the sink. "Maybe."

There was a box of hair dye—radiant copper—along with snippets of hair on the floor, where Lucy had clearly tried to change the color and her look. She'd started to wipe up her mess, but for some reason, she'd left in a hurry before she had time to completely cover her tracks.

Something—or someone—had spooked her?

Nikki glanced down at the metal trash can next to the sink cabinet, hesitating before pulling out a blue box.

"Jack . . . take a look at this."

Jack walked in from the other room, then stopped as she pulled out the slender test kit with her gloved hand and held it up between them. "Lucy's pregnant."

"Maybe this is part of the reason why she's running. Her house was trashed, her husband's dead . . ."

"So either Lucy killed her husband and ran, or someone was after them both, and she somehow managed to escape."

"Give me a second, Jack."

Nikki hurried down the hall to catch up to the housekeeper. She glanced at the woman's name tag. Knowing the manager, there was a good chance he was paying her under the table and she was working long hours for little pay.

"Maria?"

"Yes." The woman nodded, a hint of fear in her eyes.

"My name is Nikki Boyd. I'm a detective with the Tennessee Bureau of Investigation. I look for people who are missing."

Maria looked past her down the hall. "I am sorry, but I must finish up my shift. My boss gets angry if we spend time talking to the guests."

"I'm not a guest, and I'm not here to get you into trouble. This will only take a few moments. Please. Someone called in a tip to our missing persons hotline, trying to help a young woman who stayed here last night. I need to know if that was you."

Maria grabbed a stack of towels from her cart and pulled them against her chest. "I don't know about that."

"Maria, please. We think this woman's life is in danger. And we know that someone from the hotel called in the tip. Whoever called in that tip wants to help her. And so do I."

Maria set the towels back down. "She checked in last night. Seemed dressed too nice to stay in a place like this, which was why I noticed. I could tell she was scared of something. I tried to be nice. Asked her if there was anything I could get her, but she said she just wanted to be left alone."

"Did she say anything else to you? Where she was going? What she was afraid of?"

"No. Like I said. She just wanted to be left alone."

"Did you call the police, Maria?"

"No, but . . ." Maria glanced down the hallway. "She . . . she was with someone."

"Someone checked in with her?" Nikki asked.

"No . . . he came in later."

"Do you remember what he looked like?"

"He had long, dark hair and tattoos on his arms."

"Do you know why he was meeting with her?"

"I see a lot of couples come in for an hour or two, then leave, but she didn't seem like that kind of person. Besides that, he didn't stay long. He came in with some food, then left about fifteen minutes later. But he looked . . . worried."

"Did you happen to overhear a name?" Nikki asked, realizing she was pushing her luck.

"His name is Gage," Maria said. "My boy-friend got a tattoo from him last year and recommends him to everyone. His shop isn't too far from here."

Nikki grinned. Bingo.

12

Nikki pulled into one of the empty parking spaces next to a local tattoo parlor a mile and a half from the hotel. She eyed the dimly lit exterior of the shop that was in dire need of a paint job and hoped the inside was cleaner than the hotel they'd just left.

"Ever thought of getting a tattoo?" Jack asked as they walked up the narrow sidewalk.

Nikki noted the flashing red TATTOO sign next to the front door and laughed. "I'm not sure which would scare me the most. The needle or my mom's reaction. She calls them 'job inhibitors.' I thought she was going to faint when my brother came home with one."

"Now that's funny. My mom had half a dozen tats the last time I saw her."

Nikki stepped inside the shop in front of Jack. Surprisingly, the inside of the place looked both clean and uncluttered with its black tiled floor and indigo walls. Books of tattoo designs lay in stacks along a rectangular table, while intricate, colored designs hung on the walls. On the far side of the small room, a woman with tattoos up her arms and at least a dozen piercings worked on an intricate tat on a client's back to the constant humming of the tattoo machine.

A man matching the description the maid had given looked up from a second workstation before shooting Nikki a broad smile. His white tank top showed off body art covering his arms and chest, and on his head was a black fedora. "Wait. Don't say anything. Let me guess . . . a row of hearts along your shoulder blade."

Nikki's eyes widened, taken off guard by the comment. "No . . . I'm not here—"

"Second guess." He tilted his head and steepled his hands in front of his face. "Definitely not a skull or a pop-cultural reference. Maybe something sentimental. What about a favorite quote or a dragonfly?"

"I think you should go for it, Nikki." Jack nudged her, clearly amused. "A dragonfly on your ankle or shoulder blade would be cute."

Nikki smiled back at the man, then held up her badge as Jack chuckled beside her. "We're looking for Gage."

"That would be me." He took a step back and held up his hands. "I'm going to take a wild third guess here and venture that neither of you are here for a tattoo."

"Third time's the charm," Nikki said. "I'm Special Agent Boyd and this is Agent Spencer."

"Wait a minute." Gage glanced across the room to where the other artist had stopped her work to watch what was going on. "I paid my dues in prison and now run a legitimate business. I've been approved by the health department, have a current license, and—"

"Relax," Jack said. "We're not here to arrest you. We just want to talk to you about Lucy Hudson."

"Lucy?" The man's shoulders dropped. "Do you know where she is? I've been trying to get ahold of her all day."

"We were hoping you knew. She's been reported missing. We understand the two of you are friends and that you saw her last night."

Nikki tried to read Gage's reaction. He didn't look surprised, but his expression remained guarded.

"Yeah. We're friends. Good friends. The two of us go all the way back to high school."

"And the last time you saw her?"

Gage glanced across the room to where his colleague was still watching them. "Why don't we talk in my office. It's a bit cramped, but it will be more private."

The tattoo machine started buzzing again as the two followed him inside the other room. Nikki sat down on a stool next to Jack. The walls here were also covered with dozens of prints, every-thing from simple phrases and drawings to more elaborate full-color designs. And as much as the whole process of permanently marking her body with something she might hate in ten years didn't appeal to her, the man was clearly an artist.

"Are these all your own designs?" she asked.

"Yeah." He flipped around a metal chair and straddled it. "Pretty much everything we do here is original."

"You're good," she said, hoping to break the ice between them. "Very good."

"Thanks." He shrugged off the compliment. "You're looking for Lucy?"

Nikki nodded. "We understand you saw her last night."

"I did. She showed up out of the blue. I hadn't seen her for . . . I don't know . . . at least six months. But when she called me, I could tell she was upset about something. She said she needed to talk."

"So you went to see her?"

"Yeah. She told me she was staying up the street at this sleazy hotel. Man, that place is such a dump. Cops must go there at least two or three times a week. So I was worried. Said she could crash at my place, or I'd give her money for a nicer hotel, but she said money wasn't the problem. Said she was looking for a place where there weren't any security cameras. A place where she could stay a couple nights and no one would ask questions."

Nikki glanced at Jack. Lucy had definitely chosen the right place. And so far their theory was holding up. Lucy was on the run and trying to avoid a paper trail.

Nikki gripped the sides of the stool. "Why did she want to see you?"

"Like I said, Lucy and I go way back. Before she even knew Mac. We've always been close."

"Were the two of you ever romantically involved?" Jack asked.

"Lucy and me?" Gage slapped his thighs. "No way. I was more like a big brother. Our paths crossed for the first time in the foster care system when we were teenagers, and we've managed to stay in touch ever since."

"Did you ever meet Mac?"

"A couple times, but she didn't want him knowing everything about her old life. She wanted to keep those two worlds separate. And frankly, I understood. It's hard to blame her for wanting to step away from her past. She had a chance to start a new life when they got married. Before that, she hung around with a pretty rough crowd with some seriously messed up dudes. Mac kind of saved her from all that."

"Why did she need your help?"

"When she called me, she was completely freaked out. Told me she was afraid that something horrible had happened to Mac, and she was convinced someone was after her as well. She didn't know if he was dead or alive, and she didn't know who else to turn to."

"She was right," Nikki said, surprised he hadn't found out on the news. "Someone murdered Mac last night."

Gage gripped the back of the metal chair and shook his head. "You don't understand how that's going to crush her. She talked about him constantly. About how well he was doing at his job. How they just bought a house and were planning to have a baby . . ."

"Do you believe there's any chance that Lucy was involved in Mac's death?"

Gage frowned. "Lucy? No way. But I don't understand. I thought you said she was missing."

"She *is* missing. But her husband is dead. We have to look at all the options."

"You've got it all wrong. There's no way she'd have done anything to hurt Mac. Personally, I thought he seemed a bit uptight, but there was never any doubt she adored him."

"I need to know everything she told you."

Gage took off his hat and tossed it onto the table beside him. "She told me that Mac had been acting strange the past few weeks. A couple days ago, she confronted him. Thought he might be having an affair or something. But he told her that something was going on at his job. He works for some big company and believed there was something corrupt going on there."

"Specifically?"

"Said he mentioned something about counterfeit drugs, but he wouldn't tell her specifics. Said that the less she knew, the safer she'd be. But apparently it was something big he was about to expose and a lot of heads were going to roll."

Which would have given someone motivation to stop him. But who? Mac was dead, George was dead . . .

"Did he have evidence?" Jack asked.

"He'd hired some private investigator to help get him proof, but she wasn't sure what he'd found out or who was involved."

George.

"Then what did she want from you?" Nikki leaned forward, trying to put the pieces together. "Money?"

Gage shook his head. "No. She said she had enough money. She wanted the name of a . . . contact of mine."

"And who is this contact of yours?"

"Listen . . ." Gage squirmed. "I'd do anything for Lucy. I meant it when I said I was going straight, but I still have a few . . . questionable connections from my old life."

"Lucy's life is at stake," Nikki said. "That's all we're here for."

Gage grasped the back of his neck. A vine tattoo ran down to his collarbone with vibrant blues, yellows, and greens. "Fine. He makes fake identities."

"Why did she want a fake identity?" Jack asked.

"After Mac called last night, she wanted options. And she knew I had connections."

"Wait a minute." Nikki glanced at Jack. Gwen had checked through Lucy's phone records. There had been no calls that had come through from Mac's cell phone. "When did he call her?"

"Last night. I'm not sure what time. She said she was at the pharmacy picking something up and he called. That's how she knew he was in trouble. But the connection got cut off. She hadn't been able to get ahold of him since. Now I know why."

"What did he say to her?"

"Told her they were putting their plan in action."

"What was the plan?"

"He'd started doing all this prepper stuff. You know, like people gearing up for the end of the world, except he was preparing to disappear. So he had this plan set in place in case they needed to escape. A car filled with emergency supplies like cash and weapons. I'm not sure what all. But stuff they'd need if they had to run."

"Where was she supposed to go?"

"If they weren't together, they were supposed to meet at a truck stop outside of town, but he never showed up. And Lucy didn't want to leave on her own, especially when she was convinced he was in trouble."

"Who was he running from?"

"Lucy didn't know. I guess he thought the less she knew, the safer she'd be, but it doesn't seem to be turning out that way. Apparently someone in the company he worked for. Mac hid the evidence somewhere that he was gathering for proof."

"Did she know where he hid the evidence?"

Gage shook his head. "No, but she really wanted to find it. Thought it might be something she'd end up needing. You know . . . for insurance."

"And you don't know where she is now?"

"She told me to call her this morning, but I haven't been able to get ahold of her."

"Why run? Why didn't she just go to the police?"

"I told you, she'd had a tough past." Gage stood up and shoved the chair back under the desk, then leaned against it. "Let's just say that it's hard for her to trust the police."

"But what about you? You didn't think about calling the police?"

"I did, actually. I thought—in this case anyway—that would be the best thing."

"But she didn't agree."

"Like I said, she was totally freaked out. She didn't know who to trust. And I don't exactly blame her. She realizes someone's after her husband and that the people after him are more than likely after her as well. And if they find her . . ."

"How can we find her?"

"I wish I knew. Last night she promised me she'd wait around until this morning. I thought I could pull a few favors in from some friends and come up with a plan, but I needed some time. When I called her this morning, she never answered." He shook his head. "But I don't think she'll leave town until she finds the evidence Mac hid."

"Did she know her husband had been shot?" Nikki asked.

Gage shook his head. "No. Like I said, she just knew something was wrong when he wouldn't answer."

The knot tightened in the pit of Nikki's stomach. "I know she's running, and I know she's scared, but we can help her. If she calls you again, please have her contact me."

"I will, I promise, but please . . ." Gage pushed away from the desk. "You've got to find her before they do."

Nikki headed for her car with Jack, her mind still shuffling through the pieces. Mac had contacted Lucy, and even if he hadn't told her he'd been shot, it wasn't going to take long for her to figure it out simply by watching the news. But she wasn't the only one after whatever it was Mac had. Presumably that's what the two men at their house were after. But if it wasn't at their house, then where was it?

"So Mac finds out someone's making counterfeit drugs at Byrne Laboratories," Nikki said, "and he's about to blow the whistle when someone finds out and tries to keep him quiet."

"Except he knows someone will be coming after him, and he's prepared."

Nikki's phone rang, and she pulled it out of her pocket. It was Gwen. She put her on speaker.

"Nikki, I just got an email from the reporter, Mallory Philips. She's on a flight back to Nashville from LA. She wants to meet with you in the morning. Alone."

Nikki unlocked the car, then stopped beside the driver's door. "Why me?"

"She didn't say. Just that it was urgent."

Nikki hesitated. She didn't have time to chase another dead end. But if this was a valid lead, she also couldn't afford to miss whatever information the reporter might have.

"You think she's legit?" Nikki asked, sliding into the car as Jack got in on the passenger side.

"I looked her up online. She's a freelance writer who works for a number of publications. She's written some articles on counterfeit drugs over the past few years."

"Does she think Mac was involved in counterfeiting drugs?"

"I get the impression he might have been collecting evidence and she was helping him. It was scary, actually. Some of the things she's researched. If what she says is true, approximately three-fourths of counterfeit drugs come from overseas—up to fifty percent of what is sold in some countries."

"Isn't that going to kill people?" Jack asked.

"It does, but according to the articles she's written, most of these deaths go unreported."

"What about here in the US?" Nikki asked.

"It's not as common, but that doesn't mean it doesn't happen. Especially when a large percentage of the active ingredients in prescription medicine are made overseas. She listed a couple cases of high-priced cancer drugs and contaminated steroid injections where dozens died."

Nikki frowned. If this was what Mac was investigating, they were looking at a problem far more extensive than a simple domestic situation. "What time does her flight get in?"

"It's scheduled to arrive at ten, but give me a second . . . the flight's fifteen minutes late."

"I've got an even better idea." Nikki glanced at her watch. She had just enough time to drop Jack off and meet the flight if she wanted to see Mallory Philips tonight. And if the reporter really did know something about Lucy, it would be worth it. "Send her another message and tell her I'll meet her at the airport."

13

10:26 p.m.
Nashville International Airport

Nikki glanced at her watch as she hurried from the short-term parking lot toward baggage claim. A two-car accident on the freeway had gotten her there later than she'd planned, but hopefully Mallory had received Gwen's message and would wait for her.

Inside the glass doors of the baggage claim area, she scanned the crowd huddled around the carousel waiting for their bags while Ronnie Milsap played in the background. According to the digital arrival screen, Mallory's plane had landed fifteen minutes ago. If she had checked luggage, she should be here. Nikki pulled out her phone for a second look at the photo Gwen had sent her, then glanced toward the exit. There was always the chance she hadn't checked any luggage, which would mean she'd head straight for her car.

Someone standing on the edges of the crowd caught her attention. A man with reddish-brown hair hung back, wearing a brown bomber jacket and a pair of earphones. He was probably waiting for someone like she was, but something still felt off. She tried to shake the unease and went back to looking for Mallory. Because it had simply been one of those days that had brought her to the edge both physically and emotionally. This airport served thousands of passengers on a daily basis. There was nothing unusual about a man standing in the airport, waiting.

Nikki finally spotted Mallory heading for the exit as the crowd began to thin. Midthirties, long, dark hair pulled back in a ponytail just like in the photo, and pulling a silver hardback suitcase. Nikki glanced to where the man had been standing, but there was no sign of him now. She let off a short huff of relief, then hurried toward the other side of the carousel, hoping to catch Mallory before she slipped outside.

Halfway toward the doorway, she saw him again. Stopping when Mallory stopped, walking just a few feet behind her. Keeping his distance, but definitely following her.

Nikki picked up her pace to a slow jog until she was right beside Mallory. "Mallory Philips?"

The woman grasped the strap of her pink computer bag that was slung over her shoulder. "I'm sorry, do I know you?"

"Keep walking." She pulled out her badge. "I'm Nikki Boyd. Special Agent with the Tennessee Bureau of Investigation. You asked to meet with me. I left a message on your phone."

"I'm sorry. I haven't even turned on my phone yet to check my messages."

Nikki glanced behind her. The man had slowed down, as if he was trying to figure out what to do. "Listen, I know you're going to have questions, but I need you to come with me. Now."

Mallory paused at the pedestrian crosswalk and caught Nikki's gaze. "I don't understand. What's wrong?"

"You're being followed."

"What are you talking about?"

Nikki pressed her fingers against the woman's arm and started walking toward where she'd parked her car. "Just stay up with me. There's a man behind us wearing a brown bomber jacket. Have you ever seen him before?"

Mallory glanced behind her. "No. But it wouldn't be the first time I've run into a crazed stalker. It kind of goes with the territory of my job sometimes."

"Who knows you were coming back to town tonight?" Nikki asked, looking for security. On her own, she'd go after the man, but right now her number one priority had to be ensuring Mallory's safety.

"I don't know," Mallory said. "I didn't exactly keep it a secret. I've been doing a lot of posting on Twitter."

Nikki glanced behind her again, feeling an eerie sense of déjà vu sweep over her as they stepped into the parking garage. Her shoes echoed against the concrete. Shadows hovered around them. Had Mallory's connection to Mac and Lucy put her life in danger as well?

"I don't see him now," Mallory said.

"I don't either," Nikki said. But that didn't mean he wasn't still out there. "Is your car here?"

"Yeah. In economy parking."

"I can arrange for someone to come get it, but in the meantime, I think you should come with me."

"Wait a minute." Mallory stopped beside a black Hummer. "I need to know what's going on."

"You know Mac and Lucy Hudson?" Nikki said.

"Yes. In fact, I was supposed to meet with Mac tonight, but I ended up having to take a later flight. I haven't been able to get ahold of him."

Nikki felt her stomach drop. Mallory didn't know Mac was dead.

"I'm sorry. I guess I assumed you knew." Nikki hesitated, wishing she didn't have to drop a bombshell. "Mac was found murdered this morning."

"Oh no . . ." Mallory's chest heaved.

"Are you all right?"

"He's dead?"

"I'm sorry. We're still trying to figure out who killed him."

"You don't understand. He knew this was going

to happen. Even thought someone was following him. They have the resources and the motivation to bury this. That's why he was making plans to run." Mallory's voice was laced with panic. "Where's Lucy?"

Nikki started walking again. "She's missing."

"Whoever killed her husband . . . they're going to find her."

"Not if I have anything to do with it."

Nikki popped open the trunk for Mallory's suitcase, then motioned for her to get into the passenger seat. She had dozens of questions to ask, but she wasn't going to be able to relax until she had Mallory out of there. She shifted into reverse and quickly left the parking garage, heading back toward the highway and hoping her concerns were groundless.

"Where are we going?" Mallory asked.

Nikki caught the fear in her voice. "Back to my precinct. You'll be safe there."

Forty minutes later, Nikki slid a cup of coffee with extra cream and sugar across the conference room table toward Mallory, then sat down across from her. They'd driven to the precinct without saying much beyond basic small talk. The young woman was clearly shaken, and Nikki had decided it was better to give her some time to relax so she'd open up with her now.

"I really don't need any caffeine this late at

night," Mallory said, taking a sip, "but I'm so wired at this point, I don't think it matters."

"You okay?" Nikki asked. "You mentioned back at the airport that you'd been stalked before. Have you been threatened as well?"

Mallory shrugged. "A couple of times. I end up stepping on a lot of toes while digging up information some people don't want uncovered."

Nikki sat back in her chair and pushed away the fatigue threatening to take over. The past fifteen hours had pushed her, but her work was far from over. "Can I ask you a question before we get started?"

"Sure."

"Why did you insist on talking to me alone?"

Mallory cupped her hands around her coffee. "After your partner called me this morning, I did a little research. I found out that your sister went missing ten years ago. Taken by the Angel Abductor."

"You would have had to do a bit of digging to find that out."

"I'm good at digging. That's my job."

"Yes, but I'm not sure what that has to do with Lucy Hudson," Nikki said, wanting to put the pieces together.

"Nothing. Not directly, anyway. But I wanted to talk to you, because you understand what it means to lose someone you love, and I need someone who will be sympathetic. Most people tend to think I'm either paranoid or crazy when I start telling them about the issues with our drug supplies."

Nikki folded her hands on the table, still not certain where this was going. "Gwen looked up some of the articles you've written. She said you'd written quite a few on the problem of counterfeit drugs. You throw out some pretty heavy accusations."

Mallory leaned forward. "They're not just accusations."

"And your connection with Mac?"

"He read those same articles and contacted me."

"So Mac believed someone in his company was making counterfeit drugs?" Nikki asked.

Mallory nodded. "Drug companies work hard to combat counterfeiting, so these guys are getting more and more sophisticated. Unless you're a trained expert, it's almost impossible to tell the difference. But Mac was that expert. And he was trying to find enough evidence to prove it was happening at Byrne Laboratories."

"Okay," Nikki said. "So walk me through this. What exactly are we talking about?"

"Counterfeit drugs are drugs that have the wrong ingredients or are lacking the active ingredients."

"So the manufacturer skimps on the ingredients to up the profits," Nikki said.

"Exactly. And the way to make the most money is to get your counterfeit drug into the legal supply chain here in the US."

"And that's possible?"

"It's not as prevalent as it is in other countries." Mallory took another sip of her coffee. "In places like Africa, some believe that up to seventy percent of the market is counterfeit. The cheaper a drug can be produced, the higher the profit margin."

Nikki shook her head, trying to fathom the consequences if what she was saying was true. And trying to see how all of this was tied to Lucy and Mac. "What exactly did Mac know?"

"He believed someone found a way to breach the supply chain here in the US with a counterfeit antibiotic called Aryox."

"You have proof?"

"Mac was working to get proof inside the company." Mallory drummed her powder-blue polished nails against the table. "I believe at least five people are dead from this antibiotic, including three children. And more than likely that's just the tip of the iceberg. There are others out there, I just haven't found them yet."

Nikki felt a chill run through her despite the warmth of the room. If what Mallory was telling her was true, they were looking at a clear motive to want to keep this quiet. And motive enough to kill Mac, Lucy, and possibly even Mallory.

"Say for instance you need to renew your heart medication," Mallory continued. "You go to your neighborhood pharmacy to fill your prescription. You expect to leave with a lifesaving drug. But what if someone decided to take a shortcut with the ingredients in that tiny orange pill?"

"Someone dies," Nikki said.

"Exactly. And these aren't just statistics." Mallory grabbed the pink computer bag beside her, pulled out a photo of a young girl, and set it on the table between them. "This is Audrey Knight. She's four years old and lives here in Nashville. Two weeks ago, she was diagnosed with an ear infection. Her mother took her to her primary care doctor, who prescribed antibiotics. Five days ago, when she should have been playing with her friends at preschool, she was taken to the emergency room. She's currently in a coma."

Nikki stared at the photo of the little girl with blond pigtails and bright blue eyes, smiling at the camera. "And you think this antibiotic—Aryox—is to blame?"

"I've been in contact with the doctor and her mother, and everything about this case fits," Mallory said. "You have to understand that counterfeit drugs are a billion-dollar industry across the globe, and when the formula of the drug is incorrect, you're not getting the right dose of medicine."

"So when your child takes an antibiotic for an ear infection"—Nikki tapped her finger against the photo and frowned—"she ends up lying in a coma in ICU."

"Exactly. It's like art forgery," Mallory said.

"The pill always looks identical to the real medication—either brand name or generic—but that's where the similarities end. The counterfeit ones can sometimes contain ingredients like chalk, flour, sugar, or even floor wax."

Nikki took in the information, still not ready to make a judgment, but definitely willing to keep an open mind. "Here's what I don't get. Surely it isn't the intent of the counterfeiters to kill off their patients. Seems like that would be counter-productive. What if there was an autopsy and authorities discovered the counterfeit?"

"That's true, but in the end it all comes down to money. And not only is it easy money, but even if they're caught, they know they'll be back on the streets with little punishment because of the lax laws that are in place."

"So what are the drug companies doing about this?" Nikki asked.

"Here in the US they spend enormous resources to fight the counterfeiting, including hiring private investigators and security teams. But as soon as they shut down one factory, another one opens up. In other countries, they work on licensing and regulating drug vendors, along with educating consumers and disrupting fake drug criminal networks. Some countries are even putting into place mobile phone verification programs where the consumer can find out by text whether or not the drug is real."

Nikki looked again at the photo of Audrey. "How did you find out about her?"

"Her mother believed something wasn't right and started doing her own investigation on the internet. Two days ago, she called me. She's looking for answers and hoping it's not too late to save her daughter."

"This is somehow personal to you, isn't it?" Nikki asked.

Mallory's fingers tightened around her coffee cup as she dropped her gaze. "I lost someone. We were never able to prove if there was a problem with the medication, but I'm positive that's what it was. And now, I don't want someone else to go through what I did."

"I'm sorry."

Nikki knew how easy it was for the past to motivate the present. How Sarah's disappearance had been enough to change the direction of her life. And even ten years later, she had no intention of simply walking away.

"Do you know where Mac kept his evidence?"

Mallory shook her head. "No, but it needs to be found, so whoever's behind this can be stopped. Plus there needs to be a push to put a ban on the drug by the FDA before someone else dies. Before Audrey dies."

"That's going to take time," Nikki said.

"You don't understand. There isn't time." Her voice rose to an almost frantic pitch. "A girl is dying, and someone has to put a stop to this, because she isn't going to be the only one."

"I promise I'll do everything I can to find both Lucy and Mac's evidence."

"What about getting the FDA to reevaluate the drug?"

Nikki sensed and even understood the other woman's frustration, but she was talking about going up against a pharmaceutical company and banning a drug already approved by the FDA. And whether or not the executives running the company knew what was going on, if all her accusations were true, there had to be people on the inside involved who had already made it clear they intended to do everything in their power to stop anyone who got in their way. It was going to take far more than a few phone calls to put a stop to this.

"I don't know a lot about the process," Nikki said, "but I know the FDA is active in identifying and understanding the effects of a drug. And if a health risk is detected—"

"If a health risk is detected? A little girl might lose her life because of this." Mallory grabbed her purse and headed toward the door. "I thought you would be different, but you don't really get it, do you. And that's the problem. This isn't going to stop if nothing changes."

Nikki stood up. "Mallory, wait. I meant what I said. I will look into this situation and do everything I can, but I don't think it's safe for you out there right now. There are at least four people dead, plus Mac. And if what you say is true, they're going to do whatever it takes to stop this from coming out."

"I'll be fine." Mallory swung open the door to the conference room, pausing to catch Nikki's gaze. "But I'm going to figure out a way to put a stop to this."

Nikki stepped into the hallway behind Mallory, who was already on her cell phone. When she ended the brief call, Nikki offered to have someone take her to her car, but Mallory brushed her off and walked out. Wondering how their conversation had gone from good to bad so quickly, Nikki made her way to the squad room where Gwen and Jack were busy running down leads.

"Everything okay?" Gwen asked as Nikki sat down at her desk.

She picked up a pen and tapped it against the desktop. "She believes that Mac was about to blow the whistle on a counterfeit drug ring that had managed to infiltrate the legal supply line at his work. She told me he was working on putting together his evidence and had made a plan for him and Lucy to escape if it came to that."

"That would explain the ditched car and the hair dye," Jack said. "And how she's been able to get around without using her credit cards."

"Exactly. Though their plan didn't exactly go the way they'd hoped."

"Where's his evidence?" Gwen asked.

"I don't know, but we need to find it."

Because time was running out, and whoever was behind this was desperate to tie up all their loose ends. And if they found Lucy first, they wouldn't hesitate to kill her.

14

12:17 a.m., Friday
Outside Nikki's loft apartment

Nikki slipped out of her Mini Cooper, then glanced at her watch, surprised it was already almost half past midnight. Exhaustion had managed to leak into every pore of her body, soaking into her muscles and joints. But it was more than just the physical demands that had come with the day. The case had taken a toll emotionally as well.

Gwen had seen the shadows beneath her eyes and had insisted she go home and sleep a few hours. As much as she wanted to continue working the case, she knew Gwen was right. They still needed to pay a visit to Mac's boss and follow up on Mallory's claims that a counterfeit drug ring was behind Mac's death, among a dozen other things, but more than anything, they needed to find another clue that would lead them to Lucy. And in order to do that, she needed to be able to think clearly.

She locked her car, then headed for her apartment building. A street lamp shone above her as she crossed the parking lot, casting a long shadow next to her. Besides the noise of a few passing cars, the night air was still, but all she could think was, where was Lucy tonight? Had she checked safely into another cheap hotel, or—as much as she wanted to ignore the niggling thought—had they managed to find her and kill her?

Someone moved in the shadows near the entrance of the building. The tiredness that had come over Nikki quickly slipped away. Whoever had killed George might not be after her, but that didn't mean she was planning to take the chance of getting caught in the line of fire again.

"Nikki?"

She let out a sigh of relief at the sound of Tyler's voice.

"Hey . . ." She stopped a few steps from him, surprised he'd come by so late. "I didn't expect to see you tonight. Especially not this late."

"I know, I just . . ." He looked at her as if he were trying to come up with an excuse as to why he was here. But he didn't need an excuse to see her.

"You okay?" she asked.

"Yeah." He shoved his hands into the front pockets of his jeans. "I was just out for a drive and thought I'd stop by and see if you were home yet. I didn't see your car, so I decided to wait around."

She smiled at him, not surprised at the automatic calming effect his presence had on her.

"Where's Liam?" she asked.

"Spending the night with my mom. They're planning to go to the zoo tomorrow. I think he'd live there if they'd let him."

Nikki laughed. "She's great for him. For both of you, really. But do you know what time it is?" She stifled a yawn. As glad as she was to see him, all she really wanted to do was crawl into bed and sleep for a few hours.

"Late. I probably shouldn't have come. It's just that I've been trying to call you for the past couple hours, and I couldn't get through." He shot her a sheepish grin. "I was worried."

"Sorry. I was in an interview and turned off my ringer."

She searched his face, trying to read his expression. This was more than just him being worried about her. Today had brought with it memories from the past of both Katie and George. And she knew those memories would be overwhelming at the least. Painful, too, as he continued to process what had happened. Moving on from a loss was never easy. Especially with constant reminders of that loss.

And today had been one of those days.

"You couldn't sleep, could you?" she said, noting the dark shadows beneath his eyes.

"No . . ." He let out a soft chuckle. "But I feel also like I put you in a bad place today. I know your boss wasn't too happy with you for insisting you stay on the case when I was involved."

"None of what happened today was your fault. And in the end he trusted me to handle things without getting involved emotionally. Everything's okay."

"Good."

Over the past year, she'd learned to read his moods. Learned to tell when he wanted company, and when helping the most simply meant being there and not saying anything. And she'd discovered how much she enjoyed his company even when it just meant sitting together on the couch and catching a movie. But tonight he'd sought her out, and she didn't buy that he was here just to make sure she was okay. At least not completely.

"What's really going on?" she asked.

"Honestly . . ." He caught her gaze beneath the yellow light of the street lamp. "I've been worried about you. The boat. The sniper. George getting shot right beside you. And then I saw on the ten o'clock news that two detectives got fired on in a parking garage. That was you, wasn't it?"

She bit her lip and nodded. He understood her well enough to know that beneath the veneer of professionalism she kept intact were layers upon layers of emotions she worked every day to keep contained. Layers all wrapped up in anything but a neat and tidy package. But that was life. And she'd decided years ago she was willing to deal with the emotional consequences her job brought with it.

"I don't know what's going on," he continued, "but clearly this is bigger than George doing late-night surveillance."

She nodded. "Yes. It is."

"I just wanted to make sure you got home okay. When you didn't answer . . . I don't know, I started imagining the worst."

"I'm fine, Tyler. Really. This is my job and I'm good at what I do. You don't have to worry." She stopped herself from brushing her hand down the side of his face, wanting—needing—to connect with him. "Katie was the worrier."

She bit her lip again, wanting to take back the words the moment they came out. "I'm sorry."

"Don't be. Katie would have been the first to admit that. She's the one who wanted me to leave the military. She couldn't handle not knowing if I was going to come home alive or in a casket."

While she and Katie had been best friends for

what had seemed like forever, the biggest differ-ence between them had ended up being Nikki's job. Katie had never understood her desire to switch careers a year after graduating with her teaching degree. Especially to such a high-risk job. But while Katie loved her quiet life of domestic bliss, as she used to call it, Nikki had found her calling making the world a safer place. Not that she didn't want the things Katie had for herself someday—a husband, children, maybe even a house in the suburbs—but she was learning to find contentment in who she was, where she was.

Which was ironic, in a way. Her and Tyler's mutual need to fight for justice was what gave them so much in common and had become a huge part of what had made her fall in love with him. He'd found fulfillment in the military. She'd found hers chasing down bad guys. And together they'd filled that extra need for an adrenaline rush by rock climbing and rappelling whenever they could get away together for a few hours.

She reined in her thoughts. She wasn't going to go there. Not tonight.

A car sped past them and her muscles flinched automatically. She drew in a slow breath. They weren't after her. Her life wasn't in danger. All she needed was a few hours of sleep, then she'd be back on the job, looking for Lucy.

"You know you didn't have to ensure my safety," she said, shoving aside the fatigue and any lingering traces of apprehension. "I really am fine. Just tired."

"I know." He ran his hand down her arm, leaving the heated imprint of his presence behind as he pulled away. "But I would feel better knowing there's a former special ops leader watching your back."

Nikki laughed, knowing there was no one she'd rather have watching out for her, but he was worrying about nothing. "It's been a crazy day, but they're not after me, Tyler. Not this time."

"You might be right, but they're after anyone who tries to unearth the truth. And I'm not convinced that excludes you at this point."

She didn't blame him for being concerned. Six weeks ago, someone had been after her and she'd come close to losing her life. Tyler had been there to witness everything. But this time, the case wasn't about her.

"We learned a few more things tonight. We believe Lucy's disappearance—and Mac's murder—is related to a counterfeit pharmaceutical drug ring."

"Wow," he said. "Then this really is bigger than George's involvement. Just promise me you'll be careful. George is dead. If anything happened to you . . ."

Nikki felt her breath catch as familiar longings pushed their way to the surface. She wanted him to tell her that his feelings toward her were shifting. That she wasn't just Katie's best friend. That it was more than friendship he felt. More than just a brotherly sense of protection.

The streetlight left shadows on him as she studied the familiar edges of his face, leaving her heart spinning toward that place she knew she couldn't go. Not yet. If she did . . . when she did . . . it was going to be on his timing.

"You okay?" he asked.

"Yeah." She smiled. "You'd better go. I'm not the only one who needs some sleep."

"Let me walk you up. Make sure there's no thugs lurking in the shadows."

She shook her head, wishing he would stop playing with her heart. But he didn't even know what he was doing. "Go home, Tyler. And when you get a chance, tell Liam I haven't forgotten about our last Wii game. He owes me a rematch."

"I know he'd like that."

"I'll even throw in a pizza," she offered, not really wanting him to go yet.

"What about that chocolate tart you made me awhile back?" He flashed her that familiar grin that made her heart melt. "I'm telling you, I dreamed of that for weeks."

She caught the tinge of flirting in his voice, the grin still on his face. She wished he'd pull her into his arms and kiss her so she could forget about everything that had happened today. Wished it was her he dreamed about at night when they weren't together and not her chocolate tart.

"You're starting to push it," she said, forcing herself to keep the tone of her own voice light. "But I might be able to come up with something."

Tyler laughed. "If not, I suppose I could try my hand again at some Rice Krispies treats."

"Forget it," she said, matching his laugh. "Let's just both admit it, cooking isn't exactly your forte. Only you could make Rice Krispies treats that are the consistency of a . . . brick."

"They weren't that bad."

"Yeah, they were, and you know it."

She fiddled with the button on her blazer, enjoying the comfortable banter between them. The way he looked at her. The way his smile made her feel after a hard day. This was what she wanted to come home to at night. Tyler . . . Liam . . .

"Maybe that's why I've been dreaming of your tart," he said. "The only decent homemade meals I get are from you and my mom."

"You actually think making me feel guilty is going to work?"

His smile widened, making her heart tremor. "I'm not below trying, and I'm pretty sure Liam would back me up on this one."

She laughed again. "Whoa . . . time out. Now you're really playing low ball."

Nikki swallowed hard as she studied the curve of his lips . . . the strong line of his jaw . . . the warmth of his eyes. She was playing with fire, but she loved seeing him smile. And knowing she was the one who'd put that smile there was too tantalizing to make her want to stop.

"I'll check in on you tomorrow," he said, his expression sobering. No matter what either of them said, the reality of what had happened today still hung between them.

She nodded, knowing if she said anything more, her voice would betray her. He leaned forward and brushed his lips across her forehead, allowing her to breathe in the familiar hint of orange and spices from his cologne. Her heart quickened and she pulled away. How much longer was she going to be able to keep her feelings from him?

"Good night, Nikki."

She caught his gaze one last time, trying to determine if she'd seen something in his eyes, or if she was simply imagining it.

She watched him walk back to his car, hesitating as he slipped into his silver Honda Accord. How was it that she could find the courage to deal with an active shooter, but the thought of telling Tyler what she felt terrified her? Maybe she had no right to feel what she did for Katie's husband. But try convincing her heart to walk away.

She headed toward her apartment, knowing she needed to tell him the truth.

Nikki unlocked the front door and stepped into the one-bedroom loft near the heart of Nashville she'd invested in three years ago. Coffee shops and music, tree-lined streets, and a nearby park had proven to be the perfect neighborhood setting, but it was the loft itself that had sold her on the location. Twelve-foot ceilings, exposed brick walls. Katie had helped her choose items off of eBay and local flea markets and turn it into a place she loved.

Jade, her Russian Blue cat, rubbed her silky coat against her legs for attention as Nikki pulled the keys out of the door and reached for the light switch.

The upstairs floor creaked. Nikki drew her hand back and reached for her weapon.

Someone was inside.

15

12:37 a.m.
Nikki's loft apartment

Nikki grabbed her gun from her holster. With the light still off, the room was lit only by the out- side street lamp filtering through the large window at the foot of the staircase. She cleared the downstairs quickly before heading to the stairs, with Jade still vying for her attention.

Avoiding the second step from the bottom that always creaked, she slowly made her way up the stairs. Maybe Tyler had been right and she'd misjudged the situation. Whoever was behind Mac's murder was clearly willing to stop anyone who got in the way. But did that include targeting the authorities involved as well?

At this moment, it didn't matter who was right. She could see the faint glow of light from around the edges of the bathroom door. She never left that light on when she went out. Someone was in there.

"Whoever you are, step out of the bathroom now. Hands up."

The door swung open slowly, spilling light onto the landing.

Nikki took a step backward. "Luke?"

"Whoa, put that thing down." Her younger brother stepped out of the bathroom with one of her towels wrapped around his waist, dark hair still wet from the shower. "Who were you expecting?"

She let out a whoosh of air, realizing she'd been holding her breath. "What in the world are you doing? You almost got yourself shot."

"Sorry." He tugged the towel around his waist tighter and grinned. "You gave me a key."

"I gave you a key to feed my cat when I'm gone."

"I sent you a message on your phone when I got here."

She pulled out her phone and saw the missed

messages from Tyler and Luke. At least he'd called, but she didn't have the time or energy to play games tonight. "What's going on, Luke?"

"Let me get dressed," he said, disappearing back into the bathroom.

"Luke . . ."

She folded her arms across her chest as the door shut behind him. Putting off the inevitable had always been her brother's way of coping. Whether it was a conversation or figuring out where he was going to get money for rent, he'd always been good at avoiding conflict and ignoring problems. But ignoring problems rarely made them go away. On the other hand, his knack for floating through life without worrying about the future had given him the courage to ignore all the negative advice and to take a leap of faith and follow his dream.

Luke stepped out onto the landing a minute later, wearing plaid pajama bottoms and a gray T-shirt. "I'm behind on my rent and need a place to stay for a few days."

"Meaning you got kicked out of your apartment."

Again.

"It's not a big deal," Luke said, heading down the stairs past her. "You don't mind me hanging around a few days, do you?"

"Wait a minute . . . it's not a big deal? Maybe that's your problem, because it *is* a big deal.

You're twenty-eight years old and you're still struggling to pay the rent."

"Stop sounding like Dad." Luke stopped on the landing. "I just need a few days to get back on my feet. That's all I'm asking for. I'm not asking for money. Just a place to stay."

"Okay. But one more question. Are you still clean?" Eight months ago, he'd joined Alcoholics Anonymous to help kick the alcohol addiction he'd picked up after college. It had become an unwanted addition to her mom's already long list of worries for her children.

He walked back up the stairs, laid his hands on her shoulders, and caught her gaze. "I'm absolutely clean, and this lack of housing is just temporary. I promise, Nikki."

"Okay."

She glanced into the bathroom, surprised he'd actually hung his damp towel on the rack, hoping he was telling the truth. She paused before following him downstairs. Black claw-foot tub, white tiles on the wall with dark grout, wood floor, candles, and a Moroccan rug for color. Another room with Katie's touch.

Another reminder of today's events.

And the reason she was on edge. She'd watched Katie deal with her father's bad choices, and now George's bad choices had gotten him killed.

She headed back downstairs, wanting to make sure Luke was telling her the entire story. He had quit his job as an accountant three years ago to chase his dream of becoming a full-time musician. Her family had been both supportive and cautious at the same time. To his credit, Luke had an amazing ear for music and could play half a dozen instruments. But so could every other aspiring musician in the city. Which was why, while she believed in his talent, in her opinion it seemed like his chances of winning the lottery were greater than making it big on the Nashville music scene. And for starters, making enough to pay the rent.

"Mom still has your old room intact plus your own bathroom," she said, scooping Jade off the bottom step. "All I have is a couch."

"The couch is fine, and I don't mind sharing the bathroom if you don't." Luke shot her one of his lopsided grins.

"Save the charm for your fans, Luke." She set Jade down beside her food bowl, then filled the empty dish with her favorite tuna-flavored kibble. "What did Dad say?"

Luke leaned against the kitchen island. "The last time the topic was brought up he said he was done bailing me out. But seriously, Nikki. All I need is a couple more days to find myself a new place."

Nikki felt her defenses wavering. This wasn't the first, nor would it be the last time she heard those words. But as much as she loved her little brother, she needed to make sure she didn't enable him. "You can stay, but I'm in the middle of a case. I just came home to catch a few hours of sleep. You're going to be on your own."

"Not a problem. I've got a couple gigs lined up this weekend. All I need is a few days. I promise."

He played several times a week, but between irregular wages and tips, she knew it didn't always cover the bills.

"You believe me, don't you?" he said. "That I'm clean. I haven't missed an AA meeting in months. I'm doing it right this time, Nikki, I swear. But even with all the shows I manage to play, I'm always behind. And I don't want to go back to sitting in front of a computer all day."

She let out a deep sigh. "I know."

"Do you mind if I eat something?" he asked.

"You can check the fridge for leftovers, but I don't think you're going to find much."

Avoiding a diet of fast food had become a priority for her, but grocery shopping was one of those things that typically got sandwiched in between cases or after a late workout at the local gym. And a trip to the store was overdue.

Luke stood in front of her open refrigerator. "Hummus, low-fat yogurt, almond butter, pomegranate concentrate, garlic, some eggs, and a bunch of veggies . . ." He turned and looked at her. "Seriously . . . What do you eat?"

Nikki laughed. "I said you wouldn't find much. Unless you want an omelet or can come up with something else creative, you're going to have to call for delivery, though I'm pretty sure nothing's open this late."

"What's this?"

Nikki glanced at the container he'd pulled out. "I forgot some of that was left. It's risotto."

Two nights ago she'd been watching some cooking show, trying to unwind, and decided to try the dish herself. The result had been better than she'd expected.

"You actually made risotto?" he asked, grabbing a fork out of the drawer. "What's in it?"

"Leeks, bacon . . . fresh peas."

"Seriously?"

Nikki laughed as the tension in her neck started to release. "Cooking relaxes me. And unlike some people I know, my diet isn't limited to the Boyd family restaurant and takeout."

"Dad might take offense to that statement. You know how he feels about his barbeque." Luke took a bite. "Hey—this is actually pretty good."

"You sound surprised."

"Well, I already knew that you inherited Dad's cooking skills, though maybe a bit more on the . . . refined side."

"Thanks . . . I think."

"Don't worry. That's a good thing. Not that I don't love Dad's cooking as well." Luke set the half-empty bowl on the bar, then sat down on one of the metal stools. "Thanks, Nikki. For everything. You've always been there for me."

"You're welcome."

She shot him a smile before rummaging through the fridge herself. Dinner had been hours ago, but at the time she'd felt more tired than hungry. Not finding anything she wanted, she reached for a cup of tapioca pudding from the cupboard.

"Do you want some of this?" he asked, taking another bite.

"Thanks, but this will do. Don't you want to heat that up?"

"Unlike you, I live on takeout and Dad's barbeque. It actually tastes fine to me."

"Be my guest." She grabbed a spoon and pulled off the top of her pudding cup.

"You look exhausted," he said, catching her gaze.

"Fatigue is a perk of the job."

"I have a feeling Mom wouldn't like that statement. You okay?"

She took a bite of the pudding, her favorite comfort food. "I will be. As soon as I find the woman I'm looking for."

"I saw something on the news about a missing schoolteacher," he said. "Is that the case you're working on?"

"Yeah. But it's gotten . . . complicated."

"Complicated how?"

She took another bite, not wanting to go into the details of the case. "Tyler's involved."

"Tyler? How's that possible?"

"It's a long story, and only indirectly, but it's been hard on him. The day managed to dredge up a bunch of memories."

It had dredged up memories for both of them, actually.

Luke stopped eating to search her expression. "How is he? I know he's had a rough year."

"Still trying to let go and figure out how to navigate life without Katie."

"He needs someone like you." Luke dug back into the risotto. "And I don't mean someone to bring him and Liam takeout on a Friday night."

She shook her head. She wasn't going there. Not tonight. "Tyler needs time to heal. Not another relationship."

Luke held up his fork and pointed it at her. "I still say he needs someone like you."

"You sound like Mom," she said, scooping up the rest of her pudding before tossing the empty cup into the trash. "Always worried about my marital status."

Luke laughed. "Trust me. You're not the only one. Though I have a feeling she's more worried about the unstable state of my career than my state of singlehood at the moment."

His phone buzzed. He pulled it out of his back pocket, checked the caller ID, then shoved it back into his pocket.

"You're not going to answer?" she asked.

"It's nothing." His shoulders stiffened as he took the last bite of the risotto.

She knew him well enough to know he was hiding something. "What's wrong, Luke?"

"I said it's nothing." He grabbed his bowl and went to rinse it out in the sink, his entire demeanor changed.

"You're back with your old friends, aren't you?"

She knew he wasn't going to like the direct question, but there was no use skirting around the issue. She couldn't help him if she didn't know the truth about what was going on. And as much as she wanted to trust him, she knew him well enough to realize how easy it was for him to slip back into old habits. And where those habits could take him.

"I said I was clean," he said.

"That's not what I asked you."

"Yeah. You're right." He turned around, the smile from earlier gone. "I crashed at an old friend's place earlier this evening. Next thing I know, the police are raiding the apartment with a warrant."

Nikki felt her heart sink. This was exactly what she'd worried might happen. "What did you do?"

He set the dish in the dishwasher. "Ran out the back door and managed to avoid getting arrested."

"You ran out the back door. So now the police are looking for you?"

"I don't think so. But the guys I was staying with are looking for me. I think they believe I ratted them out. I can't get blamed for this, Nikki. Not by them and certainly not by the police."

"You're twenty-eight years old, Luke—"

"I didn't do anything wrong. I was just in the wrong place at the wrong time."

"But this isn't the first time you've been in the wrong place at the wrong time. At some point you're going to have to grow up and take responsibility for your actions. To pay attention to who's around you." She knew she sounded like a parent, but she didn't care. "I already asked you if you're using again—"

"I swear I'm clean." He braced his arms against the counter. "I haven't used in months."

But as much as she wanted to, she wasn't sure she could believe him.

"I'm sorry," he said.

"So am I. But it's time you grew up, Luke. You're family. And you know I'd do anything for you, but I won't protect you from consequences. That doesn't help in the long run."

She knew what could happen out there. They'd already lost Sarah. She wasn't going to lose Luke as well.

"Nikki—"

"We'll talk in the morning, okay, and figure something out. I'm in the middle of a case, and it's been an exhausting day. I've got to get some sleep."

"And tomorrow?"

"I'll go down to the police station with you, we'll tell them what happened. Because either one of these guys is going to try and put the blame on you, or they'll find evidence that you were staying there. And that's when things are going to get a whole lot worse. And frankly, it's the right thing to do."

"I don't know if I can—"

"You have to, Luke. We'll go down and talk to them together."

"I really am sorry."

He shot her that guilty look she knew all too well. Like when he'd been caught opening up his presents before Christmas morning. Or when he'd eaten the last of Dad's ice cream. But this was far more serious than a bowl of Ben and Jerry's.

She drew him into a bear hug. "You know I'm always here for you. If you get into a situation you don't know how to handle, please . . ." She took a step backward and caught his gaze. "Come to me before it gets this far."

"Okay."

"You know where the extra sheets and blankets are. I'll see you in the morning. I'm planning to be out of here early, but you can call me when you wake up, and I'll meet you at the station."

Upstairs, Nikki quickly got ready for bed, then slipped between the sheets, feeling the pressure of being pulled in too many directions. She could still feel the warm imprint of Tyler's hand on her arm. Still smell the lingering scent of his cologne, before her body finally gave in and she fell into a dreamless sleep.

The shrill ring of Nikki's phone woke her up at half past five. Gwen's name showed up on the caller ID.

"Gwen?" Nikki struggled to push aside the heavy fog that hung over her. "Didn't you go home last night?"

"I caught a few hours' sleep here at the station. One of these days I'll get smart and buy myself a place closer to work like you did. But that's not why I called. We've got a situation."

Nikki sat up in her still-dark bedroom, fully awake now. "What's going on?"

"We just got a call about that reporter you spoke to last night. She's up on the roof of a condo complex, with a hostage."

Nikki felt her stomach drop. "A hostage?"

"I'm sending you the address now. I need you to talk some sense into her. She's asking for you. Says she has more information about Mac."

"Do you think she found the evidence we're looking for?"

"I don't know."

She glanced at the address Gwen sent her. "I'll be there in five minutes."

Nikki pulled on a pair of dark-wash jeans, a brown lace camisole, and a cream jacket before slipping quietly down the stairs, trying not to wake up her brother. She glanced at the couch where her brother had slept.

Luke was gone.

16

6:01 a.m.
Sierra View Condos

Nikki stepped into the elevator that led to the roof of the condo, a twelve-unit residential building in the heart of Nashville, with Jack; Lieutenant Porter, the officer in charge of the incident; and a fourth officer. Once filled with corporate offices, the building had been converted a few years ago into ten stories of high-end condominiums, boasting incredible downtown views and a stunning rooftop garden.

From what she knew about Mallory, though, she doubted the freelance reporter could afford one of the upscale units. Which in turn raised the question of how she'd been able to get into the secure building.

But there had been no time to investigate the circumstances or strategize the best approach to take with Mallory. No time to figure out where her own brother might be. There hadn't even been time to pick up an espresso on the way that would help carry her through the next few hours. All she really knew was that the situation had been set on her shoulders. She needed to find a way to get answers and come to a quick resolution before someone else got hurt.

"I understand you met with this woman last night," Porter said, handing her an earpiece so they could communicate while she was talking to Mallory.

Nikki nodded.

"Then you probably know more about her than any of us do," Porter said, taking a bulletproof vest from the other officer and handing it to her.

"Your negotiating team is here?" she asked, slipping on the vest.

"Yes, but you're the one she wants to talk to," he said, hands behind his back. Expression stoic.

"What about the hostage?" Nikki watched the numbers on the digital counter. Six more floors. She needed to pump him for as many details as possible.

"According to the manager, he lives in the building. His name is Adi Patil. Senior VP of Development for a pharmaceutical company called Byrne Laboratories."

Nikki looked at Jack. "The same company Mac worked for."

Things were definitely getting interesting.

"The manager is going through the security

footage right now with one of my officers to find out how this Philips woman got into the building. All we really know right now is that she got in, pulled a gun on Patil, and forced him to the rooftop. They've been up there about thirty minutes now. We called your department when she started asking for you."

Nikki tried to calm her wound-up nerves.

I'm not sure I'm the right person to do this, Jesus. Another life at risk. Another huge unknown. I'm good at sorting through facts, looking at the evidence, and finding the connections. Right now we need to find Lucy, but instead, I feel like this case has me running in a hundred different directions, and I don't know how it all fits together.

Just like her personal life.

Wind whipped through her jacket as Nikki stepped onto the rooftop that was bathed in the soft, orange glow of sunrise. Groups of comfy chairs and tables, along with potted ornamental plants, filled the space. But Nikki's attention shot straight to where Mallory stood near the edge of the roof, holding a gun against the back of an older man's head. He was kneeling in front of her, hands zip-tied behind his back; his expression was one of complete terror. Late forties, possibly early fifties, with black hair and an expensive charcoal-colored suit.

Nikki walked slowly across the roof, still

working on a strategy to ensure everyone got out of this situation alive. Mallory was looking for someone to blame, and whether or not Patil was actually guilty more than likely didn't matter to her at this point. What did matter to her was that someone paid for what had happened to Audrey and anyone else she believed had been affected by someone who put money above the price of a human life.

And that person at the moment was Adi Patil.

"Mallory? It's me, Nikki." Nikki stopped about fifteen feet from where the woman stood. Close enough to be able to talk comfortably, yet not close enough that she would feel threatened. "They told me you asked for me. I'd like to help."

Mallory nodded, and Nikki didn't miss the tremor in the hand holding the gun. She needed to get Mallory's finger off the trigger.

"Mallory . . . Can you tell me what's going on?" Nikki asked.

Mallory's gaze shifted. Jaw tense. Shoulders sloped. "I didn't want this to happen, but I didn't have a choice. No one will listen. I need someone to listen, or someone else is going to die."

Nikki chose her words carefully. "I promised you I'd help, and I meant it. But not this way. Why don't you give me the gun, so we can talk about what's going on without the risk of someone getting hurt. I know that's not what you want. You want to save people. Not hurt them."

"It's too late to play nice," Mallory said.

"Then tell me what's going on. Please. I promise I'll listen again."

"Tread slowly," Porter said into her earpiece. "The harder you push, the more likely she'll be to resist."

She could see the anger in Mallory's eyes, coupled with the same determination she'd seen in her last night. She was clearly unwavering about her desire to find out the truth, but at what cost?

Mallory wiped the back of her free hand against her forehead where beads of perspiration had gathered. "I don't know why I asked you to come."

"Because you know I do care, and I am listening," Nikki said. "But first, Mallory . . . I need you to let Mr. Patil go. We can talk and figure this out together. Because if what you believe is true about the drug supply being compromised, I want it stopped as much as you do. And we will do that. But not this way." She took a calculated step forward.

"Step back." Mallory's voice rose as she shifted the gun toward Nikki, then back at Patil. "I will shoot him."

"Okay." Nikki held up her arms and moved back to where she'd been standing.

"Don't get flustered," Porter said. "You're doing fine."

Nikki took a deep breath. "Tell me what he has to do with the situation."

"Adi Patil is one of the researchers at Byrne Laboratories. But he doesn't just develop new drugs . . . he's allowed at least one of them to be copied with fake ingredients. Ingredients that don't have the correct formula and that can kill innocent people."

"That's not true—" the man started.

"Shut up." Mallory's hand tremor was getting worse as she pressed the gun to his head. "Do you know how much it costs to buy a condo in this building? Just over two million dollars. And while he's driving his hundred-thousand-dollar BMW to his golf games and charity events, people are using his products and dying."

"I don't know anything about tainted drugs." Patil's voice shook. "And if there was a tainted drug in our supply chain, the FDA would have us shut down in a heartbeat."

"Be quiet." Mallory grabbed his hair, forcing his head back.

"Mallory, if he's done something illegal, I promise we'll find the evidence we need to ensure he's convicted and punished. But you don't have to handle this on your own."

"*If* he's done something illegal?"

"Keep her talking, Nikki," Porter said. "You're doing fine."

"I know it feels as if your hands are tied," Nikki said. "We just need evidence, Mallory."

"I have evidence." Mallory let go of Patil's hair

and dug into her front jeans pocket. She pulled out a piece of paper. "This is the report of the drug content I just received by fax from a friend of mine. According to these results, the antibiotic produced by Byrne Laboratories and prescribed to Audrey didn't meet the FDA's specifications."

"That's not possible," Patil said.

"Except it is. And I can give you even more evidence. Audrey—the little girl who took the antibiotics—she died two hours ago. She was four years old. Did I tell you she has a baby brother on the way? Now he'll never know his big sister. All because of this man's greed. But even with all of your promises to help, you couldn't stop Audrey from dying, could you? Her parents have to plan a funeral now, something that never should have happened."

"I'm so sorry," Nikki said.

A rush of emotion swept through her at the news, but another piece of the puzzle had slipped into place. Audrey's death had been the trigger that had set off this chain of events. Nikki glanced at Jack, who stood near the exit. He gave her an encouraging nod.

Nikki drew in a slow breath, then turned back to Mallory. "No parent is supposed to suffer the loss of their child like this, but I need you to trust me when I tell you, we're doing everything we can to figure out who's involved in this."

"The problem is, whatever you're doing isn't

enough. If you were doing everything you could, then Audrey would still be alive. And what about the next person who dies? And the person after that. When is it going to stop?" Mallory shook her head. "You're just like everyone I've spoken to. And then in the end, those who do get caught receive nothing more than a slap on the wrist, while people like Audrey are dying. Something has to be done, and if you won't do anything to stop them, then I will."

Nikki decided to change her strategy. "Who did you lose, Mallory?"

She drew in a deep, ragged breath. "My sister."

"Can you tell me about her?"

The expression on Mallory's face softened. "Mary was five years older than me, but I was the one who took care of her when she was sick. Do you know what happens when a diabetic stops taking insulin? Within three days she went to sleep and never woke up. She had two little girls and had so much to live for, but instead she died from kidney failure, because her insulin was made from fake drugs."

"And you want someone to pay for her death," Nikki said.

Mallory nodded.

"Give me something I can pass on to the DA, Mallory. Anything that can tie Patil to this."

"He's too smart for that."

"Then let the justice system work. We'll find

the evidence we need—the evidence Mac had—and put an end to this."

"What if the justice system doesn't work?" Mallory said. "What if the only way to bring about justice is by putting a stop to it myself? I've tried to do things the *right* way and nothing's changed."

"Mallory, I agree that if all of this is true, then he deserves to be punished, but you know this isn't the way. Revenge is never the answer. He will have a fair trial, and pay the price for any involvement." The knots in Nikki's stomach tightened. Revenge might not be the answer, but she knew the pull of that desire all too well. How many times had she fought for the chance to take things into her own hands? How many times had she imagined what she wanted to do to the Angel Abductor if she ever found him?

"You arrest him," Mallory said. "He gets a slap on the wrist, and more people die. There are no stiff punishments for this kind of crime. No way to truly put a stop to what is going on."

"Here's what I do know, Mallory," Nikki said. "I know how bad it hurts to lose someone you love. I know how much you want revenge right now, and how hard it is when you can't get it. But taking the situation into your own hands and playing judge and jury . . . This isn't the answer."

"Then what? Is the answer to do nothing? Just let the system take care of things? It doesn't work that way. My sister died. Audrey died. And they're going to keep dying until someone stops them. I have to stop them."

Nikki shook her head. "By killing this man?"

"Then convince me that you can do something. Make him tell everyone here what he did. How many people have died from fake drugs. How many people he's tried to silence like Mac and Lucy."

Mallory was shaking more now—not just her voice but the gun she held. Nikki was desperate. *We need this to end without any casualties, Lord. If Mallory's right, then we need justice, but not this way.*

"Tell them," Mallory continued, talking to the man in front of her. "Tell them how it was an easy way to make money with little risk. Do you ever think about the people who take your drugs? The men and women and children who have died because of what you've done?"

"I don't even know your sister—"

"Just like you didn't know Audrey or the hundreds of others your medicine affected."

"Mallory—"

But she wasn't finished. "Tell them the truth. Tell them how the medicine you make is produced by cutting corners. How you found a way to infiltrate the US supply chain with your counterfeit drugs."

"No," Patil said. "You can't prove any of this."

193

"That's where you're wrong. This is nothing more than a game to you, isn't it? You can come home to your luxury condo every night and never once think about the men and women whose lives you are ruining."

"No—"

"Because for them, it's just like playing Russian roulette. You go to the pharmacy, buy the medicine you need, but if you pick the wrong box . . . you die. That's what happened to my sister. And now it's happening again. Have you ever played Russian roulette, Adi Patil?"

"No." His voice was shaking. "Please . . . please don't shoot me."

Mallory pulled the man to his feet so he was between her and the officers and moved closer to the edge of the roof.

"Mallory . . ." Nikki took a step forward.

"What do you think will happen if I squeeze the trigger right now, Patil?"

"What do I do?" Nikki asked Porter. "She's going to shoot him."

"We need a clean shot," Porter responded.

Nikki leveled her gun, aiming at Mallory, but Patil was in the way.

"Mallory, think about what you're doing. This isn't the way this needs to end." Nikki weighed their limited options. In her own mind, Mallory had to know she'd crossed the line. Knew there was no way for this to end well. Which made her unpredictable *and* upped the odds she was going to pull that trigger. "Put the gun down, Mallory."

Mallory stood behind the man, preventing any clean shots.

"Mallory . . . I know you're upset, and you have every right to feel that way, but this isn't how we're going to find the answers to anything."

"If that's true, then why is he still working? Why is he still out there providing drugs to people? They think it's safe. They think it will make them better, but it won't. It will kill them."

"But you don't have to be the one to make him pay. That's why I'm here."

Mallory pulled back on the trigger until the hammer was fully cocked. "He deserves to die."

"Don't do this, Mallory."

Mallory pulled the trigger. The hammer slammed forward with a loud click, followed by an eerie silence.

The chamber in the cylinder had been empty.

Nikki let out a whoosh of air. Patil was crying, his face blotchy from uncontrolled tears.

If the gun wasn't loaded . . .

One of the men behind her signaled.

"Stay back. All of you," Mallory shouted, then fired the gun again, shattering one of the clay pots. "If no one is going to stop them . . . I will."

Ten stories up, the wind blew across the roof. Mallory took another step toward the ledge, forcing Patil to come with her.

Nikki felt a surge of adrenaline. "Mallory, wait . . . you don't want to do this."

"That's where you're wrong. Maybe someone will listen now."

Nikki watched helplessly as the reporter stepped backward and plunged over the edge of the building, taking Adi Patil with her.

17

6:26 a.m.

A car alarm went off ten stories below. Nikki yanked out her earpiece, then stumbled back from the edge of the roof as a heavy numbness seeped through her. Mac was dead. Audrey was dead. And now Mallory Philips and Adi Patil were dead.

Her mind began processing every word she'd used to try to change Mallory's mind. Her tone of voice and body language. Her job in coming here had been to change Mallory's mind. To stop her from hurting herself or anyone else in the process. But beyond knowing now what Mac had been trying to find, they were still no closer to finding Lucy. And until they found that evidence—and Lucy—the woman was as good as dead.

Lieutenant Porter stepped up beside her and

laid a hand on her shoulder. "You played it by the book and did everything exactly the way you should have."

"No." Nikki shook her head, the shock of what had just happened beginning to surface. "I was brought here to find a way to stop her. And that didn't happen."

"Don't even go there," the lieutenant said. "In situations like this, there is only one person who can decide the outcome. And today that was Mallory. This was her decision. And it was a decision she'd probably already made before you showed up."

"Then why did she want me here?"

"Like you said last night," Jack said, stepping up next to them. "She wanted someone to listen to her. Maybe this was the only way she thought she could get everyone's attention."

"A slot on the nightly news would guarantee exposure, and she knew it," the lieutenant said.

"And as horrible as this is, like the lieutenant just said," Jack offered, "what happened today was Mallory's decision. Not yours."

"And Audrey's death was the final straw," Nikki said.

She knew they were right. Just like she knew she didn't have time to feel sorry for herself. At some point soon, they'd debrief and spend time going over every detail of what had just happened. But for now, feeling guilty or sorry for herself was nothing more than a distraction. And that was something she couldn't afford.

A uniformed officer was talking into his radio. Sirens blared in the distance. Someone shouted from the other side of the roof. Nikki blocked out the noise and glanced back to the spot where Mallory had jumped. She wanted to rewind the past thirty minutes and find a way to stop what had just happened. Find a way to convince Mallory that taking her life—and Patil's, guilty or not—wasn't the answer.

But it was too late for that.

"She was looking for justice," Nikki said, surprised at the empathy that came with those words. "That's all she wanted. Something good to come out of her sister's death. Someone saved because of what she had gone through. Audrey's death had to be another crushing blow."

"I know how strong the need for revenge can be," Jack said. "But that doesn't make it right."

"I know."

But for a moment she'd been able to clearly see herself standing in Mallory's place. She understood the need to hunt down the man responsible for her sister's death. To put a stop to more people having to suffer—like Audrey and her family. Because if Mallory's suspicions were correct, Audrey's death *wasn't* right, or fair, or just. And it was really no different than her wanting Sarah's abductor to pay. She knew that overpowering emotion that required justice, even if that meant losing everything herself.

"You wouldn't have done what she just did," Jack said, breaking into her thoughts. "That's the difference between you and her, Nikki. You've never tried to play God. And if the day comes when you do find whoever abducted your sister, you won't take things into your own hands."

"Maybe none of us know that until that moment comes and we're faced with a decision."

She wanted to believe that if faced with her sister's abductor, she'd do the right thing, but she knew how strong that feeling of revenge could be, and how, when fed, it could quickly grow to consume you. And knowing that allowed her to understand—at least on one level—what Mallory had just done.

"She was right about one thing," she said. "Maybe Patil was telling the truth and really didn't know anything about fake drugs in his company, but somewhere there have to be answers. Because if what Mallory said is true, whoever is behind this needs to be stopped."

"They will be," Jack said.

"We don't know that." Nikki slipped off her jacket, then pulled her vest over her head. "The system never found my sister. Ten years later, I'm looking for answers and wondering when we'll find closure. Wondering if there are other girls out there, missing because we never found him."

She didn't want the same thing to happen to Lucy.

A flutter of white wedged at the base of one of the plants caught her eye. She picked up the folded piece of paper.

"What exactly is that?" the lieutenant asked.

"She was telling the truth. It's the analysis of the antibiotic from an independent testing laboratory," Nikki said, reading over the paper. "So while we might not have any of Mac's evidence, we do have something to go on."

She pulled out her cell and called Gwen at the precinct. "Gwen, you said Mac's boss was arriving back in town this morning."

"Yeah . . . according to his secretary, he should be in soon. Do you want me to call and let him know you're coming?"

"No," Nikki said. "But I think it's time we paid him a visit."

Nikki and Jack stepped through the open glass doors of the pharmaceutical research facility located on the outskirts of Nashville. Inside, the lobby, with its glass walls and stark white–tiled floor, opened up four stories to a huge skylight that bathed the modern space in light.

"Wow," Nikki said, heading for the large receptionist's desk in the center of the lobby. "I wasn't expecting this place to be so fancy."

According to the information Gwen had sent

them, Byrne Laboratories was a state-of-the-art facility set on ten acres of land. Three large buildings included over five thousand square feet of laboratory space plus offices and conference rooms for the more than a thousand employees. And while this newer company might be competing with dozens of long-standing corporations, it had found a place in the market and was growing rapidly.

Nikki walked up to the sleek silver-and-frosted-glass counter, where a young woman sharply dressed in a black blazer and matching skirt stood, and held up her badge. "I'm Nikki Boyd with the Tennessee Bureau of Investigation—"

"Finally. Just a moment please."

Nikki shot Jack a questioning look as the woman motioned for them to wait, then picked up her phone. "They're here, Mr. King . . . yes sir."

She turned back to them and flashed a bright smile. "Mr. King's expecting you. He'll be down in a minute himself to personally escort you upstairs. If you wouldn't mind waiting for him by the first set of elevators just around the corner."

Nikki's brow rose as the woman handed them each a visitor's pass, her smile never wavering. "Please wear the passes while you're in the building, and you won't have any trouble with security."

"I'm sorry, Miss—"

"Carrie Jones."

"Miss Jones. Who's Mr. King?" Nikki asked.

"I assumed you knew. Mr. King is Mac Hudson's boss. Well, technically, his boss's boss." A shadow crossed her perky exterior. "You are with the police, aren't you?"

"Yes," Nikki said.

"Then Mr. King will be arriving any moment, and he can explain everything to you," she said, pointing to her left. "If you need me to take you to the elevators—"

"We'll be fine, thank you," Jack said.

The heels of Nikki's black boots clicked against the tiled flooring as she and Jack made their way to the elevators, past a row of contemporary, large-scale artwork.

"Did Gwen tell him we were coming?" Nikki asked.

"Not that I know of."

Elevator doors slid open as they rounded the corner. A man in his midfifties stepped out, wearing a dark gray suit, a paisley tie, and thick-rimmed, black glasses.

"You're with the local authorities?" he asked, popping an orange Tic Tac into his mouth.

Nikki nodded, then showed him her badge.

"I'm Dwight King." Sweat glistened across his forehead as he stepped back into the elevator, despite the air conditioners that seemed to be working overtime. "Please . . . if you don't mind, you can follow me back upstairs."

"You and your secretary seem to be expecting us," Nikki said as the elevator doors closed.

"I thought you were here about Mac Hudson?"

"We are," Nikki said.

He punched floor 4, then turned around to face them. "My secretary was in early this morning and discovered the break-in. She called the police. You wouldn't believe the mess we're dealing with up there as far as security goes. First the man's murdered, and now someone breaks into his office."

"All we know about is his murder," Nikki said. "Not the fact that his office was broken into."

King's brow furrowed. "Someone broke into the building last night and trashed his office. And then on top of that, would you believe it, I can't get ahold of one of my senior VPs. Without him here to help figure out what's missing, the next twenty-four hours are going to be a nightmare. And if our stockholders get wind of a potential security problem . . ."

Nikki glanced at Jack in the mirror.

"What's the name of your missing man?" she asked.

"Adi Patil."

Nikki let out a sharp huff of air as the elevator doors slid open on the fourth floor. This about to turn into a very bad day for Mr. King. They stepped into another sleek reception area nestled between two long halls lined with offices.

"Do you have somewhere we could talk in private?" Jack asked. "Then we'd like to see Hudson's office."

King nodded, seeming flustered as they followed him down the hallway to a corner office. Inside the large room, like the rest of the building, the tall windows overlooked acres of farmland.

"Why don't you sit down," King said, pointing to a couple of chairs across from his desk that held a laptop computer, a short stack of files, and a framed photo of him with his wife and three kids.

"You said Mr. Patil never showed up for work," Nikki began. She hadn't planned to be the bearer of bad news on top of everything that had been going on. "I'm sorry to have to be the one to tell you this, but Mr. Patil was killed this morning."

"Killed?" King pulled out a handkerchief from his pocket and blotted his forehead. "You've got to be kidding me. First Mac and now Adi . . ." He grabbed a bottle of water from a small fridge on the other side of the room. "Can I get either of you something to drink?"

His hands trembled as he opened the water bottle. His face paled.

"I'm fine," Nikki said. "But are you going to be all right?"

"Yes . . . I don't know." He took a long drink of the water, then wiped his mouth with the back of his hand. "Tell me what happened."

"We are still looking into the situation, but he was killed by a woman who accused your company of producing counterfeit drugs," Jack said.

"What?" King shook his head. "That's not possible. We spend tens of thousands of dollars every year to make sure that doesn't happen. Believe me, if someone had tried to infiltrate one of our drug lines with a counterfeit product, I'd know it."

"What kind of procedures are in place to keep something like this from happening?" Nikki asked.

"It's . . . it's similar to measures taken to prevent counterfeiting money," he said, sitting down in one of the cushioned chairs beside them. "Everything from holographic labels to infrared inks to Radio Frequency Identification. We use digital serial numbers, and in some cases, chemical fingerprints. On top of that we employ a number of security officials. It would be impossible for someone to successfully introduce a counterfeit drug into our supply chain."

Difficult, Nikki thought, *but not impossible.*

"About the break-in," Jack asked, "is anything missing?"

"Yes, but it's going to take hours to sort through the mess they left and find out exactly what. I do know his computer's gone as well as some of the files he was working on." King leaned forward, bracing his arms against his thighs as if the weight of the world had just been dropped on his shoulders. "The security implications of this situation are huge, not to mention the fact that I've just lost two of my men."

"When did the break-in happen?" Nikki asked.

"According to my secretary, sometime in the last twelve hours. My security people are going through the security feed right now to see if they can ID the intruder."

"We'll need copies of the footage," Jack said.

"Of course. I had meetings in Memphis all week and just returned to Nashville this morning to discover this. That's when I tried to get ahold of Adi, but couldn't."

"Can you tell me exactly what Mac's position was here?" Nikki asked.

"He worked in research and development. Mac wasn't the most organized person and had his own way of doing things, but he was brilliant."

"Did he ever come to you with concerns?" Nikki asked.

King grabbed another Tic Tac from his pocket and popped it into his mouth. "Mac came to me about a week ago with a number of issues regarding the company's security."

"What did you tell him?"

"To keep it quiet for the meantime, and I would look into it."

"And did you?"

"Of course. We have our own investigation

team. I called them in and asked them to look into Mac's concerns, but they didn't find anything." King shook his head. "You have to understand Mac. Like I said, he is—was—an outstanding scientist. Sorry. I'm still trying to wrap my head around the fact that he's dead. The problem was, while he was brilliant, he was also paranoid."

"Paranoid how?" Jack asked.

"He was one of those guys who believes that there's a conspiracy around every corner. I guess that's the price of being brilliant. You worry someone's going to steal your work, or, I don't know . . . worry about things that only a scientist would think of. Stuff the rest of us would never even dream up."

"What if we told you Mac might not have been paranoid," Nikki said, watching his reaction.

"What do you mean?" King asked.

"We have potential evidence from a third-party laboratory that an antibiotic produced by Byrne Laboratories doesn't meet the FDA's specifications."

"That's not possible. The lab is wrong." King combed his fingers through his hair. "You have to understand that companies like us—including our research department and suppliers—can all be targets of theft. That's why many companies— like our own—use security specifically for pharmaceutical companies. You wouldn't believe the logistics when it comes to the supply chain and our constant need to protect both our research and production. And it's all done to prevent something like this."

"Maybe, but two of your men are dead and one of the wives is missing," Nikki said. "And on top of that, someone broke into your high-security compound last night looking for something. I think it's time to consider the idea that Mac wasn't just paranoid."

Mr. King grabbed his water bottle and took another long drink. "I guess when you look at the whole picture, I believe you may be right."

"Why don't you show us his office," Jack said.

At the other end of the hall, they stepped into Mac's office. Books that had lined the shelves were now strewn across the floor along with papers, file folders, and notepads.

"What kind of security do you have for the building itself?" Nikki asked.

"Top-notch. Or so I thought. All I can figure is someone hacked into the security system or it was an inside job."

"We'll bring in a forensics team and see what they can find," Nikki said.

King rested his hand on the doorknob and hesitated. "Of course, though I'll need to make a few calls before anyone goes through his office. His research was highly competitive, which means there's classified information, intellectual property research and development—"

"In case you've forgotten, Mr. King," Nikki said, not in the mood to deal with a bunch of red tape, "two men have been murdered and your security has been breached."

Twenty minutes later, Nikki and Jack headed through the lobby and outside Byrne Laboratories' main entrance toward her car after finishing their initial investigation.

"Do you think King—or anyone else we spoke to—knows more than they're telling us?" Nikki asked.

"It's hard to tell. If someone does know something, they're going to be doing everything they can to cover their tracks."

"Like kill Mac."

"Whoever broke in had to have been looking for the evidence Mac had."

"Agreed."

"We need to find that evidence."

Jack's phone rang. He glanced at the caller ID. "Give me a second," he said.

"Holly?" Nikki asked.

"No comment," he said, moving to the back of the car to answer the call.

Nikki's phone rang as she slipped into the driver's seat. "Tyler?"

"Hey . . . How's your morning going?"

She put the key into the ignition. Just the sound of his voice managed to push back some of the frustrations from her morning. "Honestly, it's been rough."

For the past hour, she'd been able to shove aside the memory of Mallory's suicide, but she wasn't going to be able to keep it buried. At some point, she'd have to deal with the feelings surrounding the woman's death. But not until they found Lucy and all this was over.

"I'm sorry," he said. "Can I do anything?"

"I'll be okay. Days like this come with the territory. But you know that."

"Maybe we should plan another day out rock climbing," he said. "I'd say we both need some time away from all of this."

She fiddled with her rhinestone key chain. "I'd like that."

"Listen, I won't keep you long, then, but I just thought of something. Katie let George stash a few boxes here at the house in the spare bedroom. I know you haven't been able to find out where he kept his files. It might be a place to start."

"You're thinking he might have kept work-related files there?"

"It's definitely possible. I've never looked through his stuff, but we know he didn't have an office, and there was nothing on the boat. They have to be somewhere. Maybe there's something in his things that will give us a clue. I don't know . . . a storage locker, safe-deposit box . . ."

They needed those files. Needed to know who

George had been investigating when he'd been killed.

"Where are you now?" she asked.

"At home," he said. "Mom and Liam are headed out to the zoo."

She glanced at her watch. It was almost nine. "We're just leaving Byrne Laboratories. I need to drop off Jack back at the station, then I'll be on my way."

18

**9:03 a.m.
Tyler's house**

Forty-five minutes later, Nikki pulled into the driveway of Tyler's house in southeast Nashville, still trying to shake the events of the morning. She wasn't going to play the guilt game. Not this time. But that didn't stop her heart from breaking over the harsh reality that two more people were dead who shouldn't be.

Tyler stepped out of the front door as she walked past the row of newly planted petunias, impatiens, and begonias that lined the brick walkway and filled wooden planter boxes Katie had put in a few years ago. They were a reminder that it had been too long since she'd been here.

And of Katie, who'd always kept the yard looking perfect.

"Your yard looks great," she said, needing to start their conversation off with something ordinary. If there was anything left that was simply normal. Part of her still needed to be convinced that the entire world hadn't fallen off its axis. "Did you put in the flowers?"

"No. My mom came by a couple weeks ago with a friend of hers while I was cleaning out the gutters and planted all of these. Said it was time to spruce things up again. She was right."

She and Tyler had talked about how he'd had to let so many things go since Katie had died. And how hard it was to be a single father.

"What happened this morning?" he asked.

"The reporter I met with last night took a hostage from Byrne Laboratories and accused him of tainting the supply chain."

"Did she have proof?"

"Not yet. She'd tried to prove that an antibiotic given to treat a little girl was tainted. She told the crisis unit she wanted me to negotiate . . . then she jumped off a ten-story building with her victim." Nikki felt a wave of emotion. Telling him brought it all back and made it seem far too real.

"Wow." He reached out and grasped her fingers. "I'm so sorry."

"Me too." She closed her eyes and let him draw her against his chest. Warm. Protective. Calming . . .

She forced herself to step away from his embrace. "I should look at George's files."

"Of course. I know you don't have a lot of time," he said, turning to open the front door. "I'll take you up to where I've been keeping his stuff."

Nikki stepped into the house behind him. Like Katie had done with the yard, she'd been the one who made the house a home. Even a year after her death, little had changed inside. Her touch was still everywhere. From the rockers on the front porch to the collection of seashells on the mantel. There were picture frames on every flat surface and plastered all over the refrigerator in the kitchen. Photos from her and Tyler's wedding and honeymoon, baby pictures of Liam up to his last day of preschool, and every occasion in between. She'd decorated the house with artwork she picked up at local flea markets and buys she couldn't pass up on eBay. In fact, if Nikki thought about it, Katie had always been in the process of remodeling something.

Stepping into the house was always enough to make Nikki forget—at least for a few moments— that Katie wasn't coming back. She and Tyler had talked through the struggle as they'd worked together to go through Katie's personal things, then later turned the baby's nursery into a play- room for Liam. But there were other places in the house, like the breakfast nook in the kitchen she'd been working on when she died, and the upstairs bathroom, that he'd left unfinished.

"I finally got ahold of George's sisters," Tyler said as they walked upstairs. "I haven't met either of them, but I felt like the least I could do is let them know personally what happened. They're now trying to figure out what to do about funeral arrangements. Obviously there are still a multitude of questions—including who shot him."

"I'm hoping we can have some answers soon," Nikki said.

Tyler paused at the door of the extra bedroom in the upstairs hallway. "The last time I was in this room was when you helped me go through Katie's things after she died. One of these days I'll finish."

"When you're ready."

She stepped into the room behind him. This had been Katie's craft room. It was filled with storage boxes, wrapping paper, sewing supplies, and a few unfinished art projects. Some of the things he'd managed to pack up and give away to charity. The rest he'd boxed up neatly and stacked in the closet next to boxes of Christmas ornaments that hadn't been used this past December. Nikki had assured him that getting rid of Katie's things before he was ready would only make him regret his decisions one day. She'd learned that dealing with loss was a one-day-at-a-time process that was completely personal and couldn't be rushed.

She hesitated in the middle of the room beside him and felt that familiar heavy ache in her heart. With Tyler it was a balance of knowing there was nothing she could do beyond being there for him, and at the same time wanting desperately to fix his broken heart.

"Nikki . . ."

"I'm sorry. It's just that . . . I know this is hard for you. I'm sorry. I don't want to be the one to make things worse."

Tyler grabbed one of a dozen storage boxes with George's name on them from the corner of the room and handed it to her. "That's the last thing you have to worry about. You make everything better, never harder."

"Now that was a very sweet thing to say," Nikki said, grinning at him.

He grinned back. "You know, I read something that has really stuck with me recently," he said, grabbing a box for himself. "It said that moving through grief doesn't come by forgetting. You get through it by remembering. I don't want to ever forget Katie, but I am trying to move forward. I have to move forward."

"That's pretty profound." Nikki set the box he'd handed her on the floor and opened it. Inside were a bunch of miscellaneous items. A couple jars of pennies, old magazines, stacks of receipts. "Just like I don't ever want to forget Sarah."

"Exactly. I've made progress, actually. I moved

off the couch and back into our room again, and Liam's started sleeping better the past few weeks." He took another box off the stack, then hesitated before opening it. "There's something else I've been wanting to tell you as well."

She looked up at him and waited for him to continue.

"I'm not sure this is the right time, but . . . I'm thinking about selling the house."

"Selling the house . . ."

His words hit her like a kick to the gut. She searched his face. He looked resolved, maybe even relieved. She was going to have to push aside her own feelings. This wasn't about her. She'd always known there were tough steps he was going to have to take in order to move on with his life. But even though so much had changed, she couldn't see him or Liam living anywhere else. This was their home. Katie's home. To leave all of that behind . . .

"What do you think?"

Nikki grabbed another box and opened it, not sure she should answer his question. "Are you really ready to make a move? There were a lot of memories to walk away from in this house. So much of Katie."

She took a picture of Liam on his third birthday from a stack of photos in the box. Beneath the photos were letters and receipts inside an old candy box. Christmas cards and matchbooks and an old leather wallet. Nothing that seemed to be related to any of George's cases.

"I'm not trying to forget Katie. But I am trying to move on. It's been over a year now, and I need to start finding closure. I can't keep feeling like I'm in limbo the rest of my life. Liam needs me. All of me. And that's something I haven't been giving him. Katie's touch is everywhere in this house. She painted and decorated every room. Picked out where every picture should go. Even the flower garden was her domain. I need a place to start over. A place where Liam and I can make a new life together. I just don't think that can be here."

She pressed her lips together, waiting for him to continue.

"I spoke to a Realtor. She's convinced I can almost double my money, thanks to the improvements Katie made and the property values in the neighborhood. But it's not about the money. It's about finding out who I am without Katie, and even more importantly, about being the father I need to be to Liam."

Nikki dug through the rest of the box, her mind still spinning with the implications. Tyler deserved a fresh start. But if he moved away . . .

She paused for a moment as reality struck. That's what she was really worried about. Losing Tyler.

"And after you sell the house?" she asked.

"I'm not that far yet, though I do know that I'm dropping my summer classes, and I'm not planning to return to school in the fall."

Nikki looked at him, but this time his answer didn't completely surprise her. Tyler was former special ops with experience in criminal psychology, and he craved that adrenaline rush. It was something Katie had never fully understood. While she loved adventure, she'd constantly worried about his safety. And when a bullet had hit him and brought him back home from the Middle East with a Purple Heart, she begged him not to reenlist. And he hadn't. But leaving the corps meant leaving part of himself behind, even if he'd done it because he loved her.

"I know Katie was the primary force behind your going back to school," she said, "but I thought it was something you wanted to do."

"I thought it was something I'd come to enjoy. For Katie. And believe me, I'd do it all over if she were here, but she's not. I've realized that even with my experience, I don't want to spend the rest of my life sitting behind a chair talking with people about their problems."

"So what do you want to do?"

Nikki waited for his answer, trying to combat her own feelings that were pushing their way to the surface. Thoughts of herself and Tyler. Together. Starting over and being a family . . . She pushed those thoughts aside. It was going to take a long time before he was going to be able to contemplate life with anyone else, let alone her.

"I know this is going to sound crazy, but I just received a temporary job offer from a security company overseas that's interested in my services." He grabbed another box and pulled off the lid. "If I take the job, I think it might give me time to figure out what I want to do."

Nikki picked through more office supplies, a few dozen cassette tapes, and electronic cords, and felt her stomach sink. Surely he wasn't saying he was going to take the job? Liam needed him here. She needed him. How foolish she had been, expecting that when the time was right, he'd be able to put enough distance between himself and Katie and turn to her, waiting for him on the sidelines. And that he'd realize he shared her feelings.

A dozen concerns rushed through her head, but she shoved them all aside for the moment. Because this wasn't about her and what she wanted. This was about what was best for Tyler and Liam. And moving on with their lives—even if it meant without her—was what was best.

Wasn't it?

"Where would you be located?" she asked.

"Liberia. The company works alongside the State Department to improve regional stability. I'd be working with their paramilitary and local officials who need to be trained in negotiation methods and mediations."

"Wow. You'd be perfect for the job. How long?"

"I've told them the longest I could come for right now is three months. I won't agree to be there longer than that. But it would help me get a foothold into other jobs here in the US. And give me time to figure out what I need."

"Sounds like a far step from a psychologist's office."

"It is, but that's the point."

"What about Liam?" she asked, then swallowed hard. Tyler would never be able to move on with anyone until he figured out who he was now on his own. And that was something she couldn't do for him.

"Like I said, it will just be temporary. My mother will take care of him for me while I'm gone."

"So you are going?" She tried to push the emotion from her voice and concentrate on the last of George's boxes.

"They just gave me the official job offer yesterday, and they've given me a couple more days to decide, but yeah . . . I'm pretty sure I'm going to say yes."

"Liam needs his father. He needs you here with him—" Nikki closed her mouth before saying anything else. This wasn't her call. She had no business making him feel guilty about his decision. "I'm sorry. It's not my business."

"It's just three months, Nikki."

But she knew how fast kids changed. And on

top of that, Liam had already lost so much over the past year. His mother and now his grandfather. What if he thought he was losing his father as well?

"My mom's happy to keep Liam, but she doesn't think I'm doing the right thing either. I guess I was hoping you would understand. I just need some time to figure things out."

He stood beside her, waiting for her to answer. But all she wanted to do was beg him not to leave. To find the courage to tell him she loved him, and that she'd be there to help him move forward.

She looked up at him. "You know I'll support you in any decision you make."

"But you don't think going is the right decision."

"Maybe there isn't a right or wrong in this situation. And if a couple months away clearing your head will give you the direction you need, you'll end up being an even better father to Liam in the end."

An awkward silence hovered between them. If someone would have told her a year and a half ago that she was going to fall in love with Tyler, she would have laughed. But now everything had changed.

"Liam will be okay," she said. "And so will you."

"I know. Because I have to be. For him." He stuck the lid back on the box he'd been looking through. "I'm not finding anything related to George's cases."

"I'm not either." Nikki pulled out the last box, knowing she needed to let the subject go for now.

"Wait a minute . . ." Tyler pulled out a sheet of paper and a magnetic key case.

"What is it?" she asked, setting her box aside.

"It's a contract with a storage company." He opened up the key case. "Looks like it's to a storage locker. Not too far from here."

"You said he lost his house just over a year ago?"

"His wife—Katie's stepmom—kicked him out. He brought most of these boxes over then. Last I knew, he was renting a studio apartment. I thought he was still there until I found out he'd been living on my boat."

"Renting a storage locker in the process would make sense," she said.

A sound from the backyard caught her attention. She looked toward the window and frowned.

"Nikki . . . What's wrong?"

"Did you hear something?" she asked.

"No. It was probably just the neighbor's new puppy. Barks constantly, especially at night. Drives me crazy."

"I guess everything that's happened today has me paranoid." Nikki pulled back the lightweight curtains to look into the backyard just to make sure. She saw two men, dressed in dark colors and carrying weapons, breaking into the back door.

"Forget paranoia. There are two armed men breaking into your house." Nikki let the curtain fall back into place, then grabbed her phone from her pocket and called dispatch. "This is Special Agent Nikki Boyd. I'm going to need immediate backup."

19

9:45 a.m.

"Backup won't get here in time," Nikki said, already on her way out of the room. She figured they had a minute before the intruders were inside the house. Two at the most.

"I'll grab my Glock from my bedroom and meet you on the landing," Tyler said.

Nikki nodded. They needed to take them together, as soon as they opened the door.

She hurried down the narrow hall of the upstairs floor, wondering what in the world someone was doing breaking into Tyler's house in the middle of the day. But there was one question she didn't have to guess at. This was no coincidence. They'd killed Mac and George. The only thing that made sense was that they believed Tyler was somehow involved.

Thirty seconds later, Nikki edged down the staircase as Tyler fell in behind her, hoping the element of surprise would be enough. She took the last stair and moved silently toward the kitchen in the back of the house. Seconds ticked by. Their options were limited. There was little chance the intruders were going to give up without a fight, but neither did she want them killed. They needed answers, and their best bet was to immobilize them. She glanced at Tyler's profile. Intent. Focused. Extensive weapons and tactical training while he was in the military made her trust Tyler as much as she trusted her team. Completely.

They stepped into the kitchen as the back door swung open.

"This is TBI," she shouted. Gun level. Heart pounding. "Drop your weapons now, and put your hands behind your head."

The element of surprise gave them the advantage they needed, but only for a moment. The two men hesitated. Tyler lunged at the taller one, decisively disarming him before he had a chance to react.

Nikki moved toward the second man, who was shorter but stockier than his partner. Confusion briefly flickered across his face before he lunged forward and slammed Nikki into the counter behind her. She winced at the sharp impact across her tailbone, catching her balance as he lunged at her again. This time she blocked his assault with a solid blow to his kneecaps.

He groaned in pain, turned sharply, and headed back out the door.

"I've got him," Nikki shouted as she followed him while Tyler took off after the other man inside the house.

Adrenaline carried her outside into the large backyard as the intruder flew across the grass toward the back fence. She pushed herself harder, ignoring the pain in her lower back. Another few feet and she'd catch up with him. He began scaling the fence.

Grabbing the bottom of his shirt, she yanked as hard as she could, pulling him to the ground and knocking the wind out of him.

She quickly flipped him over onto his stomach and pressed her foot firmly into his back. Grabbing his gun, she removed the magazine. He squirmed beneath her.

She pressed her foot harder into his back. "Don't even think about it if you know what's good for you."

Thirty seconds later, Tyler emerged from his house, his weapon aimed at the man walking in front of him, hands handcuffed behind his back in defeat.

"Why don't you join your friend here," Nikki said.

"Things would have gone a whole lot easier if

you both had dropped your weapons when we asked the first time," Tyler said.

The man cussed, then fell on his knees.

"Who are you working for?" she asked.

"It doesn't matter," he said, his chin tilted in contempt. "Arrest us, and they'll just send someone else to finish the job. And they will finish the job."

"What job?" Nikki asked.

The man's smile broadened as his gaze shifted to Tyler. "Let's just say I wouldn't stop looking over your shoulder if I were you."

"What job?" Nikki repeated.

The man pressed his lips together, refusing to answer.

"Facedown on the ground," she said.

Nikki glanced at Tyler. The rush of adrenaline had been replaced by a wave of fear. They needed answers. Needed to know who was behind this and if Tyler's life was in danger.

Sirens wailed nearby. A minute later, two uniformed officers came around the back of the house, through the side gate. Nikki held up her badge, careful to keep her weapon aimed at the men with her other hand.

"I'm Special Agent Nikki Boyd with the TBI Missing Persons Task Force," she said as the officers approached them. "We caught these men breaking into this house. Both had weapons. I need you to take them down to the precinct and book them until I or one of my teammates can question them on their involvement with an active missing persons case we're working on."

"Yes ma'am."

The officers pulled the men to their feet, handcuffed the second one, then headed for their squad car.

Nikki stood in the middle of Tyler's backyard, feeling the drop in her blood pressure and heart rate, the aftereffects of an adrenaline surge.

"You okay?" Tyler asked.

She nodded. "Yeah, but I could use a little less excitement these last couple days."

"I agree," Tyler said. "But whoever sent them thinks I'm connected to all of this somehow, though I don't understand how."

"Maybe they thought George gave you something, and they're desperate enough to try and destroy all the evidence. Trying to tie up all possible loose ends." Panic sliced through her. If they saw Tyler as a loose end . . . "If they know about Liam—"

Tyler pulled out his phone and pressed the speed-dial button. "They might decide to use him as leverage to get to me."

"We don't know that. Not for sure."

"But I can't take that chance." Tyler caught her gaze as he waited for his mother to answer. "She's not picking up."

Nikki tried to suppress her own apprehension.

"It could be anything, Tyler. Dead battery, bad reception, ringer turned off."

But she knew that none of those explanations were going to fly until he saw with his own eyes that they were okay.

"If they find Liam—"

"Don't go there. Not yet. For now, we know they're in a public place, and they should be safe."

Tyler tried again, then shook his head. "She's still not answering."

"Keep trying. I'll have a backup team meet me there, then I'm going to see about arranging a safe house for the three of you until we figure out what's going on."

"I'm coming with you," Tyler said as they headed inside to lock up the house.

"Tyler—"

"This is my son, Nikki. I can handle myself, and you know it. I just disarmed an intruder in my house."

She shook her head, but she couldn't argue with him. Instead, she quickly called Gwen to give her an update as they headed for her car.

"Gwen's got a track on your mother's phone's GPS," she told Tyler as soon as she hung up. "And she's going to have zoo security look for them until the authorities show up."

"I can't lose either of them," Tyler said.

"You're not going to."

Nikki drove in silence to the zoo beside Tyler, trying not to let her mind go to the worst-case scenario. They'd find them petting the kangaroos or maybe watching the monkeys. Everything was going to be okay.

"I need an update, Gwen," Nikki said as she parked in front of the zoo and hurried to the front entrance with Tyler. "Have they found them?"

There was a long pause on the line.

"Gwen . . . give me something."

"I just got a call from security," Gwen said. "Virginia Grant's phone was turned in, but so far they haven't been able to find her or Liam. I'm sending in more uniforms so we can coordinate a search. One of the senior staff members will meet you at the gate."

Nikki's heart pounded. She reached out to Tyler, lacing their fingers together. "Someone turned in your mother's phone."

Tyler's face paled as they quickened their pace. "Nikki—"

"They're already looking for Liam and your mother. We're going to find them."

This has to end okay, God. Please . . . Don't let anything happen to them.

Nikki released Tyler's hand, then flashed her badge at the young man working at the front entrance. "I'm with TBI. I'm supposed to meet someone from your management team."

"I'm Michele Rowland with the zoo's senior management team. You can call me Michele." A fortysomething-year-old woman wearing a zoo staff polo shirt and khaki pants walked up to them, her expression grim. "We've just been updated on the situation and want you to know our staff is available to help in any way we can. We already have the staff looking for the pair."

"I appreciate it," Nikki said, following the woman away from the ticket counters.

"I believe this is her phone," Michele said, handing it to Tyler. "It was turned in about fifteen minutes ago to our lost-and-found."

"Yes," Tyler said. "This is hers. What about her car?"

"Her car's still in the parking lot. We checked there first." Michele's phone rang and she answered it, nodded her head a couple times, then smiled. "Got it, thanks."

"Looks like we found them," she said, hanging up her phone. "We can take one of the ATVs we use for getting around to get there faster."

Tyler let out a sharp breath of relief. "How far?"

"Not far at all. They're at our Critter Encounter exhibit."

"Liam's favorite spot," Tyler said.

A couple minutes later, Nikki caught site of Liam's blond hair and Tyler's mom, who was wearing a lime-green capri pantsuit. Two local law enforcement officers stood beside them. As they stepped out of the ATV, Nikki glanced around the fenced-in, open space where several families with small children were enjoying interacting with the animals. Maybe they'd worried for nothing.

"Liam?" Tyler called out to his son.

"Daddy!"

Liam ran, then jumped into his dad's arms, a huge smile on his face. "You wouldn't believe what we saw. And I just got to pet an alpaca. Do you know what that is?"

He started bubbling on about a baboon they'd seen and a poison dart frog, but Tyler's mom wasn't smiling.

"Tyler?" she asked. "What in the world's going on?"

"Nothing. Everything's fine." Tyler looked at Nikki, then back to his mother. "I couldn't get ahold of you. I got worried."

"So you bring out the entire police department?"

"Yes . . . no . . . I just wanted to make sure you were okay."

"We're fine."

Nikki pulled Virginia aside while Liam continued telling Tyler his story.

"This has to do with George, doesn't it?" Virginia asked.

Nikki nodded. "We were at Tyler's house, and there was a break-in."

"A break-in?"

"We think that whatever George was investigating got him killed."

"And now they're after Tyler?" Virginia asked.

"It's a possibility we can't ignore. Have you seen anyone acting suspicious? Anyone that stood out?"

"No. I . . . Wait . . ." Virginia clutched her handbag against her. "There was this man. I saw him a few minutes ago. I didn't think anything about it at the time, but he might have been following us. He walked away as soon as those officers approached us."

"Can you describe him?"

"I don't know . . ." She glanced around, flustered. "I guess he was average height and wore a . . . brown bomber jacket. Auburn hair. He had some sort of tattoo on the back of his hand. I only noticed him because you don't see a lot of single guys walking around the zoo. Mainly families, women with kids, older couples . . . But that doesn't make him guilty."

The hair on the back of Nikki's neck stood up. It was the same description as the man she'd seen following Mallory at the airport.

Nikki glanced around the enclosed area for anything or anyone that looked out of place. It was just like Virginia said. A couple families with preschoolers were having fun with the animals. No one suspicious. But that didn't mean Tyler and his family were safe. She wasn't going to stop worrying until they were out of the open, and out of danger. Or at least until they had a chance to question the men who'd broken into Tyler's house and had some answers.

Tyler's mom grasped Nikki's arm. "Do you really think someone's after my son?"

"I don't know yet, but I'm going to make sure he's safe. And make sure that you and Liam are safe as well."

"I need to talk to Tyler alone, please."

Nikki glanced at Tyler, then turned to Liam. The boy had been through enough lately. He didn't need to know what was going on.

"I heard this was your favorite part of the zoo. Want to show me one of those alpacas?"

Liam took Nikki's hand, happy to introduce her to a brown baby alpaca with a white head, while Tyler talked to Virginia.

"What else have you seen today?" Nikki asked.

"Meerkats and monkeys."

"Sounds like fun. I always loved the zoo. My favorite animal is the leopard. They're so strong and yet elegant."

But Liam wasn't smiling anymore. He let go of her hand. "Something's wrong, isn't it?"

"What makes you say that?" Nikki caught the fear in Liam's eyes and prayed for wisdom to know how to respond.

"Daddy's scared. Mamaw's scared."

She shook her head. "There's nothing you have to worry about."

"Dad always tells me not to worry, but I know he worries. Just like he still gets sad when I ask about Mama. Just like I know bad things can happen."

Nikki hesitated. There was a lot more wisdom in this six-year-old than any of them probably realized. "Like the day your mom died?"

Liam nodded. "I miss her."

She tousled his hair and crouched down beside him. "I miss her too. We all do."

"Daddy tells me I'll see her again one day in heaven. But sometimes I think I'm forgetting what she looks like."

Nikki felt her heart swell with a mixture of sadness and wistfulness. "That's why you have your pictures. And the album Mamaw made you."

Liam nodded. "Is Daddy sad today? Did something else bad happen?"

"I think he's more worried than sad. He couldn't get ahold of your mamaw, and sometimes he worries. But that's just because he loves you."

"I know he worries that something will happen to us. Something like what happened to Mama."

Nikki nodded. She wasn't the one to tell him his grandfather had died. Or even the fact that their lives might be in danger. But neither did she want to play games with him and pretend nothing was wrong. "You're a pretty wise kid, you know that?"

"Ha! I'm just six."

Nikki laughed, then pulled him into her arms and gave him a big hug.

"How come you haven't been over to our house for a long time?" he asked, stepping back.

Nikki stood up, searching for an answer. "I've been busy working. I've missed seeing you though." She frowned, knowing it sounded like another excuse.

"Are you mad at Daddy?" Liam asked.

"Mad? No. Not at all. Just . . . like I said. Busy with work."

"Daddy says you work too much. I think he misses you too when you don't come over. Kind of the way he misses Mama."

Nikki swallowed the lump in her throat as a goat nudged up behind her. She watched Liam reach out and pet it, refusing to read anything into the words of a six-year-old. She'd been a part of his life since his birth. Just like she'd been a part of Katie and Tyler's life.

She looked over to where Tyler and his mother stood. Behind them, Jack had just entered the enclosure.

"Nikki . . . You found them," he said, steering clear of a donkey.

"Hey, bud . . . ," Nikki said to Liam, "why don't you go back to your dad for a second. I'll be right there."

She waited for Liam to join his father before

turning to Jack. "We might have been right. Virginia said she noticed a man following them a few minutes ago, and the description is similar to the guy I saw at the airport. She thought she was just being paranoid, but at this point we can't dismiss anything."

"I agree."

"I think we need to get the three of them somewhere safe."

"It might take time to get something set up—"

"I've got an old friend who owes me a favor," she said. "She's got a ranch outside the city that would work."

"Who's your friend?"

Nikki shook her head. "That will have to stay confidential, but I think I can make a phone call and arrange something. She's in the music business and on tour right now."

"The place is secure?"

"The cost of fame. Closed-circuit surveillance, alarms, and a top-notch staff that can be trusted—all former military."

"Give her a call then."

Nikki nodded. "We can get them settled, then go check out George's storage unit while Gwen questions our two intruders."

Ten minutes later, with arrangements to use the house finished, Nikki slipped her phone back into her pocket. Tyler wasn't going to like the idea, at least not for himself, but she knew it was the right thing to do. Until they knew who was after Lucy —and clearly now Tyler—they were going to need to take every precaution they could until they got to the bottom of this.

"Tyler . . ." Nikki caught up to him while his mother and Liam were escorted toward one of the zoo's ATVs. The sooner they got them out of here, the better she was going to feel.

"Why do I have the feeling I'm not going to like what you're about to tell me?" he said.

"Please don't argue with me, but I've just arranged a safe house for the three of you."

"A safe house?"

"It's a friend's home, actually. She's traveling and doesn't mind. It would just be for a few days, but the place is completely private and secure, and you'd be safe until this all blows over. Plus, it's a ranch with horses and dogs. Liam will love it."

He hesitated briefly, then nodded. "Okay."

"Okay?" Nikki raised her brow. "I was prepared for a heated debate. You're not going to argue with me?"

"I've lost enough. I'm not losing them. Even if it means a day or two of confinement." They broadened their steps in order to catch up with the others. "Though I am hoping it's not going to be longer than that."

"I can't make any promises, but I'll come help get you settled."

He stopped at the edge of the enclosure. "What about you? I'm still not convinced you're safe. It wouldn't be the first time someone connected to a case you were working on came after you."

He'd been with her six weeks ago when a man had come after her, threatening to kill her. She'd almost died that day.

But this was different.

"I'm going to be okay, Tyler. We both are."

They had to be. Because the stakes had just upped another notch, and neither of them were ready to lose someone else they loved.

20

1:00 p.m.
Dee Dee's Self Storage

It was the first time Nikki had had a chance to call her brother all morning. With Tyler and his family settled at her friend's ranch, she followed Jack through the storage facility where George had rented his unit, waiting for the phone to ring. The call immediately went to voice mail.

She let out a huff of air. "Luke, this is Nikki. Just wanted to make sure you're okay. Call me. Please."

They stopped in front of number 63.

"Let's hope this gives us some answers," she said.

She slid the key they'd found at Tyler's house into the padlock of the storage unit, popped open the lock, then rolled up the steel door. Taking a step inside, she squinted and tried to adjust her eyes to the dim lighting. A wall of cardboard boxes, all labeled with a black marker, framed the front of the unit. She scooted through a small opening as Jack flipped on the overhead light.

The florescent light flickered on, illuminating the back of the unit.

Nikki's eyes widened. "Whoa . . ."

"What is it?"

"You've got to see this for yourself."

Jack squeezed into the space next to her. Behind the six-foot wall of boxes, the storage unit had been set up as living quarters, with a twin-sized bed, lounge chair, a battery-operated lamp, and a small desk. Another row of boxes were stacked four high along the back wall, along with a tool-box, a couple pieces of furniture, and three large file cabinets. More than likely, everything George had owned was sitting right here in a twelve-by-twelve storage unit.

Nikki picked up a worn copy of John Grisham's latest novel off the bed. "So George was not only using this as a place to store his stuff, but as a temporary office and living quarters as well."

"You've got to admit, it's cheaper than office space," Jack said.

"And illegal. I'm surprised the owners didn't find out and evict him." She dropped the book back onto the green-and-yellow Hawaiian bedspread. Sweat beaded at her temples, thanks to the humid, stagnant air. "I don't get it. They might not have been close, but George could have gone to Tyler or one of his sisters and asked for help. How in the world did it come to this? A fifty-five-year-old man living out of a storage unit. Makes me feel sorry for him."

She flipped open the top of a box filled with sci-fi novels. Katie would have been crushed to see this as well. She might not have liked a lot of what her father did, but had she known, she'd never have let it come to him having to live like this.

"Asking for help isn't easy for some people," Jack said, poking around the man's desk. "I don't know anything about George, but I know how it was with my own father."

"What happened with him?" Nikki opened up a second box filled with prescription eyeglasses, batteries, postage stamps, and rubber bands, and let out a lungful of air. They needed his case files. And something that would lead them to Lucy. They had to be in this room somewhere.

"When I was thirteen, my mom ran off with

another guy," Jack said. "Left my dad and us kids on our own. Three months later, my dad was laid off from his job. And yet no matter how bad it got, he refused to ask for help. I remember being down to our last box of cereal, and he was still too proud to ask for a handout from family, or anyone, for that matter."

Nikki glanced up to where Jack was looking through a box on top of a card table. "What did you do?"

"Eventually he found full-time work again, but it paid barely more than minimum wage. I started mowing lawns and buying groceries with the extra money. But it was like this elephant in the room we never talked about. Even taking money from his son was unacceptable."

"That's sad."

"Maybe, but for him it was the only way he knew how to keep his pride." Jack picked up a piece of wireless video equipment. "As for George . . . he might have been broke, but he sure had a lot of expensive equipment. Surveillance equipment, recorders, GPS trackers. And here's something else that's interesting."

"What's that?" Nikki asked.

Jack pulled a handful of slips from an envelope. "Did Tyler ever mention that George was a gambler?"

Nikki shook her head. "Not that I can remember."

"These are win/loss statements from a local casino," he said, handing the pile to her.

Nikki glanced at the dates. "These are all for the last six months or so. And it doesn't look as if he was on a winning streak."

"Let's just say he would have been a lot better off if he'd stayed away from the slot machines," Jack said, pulling another batch of slips from an envelope. "The ones here go back at least a year."

"And would help to explain his money issues and why he felt like he needed to open credit cards in Tyler's name," Nikki said. "Katie told me he was good at his job, but losing his wife, his home, and Katie must have pushed him over the edge. He starts gambling, loses badly, and can't pay his rent. He gets evicted from his apartment and, with nowhere else to go, ends up living here until he can get things together."

"Then why was he on Tyler's boat?" Jack asked.

"I don't know. It's been hotter than normal the past few days, and this unit isn't air-conditioned. It's got to be close to ninety degrees in here."

She searched through another box. A pile of small binders with handwritten notes, a box of memory cards, and half a dozen voice recorders. Photo printer, binoculars . . .

"It's going to take a lot of time to go through all of this," she said. "But there have to be photos, notes, surveillance . . . something."

At a glance, it looked like George had been

meticulous with his notes, but she couldn't see any sense of order to his filing system.

"Looks like Tyler was right, and he used notebooks or digital voice recorders."

Jack opened one of the file drawers. "Makes sense. There are six or eight memory cards here."

Nikki opened up another box, pulled out a manila folder, then paused. "Hold on." She picked up a stack of photos. "Take a look at these."

"What are they?"

She sat down on the bed, then set down two of the eight-by-ten photos. "King clearly had a secret he didn't want out."

Jack picked up one of the photos. "King from Byrne Laboratories?" He let out a low whistle. "These aren't exactly photos you want your mother to see."

There were at least two dozen photos of King with a woman outside a hotel room.

"I saw the family photo he keeps on his desk," Nikki said. "And this is definitely not his wife."

"But I'm still not connecting the dots here," Jack said, dropping the photo back onto the bed. "George said Mac hired him to see if his wife was having an affair. Why was he spying on the man's boss?"

"I don't know. Maybe this was a different case. Or maybe George lied to us. But either way, this definitely looks like blackmail," she said, pulling out the rest of the photos. "And here's another one with King and the man on the roof today."

"So who's blackmailing who?"

She shoved the photos back into the envelope. "You think George was blackmailing King?"

"It's possible. He was strapped for cash. What better way to earn a few grand."

"Maybe," she said. "But there has to be something else we're missing."

"You think it's related to our dead reporter and her counterfeit drug claims?"

Nikki nodded. "It would make sense that either King or Mac—or maybe both—were involved."

"We need to search these files, then have CSU comb through the rest. And maybe use Tyler to help us. He knew George better than any of us."

"Excuse me."

Nikki turned around. A woman stood in the doorway of the unit. Asian, midfifties, no more than five foot five, dark hair with gray streaks, pulled back in a ponytail.

"My name's Lilly Chéng. I'm the manager of this business. I'm going to need to ask what the two of you are doing here."

"Special Agents Nikki Boyd and Jack Spencer with the Tennessee Bureau of Investigation." Nikki stepped out into the sunlight where it wasn't as crowded and held out her badge. "We're following a lead for a case involving George Brennan."

The older woman clenched her hands in front

of her. "I was hoping to avoid a run-in with the law. How did you find out about him?"

"About George?" Nikki asked.

"That he was living here. I'm assuming that's why the two of you are here."

"No, it isn't, actually."

"Then why . . ." She frowned. "Wait a minute. Did something happen to him?"

"How well did you know him?" Jack asked, not answering her question.

"Not well, but he rented from us. I just saw him a few days ago. He came by for an hour or two. I think he used this place for his office as well as a place to sleep until I threatened to evict him."

"Why do you think something happened to him?" Nikki asked.

"I don't know. When I saw him, he seemed . . . agitated. Upset about something. I knew he was a private detective. Told me most of the work he did was surveillance. You know . . . shady stuff like uncovering infidelity. So I guess I figured with that kind of work, you were bound to make somebody mad at you. I felt sorry for him. Told me he'd had a string of bad luck. His wife had left him . . . his daughter had died."

Nikki glanced at Jack. The story had been all over the news, but clearly the woman had missed it. "George was killed yesterday."

"Killed?" The woman pressed her hand against

her heart and shook her head. "No . . . No . . . This is all my fault."

Nikki wasn't following. "I'm sorry . . . why is this your fault?"

She took in a shuddering breath. "I've felt awful about this for days. But like I just said, I had to confront him about sleeping here. You saw how the unit was set up. A bed, desk, office equipment. He'd been living here for weeks . . . maybe months . . . To be honest, I'm not even sure."

"When did you find out?"

"About a week ago. My husband and I recently took over managing the facility. In the process, I found quite a few discrepancies—including the fact that the previous owner was skimming money off the books. That and allowing a few tenants to live in their units. And as much as we hated having to say anything, my husband and I decided it wasn't worth the risk to look the other way."

"So what did you do?" Jack asked.

"Confronted him as nicely as I could. Told him it was not only against our policy, but that it was also illegal for him to be actually living in the unit."

"What was his reaction?"

"Initially, he was upset, and I believe a little embarrassed. At first he tried to argue with us, but my husband was insistent that he couldn't live here. I really did feel bad, but it's honestly not safe. There's no running water or bathroom facilities. The units aren't fire-rated or climate-controlled, which is why insurance doesn't allow it. There was an incident just last winter where a space heater burned down an entire row of storage units. It's just not worth the risk."

Nikki glanced back at the row of boxes. "His stuff is still here, so he obviously didn't move out."

"No. I told him if he didn't stop sleeping here voluntarily, I'd be forced to start a formal eviction process. After that he'd have three days to vacate the premises. I didn't want to do that, but the law is on my side. If he followed the rules, though, we would let him continue to store his things here."

"What did he say to that?"

"He agreed. Told me his son-in-law had a place he could stay, but that he wanted to continue storing his things here. I decided not to deny him access to the unit as long as he was only here during the hours we were open. I went as far as giving him information on a couple of shelters and charities that could help him, though he wasn't very receptive. I think I upset him. Implying he was homeless."

"When did this happen?" Jack asked.

Mrs. Chéng scratched the side of her head. "About five . . . six days ago, I guess. And he's been back several times, but never past closing. My husband made sure of that."

Nikki turned to Jack. "That's why he's been living on Tyler's boat."

"So he was killed because I evicted him—"

"No," Nikki said, trying to reassure the woman. "His death had nothing to do with him leaving. You did what was right."

"Is there anything I can do?"

"We'll be bringing CSU to go through his things. I'm also in contact with his family. I'll talk to them about moving out the rest of his things."

"He's paid up through the end of next month. That's one thing about George—according to the records, he's been renting out this place for over a year and never missed a payment."

Nikki's phone rang as the manager left, and she grabbed it out of her jacket pocket. "What have you got for me, Gwen?"

"Unfortunately, the two thugs who broke into Tyler's house still aren't talking, but I do have some information on the man who died this morning."

Nikki switched the phone to speaker. "Go ahead. Jack's here as well."

"Okay . . . His full name was Adnan Patil. Born in Delhi, but later immigrated to the US with his brother, where he finished his education. They both became US citizens about fifteen years ago. He was single, forty-two years old, and apparently brilliant. Started working for Byrne Laboratories in 2006. Over the past decade he worked on a number of projects, and for the past five years, he worked with Mac Hudson."

"What about the brother?"

"Saad Patil. Turns out the FBI has an open file on him, though I still haven't been able to dig up much information. While he's managed to avoid any run-in with the law in this country, he was questioned about being involved in a theft of two prescription drugs that were worth over three million dollars each. But there wasn't enough evidence to convict him."

"What in the world do they do with the drugs?" Nikki asked.

"According to my contact at the FBI, they either pose as distributors and try to sell the drugs to hospitals, or more likely, they would be shipped to Latin America or Asia and sold on the black market."

Nikki looked up at Jack, a sick feeling spreading over her. Mallory very well might have been on to something. "If Saad Patil has been involved in distributing counterfeit drugs, this might actually be starting to make sense. Adi Patil would be the perfect inside man, and together they'd have the skills to not only create a cheap, counterfeit drug, but also to get it placed within the US supply chain, which would increase both distribution and profit."

"But how do King and Mac fit in?" Jack asked.

Nikki leaned against the brick siding of the

storage unit. "According to Mallory, Mac was trying to find evidence of a breach."

"And," Jack said, "if we're on the right track, it wouldn't have hurt for them to have someone in upper management like King involved. Blackmail can motivate people to do all kinds of things."

"And if they have Lucy?" She didn't want to ask about what she was really thinking. Because if they had found Lucy, the odds that she was still alive were quickly fading.

"So far all they've left behind is a body trail," Jack said.

"What do you want to do next?" Gwen asked.

"Have Dwight King brought in," Nikki said. "I think it's time we finished our conversation."

21

3:04 p.m.
Precinct

Nikki stepped into the air-conditioned precinct, her mind running in a hundred different directions. She was trying not to worry about Tyler and Liam, knowing they were off the grid and surrounded by security. Trying not to worry about her brother, who she still couldn't get ahold of. And then of course there was Lucy. The deeper they dug into her case, the more layers they discovered. But nothing they'd found so far had led them to the missing woman. And Nikki was finding it impossible not to jump to a worst-case scenario in all three situations.

Because this case clearly had a far longer reach than what they'd first thought. A possible counterfeit drug, blackmail, murder, suicide . . . But while they had pieces of the puzzle, they still didn't know where Lucy was.

A young woman with short, dark hair and a furrowed brow brushed into Nikki as she hurried through the lobby. "I'm sorry. I wasn't paying attention to where I was going."

"Can I help you?" Nikki asked.

"Yes, actually." The woman shot her a perky smile. "I'm looking for Jack Spencer. I've tried to call him several times, but he's not answering his phone, and the receptionist didn't know where he was."

"Is this related to a case?" Nikki asked.

"A case? No . . . Nothing official." A blush crept across her face. "Jack's just a . . . friend of mine. We had planned to meet for lunch today, but he told me he had to work. I decided to swing by and bring him some dessert from this restaurant I discovered downtown. They have the best chocolate-pistachio mousse cake in the world."

"You brought him cake?" Nikki asked, eying the pink carryout box.

"Yes . . . but I'm sorry. I should have introduced myself. I'm Holly Logan. Jack and I have gone out a few times."

"Holly. Of course. Jack's mentioned you several times."

"Really? He's told you about me?"

Nikki tried not to notice that the woman looked more like a college coed than a professional allergist in her skinny jeans, bright-pink ribbed cardigan, and a matching oversized handbag.

She buried the thought. Who Jack dated was none of her business. "I work with Jack, actually, and he told me that the two of you had started seeing each other. He just didn't tell me you were so . . . young."

Nikki winced as the word came out before she had a chance to filter her comment, but Holly didn't seem to care.

Instead, she flipped a strand of hair behind her ear. "I'll take that as a compliment, thank you." She leaned forward as if they were simply two women gossiping about the men in their lives. "I've always preferred dating older men. They're so much more stable and confident than guys my age."

Nikki took a step back, preferring not to guess what Holly's age really was, let alone continue this line of conversation with someone Jack was dating.

"You know, Holly, I—"

"It's been a while since I've been in a relation-ship," Holly rambled on. "And you know how the first few dates can be a bit awkward. Let's just say we're still in that stage."

Nikki forced a smile. "I'm sure we've all been there."

"So do you know if he's here?"

Nikki cleared her throat. "He just dropped me off, actually. He had to run a personal errand, but he shouldn't be long if you want to wait here in the reception area."

Holly glanced at the row of chairs where a couple sat with a squirming toddler. "No, that's okay. I won't stay. I know he's busy doing cop stuff, and I don't want to bother him." She handed Nikki the box. "It sounds so cool to say I'm dating a cop. But anyway, if you would just give this to him. Tell him I was thinking about him, and sorry we missed our lunch date."

"Of course. I'm sure he'll be in touch with you as soon as he's free."

Nikki watched Holly walk away before heading to see Gwen, who was busy working on her laptop.

"Hey." Nikki dropped the takeaway box and her bag onto her desk, then leaned against the edge.

"You've had quite a day so far," Gwen said with a hint of concern in her eyes. "You okay?"

"Starting the day off with a suicide, followed

by an armed home invasion . . . I've had better days. I'm going to be doubly glad when we catch these guys. When Lucy is safe, and this is over."

"We're going to find her."

"I hope so." Nikki gripped the edge of the desk. "Has King been brought in yet?"

"No." Gwen glanced at her watch. "But I expect him in the next hour. In the meantime, I've got several things for you. Preliminary autopsy report from the ME just came in, and so far George's story is checking out. Hudson was shot in his house, then died on the boat."

"George might have been telling the truth about that, but he didn't tell us everything."

"What do you mean?" Gwen asked.

"We found surveillance photos in his storage unit that he'd taken of King with a woman who isn't his wife."

"Blackmail?"

Nikki folded her arms across her chest. "Looks like it."

"Hired by whom?"

"That's what I'd like to know."

"I could go pay a visit to his wife," Gwen said. "See if she knows anything about them."

"Perfect."

"What did I miss?" Jack asked, stepping into the room.

His phone went off as he sat down at his desk.

He glanced at the caller ID, then shoved it back into his pocket.

"Gwen was just catching me up on the ME's preliminary autopsy results," Nikki said, "but if you need to take a call . . ."

"It's nothing."

"If it's Holly . . . ," Nikki said, unable to resist giving him a hard time.

"Wait a minute. Am I missing something here?" Gwen asked. "Who's Holly?"

Nikki shot Gwen a grin. "Ask him."

She took the bait. "Who's Holly?"

"Seriously, Nikki? Remind me not to divulge my private life to you in the future."

"You still didn't answer my question," Gwen said.

"Jack went to see an allergist a couple of weeks ago," Nikki said. "Her name's Holly."

"We hit it off and have gone out a couple times."

Gwen tapped her pen against her lower lip. "Definitely sounds like a good thing, but why do I have the feeling things aren't going as smoothly as you'd like?"

"I don't know yet." Jack leaned back in his chair and scratched his wrists. "She's beautiful, fun, energetic, but lately I'm wondering if she might be a bit . . . needy."

"She came by a few minutes ago, and I met her," Nikki said, watching for Jack's reaction.

Jack sat up. "You . . . you met her?"

Nikki nodded at the pink box. "She said you had to cancel your lunch date, so she decided to bring you something."

Jack stood up and grabbed the box off her desk, opened it, then scooped up a bite of frosting with his finger. "Okay . . . this cake is good—really good, actually—but don't you think it's a bit . . . I don't know . . . creepy?"

"Creepy?" Gwen asked. "She brought you dessert. I think that's sweet."

"Me too," Nikki said.

Jack dropped the box onto his desk. "Would you think it's sweet if I told you that on Monday, she was at my house, waiting for me with dinner because I had to work late and she was worried about me?"

"Well—"

"In the past week, I've received an average of ten text messages from her a day and probably six or seven calls. She doesn't seem to realize that I can't always just grab the phone and give her my full attention."

Nikki tried not to laugh. "Okay, that might be just a little creepy, but hey, you got a slice of pistachio chocolate cake out of it. I've heard it's out of this world, but . . ." She hesitated.

"But what?" Jack said.

"She just seemed a bit . . . I don't know. Young for you."

"How old is she?" Gwen asked.

"We're six years apart. So what?" Jack tugged at his tie. "She's over twenty-one and legal."

"Six years apart?" Nikki asked.

"Fine. Nine, but who's counting?"

"Okay, you two," Gwen said with a chuckle. "There is one other piece of information I just received."

Nikki turned back to Gwen while Jack opened the box again and took another bite of his cake.

"I don't know if this is going to be of help in finding Lucy, but forensics got a hit on a partial fingerprint on the cocaine found on the *Isabella*."

"And . . . ," Nikki prompted.

"It belongs to Jason Turner."

"Jason Turner?" Jack leaned back against his desk. "The guy whose boat we commandeered? So he'd been on the *Isabella* as well."

Nikki shook her head. "The plot just keeps getting thicker and thicker, doesn't it?"

"He's got quite a rap sheet," Gwen continued. "A couple of DUIs, a drug bust . . ."

"Any of Lucy's fingerprints or DNA on the boat?"

"None, which confirms George's story that she wasn't there. Unfortunately, I haven't been able to find any footage on the marina surveillance cameras of George arriving at the *Isabella* that night."

"Homicide interviewed Turner yesterday, but they could have missed something. I think we should head over there," Nikki said, grabbing her bag. "There's a chance Mr. Turner saw something."

"DEA wants in on this," Gwen said, "but they've agreed to let you talk to him first. I'll let them know they can pick him up later this afternoon."

Jack started out with Nikki, then stopped to grab his cake. "Maybe I was wrong. Holly might be worth keeping around after all."

The smell of fried fish and hush puppies greeted them from the marina restaurant as Nikki and Jack stepped onto the dock. At almost four, the temperature had dropped slightly with an added cool breeze coming off the water. A group of teenagers laughed as they made their way up the dock.

"I've never understood the attraction of living on a boat," Jack said as they passed a boat where a couple had taken up summer residence.

"I'm not sure I do either," Nikki said, "though clearly it has its advantages for people who want a simpler life."

The *Isabella* sat in the water with sunlight reflecting off her bow. The yellow crime-scene tape had been taken down once CSU had finished their work. For Katie's sake, she wanted to believe George really had changed and had been nothing more than an innocent bystander. But she still wasn't sure. There were too many questions. And he wasn't here to answer any of them.

"Looks like Mr. Turner is in," Nikki said, as they approached the express cruiser in the adjoining slip and caught sight of the man.

At least they wouldn't have to hunt down another person.

A couple of suitcases sat near the boat's stern. Nikki frowned. Apparently the man wasn't planning to stick around very long.

"Mr. Turner." Nikki held up her badge and smiled at the man. "I'm Nikki Boyd with the Tennessee Bureau of Investigation. This is my partner, Jack Spencer. You let us borrow your boat yesterday."

"Clearly you have your own definition of the word 'borrow,' but I already spoke to an officer about what happened," he said, adjusting the brim of his ball cap.

"We understand that," Jack said, "but we'd like to ask you a couple more questions, if you don't mind."

Turner's gaze narrowed. "You're not planning to 'borrow' my boat again, are you?"

Nikki chuckled at the worried look on his face. "No, not today."

"Good, because I'm going to have to wax it all over again as it is."

"Sorry about that," she said. "I understand you're here most evenings?"

259

"Sure." Turner shrugged. "If I'm not at work, I'm usually here."

Jack glanced at the suitcases. "Though it looks as if you're going somewhere?"

"I just started a new job," he said. "I've been out of work for a while, living here on my boat. I'm moving into an apartment."

"Were you here Wednesday night, between five and eight?" Nikki asked, still not ready to buy his story. If the man was guilty, he could be running.

"Yeah. I guess."

"Did you see anyone boarding the boat next to you?"

Mr. Turner shrugged. "I'm used to seeing people coming and going all the time."

"Did you know Mr. Brennan? The man who'd been staying there the last couple weeks?"

"George? Can't say that I really knew him, but I spoke to him a few times. He was friendly. Seemed as if we were both in the same situation. Wife kicked him out. Was trying to get back on his feet. I felt sorry for him, actually."

"Did you see George arrive Wednesday night?"

"Wednesday . . . I don't remember. It's not like I keep track of who comes and goes."

"Here's the problem," Jack said. "We know you weren't completely forthcoming with the officer you spoke to yesterday. And in fact, I don't think you're being forthcoming right now either."

"What do you mean? That I have some sort of connection to that dead guy?"

"Not the dead guy. But a kilo of cocaine we found on the *Isabella*. Which makes me believe you might be lying about other things as well."

"Cocaine?"

"Drop the innocent act," Nikki said. "We know you were on that boat. Your fingerprint is the only one on the bag of cocaine, which has to be worth what . . . twenty . . . twenty-five grand?" She turned to Jack. "We could be looking at a drug deal gone bad, or—"

"Wait just a minute . . . there's no way you can tie me to murder."

"Your drugs were on the boat," Jack said.

"But to be honest," Nikki said, throwing him a bone, "we aren't interested in pursuing the drug charges. We need to find out what happened to Mac Hudson."

"I said I didn't kill him."

"Then why were your drugs on the *Isabella*?"

"Fine." Turner sighed. "I was worried about getting caught, so I hid the stash on the *Isabella*. It was just supposed to be for a day or two, but then with everything that happened yesterday . . . So much for trying to keep a low profile. With all the police buzzing around this place, I was never able to get the drugs back."

"So you saw George that evening?"

Mr. Turner's frown deepened. "Yes, I saw him, but I don't think he saw me."

"What time was that?" Nikki asked.

"It had just gotten dark, so somewhere between eight thirty and nine."

"What was he doing?"

"Helping some guy down the dock. He looked injured. I thought it seemed a bit odd, but George seemed like a nice guy. I thought he was just helping a friend."

"Was it just the two of them?" Jack asked.

"There was a third guy."

She held up a photo of Adi Patil on her phone. "Is this him?"

"No."

She swiped to the photo of Dwight King. "What about him?"

Turner squinted. "Yeah, that was the other man George was with."

Nikki smiled. Bingo. "And did you see anyone leave later that evening?"

"No, but I'd had a rough day and fell asleep early. Slept like a log. Didn't see anyone until the next morning when you all showed up."

"Have you ever seen this third guy hanging around here before?" Jack asked.

"Maybe once or twice. To be honest, I wondered more than once if George was dealing or something. He seemed to have a few shady friends. They never stayed more than a few minutes."

"Thanks for your help, Mr. Turner," Nikki said, slipping her phone back into her pocket. "We appreciate it."

Nikki turned around as two men wearing suits approached the boat.

"Mr. Turner?" one of them asked, pulling off a pair of sunglasses.

"Yeah?"

"I'm Agent Parker with the DEA." The other one held up a badge. "And this is Agent Jones. We've got a warrant to search your boat."

"Wait a minute." Mr. Turner flashed Nikki a panicked look. "You said—"

"I said *we* weren't interested in pursuing the drug charges. But they are."

Nikki and Jack walked away as the two DEA agents boarded the boat.

"I hope Mr. King is ready for his interrogation," she said, "because we just connected him to Mac Hudson's murder."

22

Nikki watched Dwight King through the one-way mirror outside the interrogation room. Even his designer suit and polished shoes couldn't hide the telltale signs of nervousness. Fingers tapping against the table in front of him. Beads of sweat forming along his brow. She was convinced King knew more than he'd told them. Someone had blackmailed him, and they needed to know who was behind the blackmail, and why.

Jack walked into the observation room, scratching his wrists, which were still fiery red. "You ready for this?" he asked.

"I'm ready for some answers."

Nikki stepped into the room, then slid into the seat across from Dwight King while Jack stayed standing beside her.

"Mr. King." Nikki shot the man a wide smile, hoping to help put him at ease. "I'm sorry we had to ask you to come in, but we had a few more questions that needed to be clarified after talking with you this morning."

"That's fine." He clasped his hands together and met her gaze. "Though I hope we can keep this short. I'm still trying to sort through things back at the office. Everything's still a mess."

"I understand. This shouldn't take long." She glanced down at her notes. "This morning you told us that Mac Hudson came to you last week with some concerns about Byrne Laboratories' security. You also said that while you looked into those claims, you didn't find anything that made you believe that there were any foundations to his claims. Is that correct?"

"Yes. Like I told you, Mac was clearly paranoid." King's Tic Tacs jiggled in his jacket pocket as his leg shook beneath the table. "As a company, we put thousands of dollars into ensuring that things like this don't happen, from our labs all the way to our transport system. So to have a breach in our system is simply not possible. We're not just some online pharmacy, shipping from overseas, selling counterfeit versions of FDA-approved medicines. We're the real deal."

"And yet Mac Hudson was obviously on to something," Jack said, "considering the fact that two hitmen were sent into his house to kill him."

"And I told you I agreed with your assessment."

"True, but here's something we didn't go over," Nikki said, leaning forward. "We believe that not only was there a breach in the supply chain, but that Mac Hudson found out that you were one of the ones involved."

"Wait a minute . . . you think I was involved in

this?" Mr. King's face reddened as he gripped the edge of the table. "You're actually accusing me of putting counterfeit drugs in the supply chain? That's crazy. Why would I do that?"

"I'm going to let you fill in the blanks for that." Any hint of a smile faded as Nikki slid a photo across the table and studied his reaction. "Do you know this woman?"

King rubbed his fingers across his mouth. "I . . . no. She doesn't look familiar."

"Are you sure?" Jack asked.

"Of course."

Nikki slid a second photo across the table. This one was of King and the woman, Delilah Frailey, with their heads close together, chatting about something as they left a local hotel.

"Care to rephrase your answer?" Nikki asked.

King's hand dropped to the table, his frown deepening.

Nikki set down two more photos, one which captured King and the woman in an intimate embrace. "I have more of these—"

"Stop. I have no idea why you dragged me down here to show me these photos. So I've been having an affair. But that's my business," he said, tapping one of the photos. "I'm a grown man, and the last time I checked, while being unfaithful to one's wife might be immoral, it certainly isn't illegal. And it certainly doesn't give you the right to treat me like I'm a criminal."

"All true," Nikki said, "but let me ask you another question. Do you know who took these photos, Mr. King?"

The man squirmed in his chair. "Probably some shady detective my wife hired to find out why I was coming home late at night."

"While that would be a plausible scenario, it wasn't your wife who had these photos taken. In fact, when she saw these pictures earlier this afternoon, it became quite clear she had no idea you were even having an affair. Though I'm sorry to say she does now."

King slammed his fists against the table. "You went and spoke with my wife about my having an affair?"

"One of my colleagues did. Which brings me to my next question," Nikki said, putting down another photo from her file in front of King. "Do you know this man? And before you answer, I would suggest telling the truth this time."

King combed his fingers through his thinning hair. "No."

"You told us that you took a flight back to Nashville this morning after a week of meetings in Atlanta," Nikki continued.

"That's correct."

"Can you tell me when you left for Atlanta?"

"Sunday night. The meetings started the next morning." King's chest heaved. "Why are you asking me all these questions?"

"We have a witness that places you at a marina with this man the night before last." Nikki pointed to the photo. "His name is George Brennan, and he is—was—a private investigator. And what makes this all even more interesting is that he's the man who took these surveillance photos of you and your mistress."

King leaned back in his chair and shook his head. "Impossible. Your witness is mistaken. I was in Atlanta until this morning. You can ask any number of my colleagues who were there. Check flight manifests. Rental cars—"

"Guess what? We've already done that." Jack braced his arms against the table and caught the man's eye. "And do you know what we discovered?"

King shook his head.

"We learned that the husband of the woman you're having an affair with—Thomas Frailey—is quite wealthy and owns a Cessna Citation Excel. That gave you access to a private plane. And while the FAA doesn't require flight manifests for private, domestic flights, we found footage of you leaving Nashville's international airport just before eight o'clock Wednesday night."

Nikki caught the growing fear in King's eyes as he spoke. "I told you I don't know this man."

Jack pulled out a highlighted phone record from the file in front of him. "We have phone records that prove you had a fifteen-minute conversation with George Brennan starting at 5:17 p.m. So when George called you and told you Mac had been shot and that he knew you were involved in a security breach at Byrne Laboratories, you were terrified, because you realized that your secret was about to get out."

"No . . . no . . . no . . . I didn't have anything to do with Mac's death."

"You might not have been involved in his death," Nikki said, "but you came running back to Nashville after George called you. I can't help but wonder what exactly he said to you on the phone, but whatever it was, it was obviously very convincing."

King stared at the table as if weighing his options. But there was no way to deny the evidence staring back up at him.

He blew out a lungful of air. "I got a call a little after five on Wednesday. I was back in my hotel room getting ready for dinner. The man said his name was George Brennan, and I could tell by his voice that he was upset. He told me he had just left Mac Hudson's home, and that Mac— along with two other men—had been shot. The other two men—men who had been sent to kill Mac—were dead."

"Why call you?" Jack asked.

"George said . . . he said he knew I was being blackmailed, and he needed some answers. I started to deny his accusations, but he knew too much."

269

"So you called your mistress," Jack said, "and arranged for a private jet to fly you back to Nashville."

"I might be involved in this mess, but I don't know all the players. They kept me in the dark on purpose, and I needed to know what was going on," King said. "George picked me up at the airport. Mac was in the backseat, in and out of consciousness. George told me Mac had made him promise not to take him to a hospital, and that we needed to find Lucy."

"Why didn't he want to go to the hospital?"

"Mac knew that's where whoever had sent those men would look for him. He was terrified that if he showed up at the hospital, that whoever was after him would find him and then be able to get to his wife. And to be honest, neither of us wanted to have to answer hospital personnel's questions. So George drove us to the marina where he had access to a boat and said we'd be safe while we tried to figure out what to do."

"Did Mac tell you what he knew?" Nikki asked.

"He was delirious. He said he had evidence someone had breached the supply chain with a counterfeit drug, and that we had to find Lucy. But then he died. I knew I had to be back for my meetings so no one could find out I'd been gone. George gave me the keys to his car. I drove to the airport, leaving George to deal with Mac, and took Delilah's private plane back to Atlanta."

"Did Mac tell you where his evidence was?" Jack asked.

"No. He was too far gone to answer any questions."

"What about George?" Nikki asked. "Didn't he know who hired him?"

King tugged on his green paisley silk tie and shook his head. "He never told me who hired him. He said he thought it was just another divorce case and that nothing was said to him about blackmail. I was contacted by email and made payments via cash drops. George told me he had thought it was just another contested divorce proceeding."

"When did you find out about the blackmail photos?"

"About a month ago, I received a set of photos, along with instructions of what I had to do unless I wanted the photos to go public. I was in a panic. I married into both money and the company. If I asked my wife for a divorce—or if she found out I was having an affair—I would lose everything. Someone must have found that out, because they needed someone on the inside who was high enough up in the company to fudge security."

"And you turned out to be the perfect candidate," Nikki said. "What did they ask you to do?"

"I received an email from them every few days, telling me what to do and reminding me what would happen if I didn't."

"But you never found out who was involved?"

"No, and I didn't want to. I figured the less I knew about the entire setup, the better it would be for me in the end."

Nikki's brow rose at his statement. The man had to be completely naive to believe a situation like this would end well.

King looked back down at the table. "I think I need to speak to a lawyer."

"That's fine. But we don't have a lot of time, because we found out about something else this morning. If our suspicions are correct, and Byrne Laboratories has manufactured or distributed a tainted antibiotic, then this isn't just a white-collar crime anymore. A four-year-old girl died this morning."

King looked back up at Nikki. She had his full attention now.

"Wait a minute . . . What are you talking about? You're accusing me of murder?"

"Surely you realized that having a counterfeit drug make it into the supply chain brings with it the potential for serious consequences. And now that's exactly what has happened."

"I told you I only did what they said. I don't know anything else. I'm not a murderer. I could never hurt anyone."

"Maybe you didn't pull the trigger in the Hudson house that night, or even administer the pill that took four-year-old Audrey's life, but things have now spun out of control, haven't they?" Nikki said. "Mac realized something was wrong and started looking into things, but you knew what was going on and did nothing. You had to have known there was the potential of people dying. But you still didn't say anything. Even when they sent in hitmen to take out Mac to silence him."

"Who else is involved in this?" Jack asked.

King rubbed his hand across his jaw. "I don't know. I'm telling you the truth. I just do what I'm told to save my family."

Nikki shook her head. "I'm not sure a jury would see it that way. They're going to see how you found a way to pocket thousands of dollars on the side."

"No . . ." King's hands had started to shake. "They blackmailed me. If I didn't do what they said, they threatened not only to make sure I ended up in jail, but to hurt my family. You have to believe that. I still love my wife, and if anything happened to my children . . . I didn't have a choice."

"That's where you're wrong, Mr. King," Nikki said, standing up to leave. "You always had a choice."

23

Nikki pulled into the driveway of the five-bedroom period farmhouse and parked her car. The setting was not only secure, but idyllic. The picturesque location was surrounded by open pastures framed by a hundred and fifty acres of thick woodlands. The perfect safe haven in the middle of a storm.

Tyler met her in the driveway.

"You're just in time," she said, sliding out of her car. "I've got a few boxes that need to be brought in."

She popped open the trunk, handed him two of the file boxes she'd brought with her for them to go through, then grabbed the last two before managing to shut the trunk with her elbow.

"This place is incredible," Tyler said as he followed her toward the wraparound porch. "When you said safe house, I expected some tiny, nondescript hotel room at best."

Nikki laughed. "I thought you might like this a bit better."

"I can't believe you've never told me you have a friend in the music business. And you still won't give me a hint about whose house it is?"

Nikki glanced at Tyler's profile. "She went by Lulu growing up. I still call her that from time to time, though she hates it, but to me she's still just a longtime friend. We went to high school together and have stayed in touch over the years, even when her parents moved back east after graduation. She returned to Nashville about five years ago to try and jumpstart her career. Let's just say it worked. As for the house, I was told that the fewer people who know who owns it, the easier it is to guard her security. Not that there aren't ways to find out in this day and age, I suppose."

"I've heard rumors that Taylor Swift bought a place out this direction."

"Nope."

Tyler sighed. "She *is* a lot younger than you."

"Thanks."

"Miranda Lambert?" he asked.

Nikki laughed again. "Enough."

"I guess it will have to be enough that the place is incredible. My mom's been making sure Liam doesn't mess up anything all afternoon."

"Tell both of them not to worry," she said as they stepped inside the front door of the house.

"They'll be fine. Mom's watching him swim right now, so he's having a blast."

"Yum," Nikki said. "Has she been cooking too?"

"She decided to keep herself busy and bake a peach cobbler."

"It smells delicious. Jack and Gwen are right behind me with a few more boxes and a couple large pizzas."

"I know a little boy who's going to be extremely happy. Swimming, pizza, and his mamaw's peach cobbler. It doesn't get much better than that."

"That's exactly what he needs right now."

"Welcome back, Nikki." Aaron Sullivan, a former Navy SEAL who now managed the security of the property as well as its employees, met them in the entrance and took one of the boxes from her.

"Thanks, Aaron."

"Why don't we take these into the dining room," he suggested. "The table in there should be large enough for you to work."

"Thanks again for helping me set this up and letting them stay," she said, giving the older man a broad smile. "I know all of this was last minute."

"It's not a problem at all. Most of the staff enjoys having people in the house, and to be honest, it keeps life around here a lot more interesting."

Nikki laughed. "And if I were honest, I'd be happy with a bit of boredom for the next forty-eight hours."

"I'm headed out to the bunkhouse for a few minutes," he said. "Just holler if you need me."

"Thanks, Aaron."

"Tell me what you've found," Tyler said once Aaron had left, setting down his boxes beside hers.

"Well, for starters, we visited George's storage unit and found a bunch of boxes, as you might have noticed. We decided to go through them here, because we could use your help," she said, knowing he was just as anxious as she was for all of this to be over. "The two of you might not have been close, but you knew him better than any of us. You might be able to catch something we would miss."

"Okay. What else?"

She caught his gaze. "We're not sure how long this has been going on, but it looks like George was living in his storage unit. A few days ago, the managers found out what he was doing and told him he'd be evicted if he didn't stop. That's why he moved out to your boat."

"Wait a minute." Tyler tapped his fingers against one of the boxes. "George was living in a storage unit? Why didn't he just come to me for help?"

"I don't know—"

"I do." He shook his head. "Because George never would have come to me for help. Especially in a situation like this. But still, if it were simply a matter of money and time to get back on his feet, I wouldn't have turned him away. He is—was—my son's grandfather."

"This wasn't your fault," Nikki said. "You and Katie both tried to help him on numerous occasions."

"I know, but I feel like I should have known something was wrong." He nodded toward the boxes. "What else did you find in the storage unit?"

"From what I could tell, probably everything he owned."

Tyler frowned. "Any answers to who's behind all of this?"

"I'm hoping we'll find them here. There's quite a bit of stuff to go through, though, so it's going to take time, but I'm hoping we can find something that will help put an end to this."

Tyler sat down on one of the padded wooden chairs and pressed his palms against his thighs. "The last time I saw George, he told me he was getting his life back together. That he had a couple cases lined up and was making pretty good money. I knew he had financial problems after the divorce, but I had no idea it had come down to him living in a storage unit."

"Jack found win/loss statements from a local casino," she said, catching the guilt in his eyes. "He might have been working again, but he'd also been gambling and from what we can tell had lost quite a bit of money. Did he ever talk to you about gambling?"

"No . . . He and his ex-wife went to Vegas at least once a year, but I never got the impression that it was an addiction. Just something they did for fun with a bit of extra cash. Beyond that, I don't know."

"I'm sorry," she said, not knowing what else to say.

"Me too," he said, looking out the window to where another car had just driven up to the house. Jack and Gwen were here. "I just wish things had ended differently between us. And even more important, differently for George."

An hour later, Nikki had yet to settle her own restlessness. The place was built like a fortress. But if that was true, then why did every sound have her jumping?

She got up from the table where she'd been going through George's file and went to the window. There were no cars on the darkened, secluded drive. No unexplainable shadows hovering in the distance. Nothing to worry about. And yet she was worried.

Nikki glanced across the room to where Tyler sat, going through more files. George had been hired by Mac, and now Mac's wife was missing, George had been murdered, a young woman was dead along with the man she killed, and Tyler's life was in danger. All separate pieces of a large puzzle, and she couldn't figure out the common denominator. She let the drape fall back, wishing it wasn't so hard to protect those she loved the most. What if she couldn't protect them? What if something bad happened to Tyler or to Liam or to Tyler's mother?

I feel so out of control, God. So frustrated over what I can't control.

Jack walked over and stopped beside her. "We've got extra officers out front, and security cameras and alarms on the house. Even if they could find us, no one's going to get in."

"I know." She stepped back from the window, but his assurances did little to relieve her worry.

She took a deep breath, inhaling the smell of coffee, pizza, and cobbler. Maybe what she really needed was another caffeine boost.

"I think Virginia just put on a new pot of coffee," she said, turning back to the work in progress. "Anyone up for a refill?"

Jack grabbed his empty cup and handed it to her. Gwen, who was on the phone, shook her head.

"Tyler?"

He glanced up from the files he was going through and shook his head too. "I'm good for now. Thanks."

Nikki took the mugs into the kitchen where Virginia was wiping down the counters while the coffeepot finished dripping. Virginia had kept the caffeine coming the past several hours while they worked through George's files, along with large helpings of cobbler and French vanilla ice cream.

Virginia brushed back a stray strand of her short gray hair and gave Nikki a warm smile. "How's it going?"

"We're still looking for that elusive piece to this puzzle."

"My father used to tell me that a strong cup of coffee could fix just about anything. That and a bowl of warm, gooey cobbler."

"Well, it's certainly helping." Nikki held up the two empty mugs, not missing the fatigue behind the older woman's smile. "You doing okay?"

"Just trying to find ways to keep busy so I don't think about why we're here."

"I can attest to the fact that your cobbler has been a big help."

"I hope so." Virginia let out a low laugh. "When I'm anxious, I like to bake. I'm seeing if I can find what I need for a cheesy sausage breakfast casserole for tomorrow."

Nikki set the mugs on the butcher-block countertop that kept with the theme of the farm-style house, along with its white cabinets, wood flooring, and cheery, red gingham curtains over the row of windows.

Virginia's bright demeanor faded. "I don't know if Tyler ever told you, but before my husband retired, he was a fireman." She finished wiping down the counter, then rinsed out the rag. "I worried about him every day he went out. And do you know what the crazy thing is? It was high blood pressure and a heart attack that killed him. Not a fire."

Just like Katie. No one expected her to die that day out on the water.

"Then Tyler went off and joined the military," Virginia continued, leaning back against the counter. "I watched Katie do the same thing with Tyler. Worrying constantly when he was gone. Knowing that when someone in their company came back in a body bag, it could be him. And then we lost *her*. Life is so . . . unpredictable."

"It is." Nikki ran her finger around the rim of her mug while the coffee finished brewing. "And that worry's hard to avoid. You loved your husband. Loved Tyler and Katie . . ."

"I guess I expected that I'd get used to them going off and putting their lives in danger on a regular basis, but I don't think I ever got used to it."

"And now this," Nikki said.

"This is different, though. My son and possibly my grandson are being targeted." Virginia shook her head. "You know what I mean. I'm a mom and grandma from the suburbs. I spent yesterday dropping off dry cleaning and library books and made a spaghetti casserole for a woman who just had a baby. And today, someone tried to kill my son, and my grandson's life could be in danger."

"I'm so sorry about all of this—"

"Don't be. It's not your fault. The other thing I worry about now is how Tyler and Liam are doing emotionally. Liam especially needs stability in his life right now. He's finally sleeping through the night and acting like a normal little boy again, but I still can't stop worrying about him. Then again, I guess as a mom and a grandma that's my job, isn't it?"

"I know if you were to ask my mom, she'd say it's impossible not to worry."

"Anyway." Virginia waved her hand in the air. "I shouldn't be dumping all this on you."

"Please. This has been a hard day, and you have every right to feel unsettled. Even I have found myself struggling. This has hit far too close to home for all of us."

Virginia caught Nikki's gaze. "I hope you know how much I appreciate you."

Nikki suddenly felt self-conscious. "I'm just doing my job."

Virginia shook her head. "I'm not talking about all that's going on right now. I also mean the way you've been there for Tyler over the last year. You've always gone the extra mile. I don't know where he'd be without you. And knowing him, he doesn't verbalize how he feels as much as he should, but you've been his rock since Katie died."

Nikki reached up to fiddle with her necklace. "I enjoy spending time with him and Liam. They're like . . . family."

The coffee stopped dripping. Virginia grabbed the pot and started pouring the hot liquid into the two mugs. "You know, if Tyler ever decides to get married again, you'd be my first choice for him."

Nikki felt her cheeks flush. Surely her feelings for the woman's son weren't obvious.

"I'm sorry." Virginia rushed on before Nikki could respond. "That was probably far too forward. I just . . . worry about him. Even though I help as much as I can, I know he struggles being a single dad. But of course his love life isn't any of my business, and I would never interfere. I just want to see him happy again."

"Me too." Nikki tried to shrug off the compliment. Virginia had no idea how close to home she'd hit. "But I think it will be a long time before he's ready to open his heart to someone again."

"Maybe." Virginia took a sip of her coffee. "I'm assuming he told you about the job offer he got."

"Yeah. We talked about it a little."

"I don't know how you feel, but while I understand his reasons, I'm not sure I agree with them."

"If he does go, I'd love to come and hang out with Liam every now and then, if you don't mind. He could even come spend the night at my place to give you a break."

Virginia smiled. "I know he'd love that. Liam adores you."

"Hmm . . . why is it that the two of you are in here together and my ears are burning?" Tyler laughed as he walked into the kitchen and pulled his mother into a gentle hug.

Nikki laughed too, hoping he hadn't overheard any of their conversation. "Trust me, we'll never tell."

"She's right," his mother said. "Do you want some coffee?"

"I didn't think so, but those files are beginning to all run together. George might have been thorough with his notes, but he definitely needed a secretary to keep him organized. I've never seen such a haphazard filing system."

"I'll take Jack his coffee before it gets cold," Virginia said, slipping out of the kitchen.

Tyler poured himself a fresh cup, then took a sip. "My mother brought up my job offer, didn't she?"

Nikki hesitated before picking up her cup. "Yes."

"And?"

"She didn't say much."

"I think the whole situation has made her more worried about me than she already was, which doesn't help."

"Of course she's worried about you. She just wants what's best for you."

"Sometimes I'm not sure what I'm doing—to even consider leaving. I keep thinking I'm making the wrong decision. Worried how it's going to affect Liam. What if he thinks I've abandoned him—"

Nikki shook her head. "Stop."

Tyler's eyes widened.

"You're a great father," Nikki continued. "And if you need to go away for a while to take care of yourself and figure things out, then that's what you need to do. Liam knows how much you love him. He's never questioned that, and he never will."

"It's just that I go to class every day, studying how to help other people heal, and I'm still hanging by a thread half the time."

"That's why you should go." Her gaze dropped and her voice came out barely above a whisper. "Go take care of yourself. Find out what's missing, then come back and take care of your son."

She looked up at him and felt her fingers tremble as she grasped the mug. It would be so easy to imagine *that* moment. Tyler returning home to Liam. Returning home to her.

"Nikki?"

She swallowed hard, trying to stifle the emotions she felt. "I just want you to find wholeness again. We all do."

"I know."

He reached out and slid his hand down her arm. She flinched. His touch had become too familiar. Too intimate. She wanted to step into his arms. Have him hold her, tell her he loved her, and that they'd find a way through this. Together. That they could be a family because she was there to plug up the holes in his heart Katie's death had left.

"Nikki?" Jack called from the other room. "I think we might have just found something."

Nikki headed back into the living room with Tyler. "What have you got?"

Gwen fanned out a pile of surveillance photos George had taken of Mac Hudson. "According to the date stamp, these photos were taken after Mac hired George."

Nikki studied the spread of pictures in front of them. All of Mac, in various locations, including Byrne Laboratories and outside his home.

"This doesn't make sense," Tyler said. "If George was working for Mac, why was George taking photos of him?"

"Someone else hired him," Gwen said.

"Wait a minute." Nikki's mind began to spin. "Maybe this does make sense. According to Mallory, Mac thought someone was following him. And we know he'd planned to run as soon as he had the evidence he needed to take these guys down."

"So who had the most to lose from Mac finding out the truth?" Gwen asked.

"More than likely the same person who hired George to take the blackmail photos of Dwight King," Jack said.

"What does seem clear is that someone hired George to shadow Mac and find out exactly what he knew." Nikki glanced at Tyler. "Which meant George was playing both sides."

"And then when he became a liability," Tyler said, "they killed him."

24

8:30 p.m.

They killed George when he became a liability.

Nikki felt a shiver slide through her at Tyler's words. They had enough information to know that whoever was behind this—whether it was one of the Patil brothers, Dwight King, or someone else—had thousands, if not millions, of dollars at stake. And beneath the money trail was the loss of human lives. If Mallory was right, patients who had innocently taken these drugs were dying. Audrey had died, and her family deserved to know why.

Nikki stared at the photos of Mac. Mallory had believed his story, and they both had been working to find evidence inside Byrne Laboratories that would connect the company to a counterfeit antibiotic. Mac's suspicions had cost him his life; Mallory had taken her own in a desperate attempt to get someone to pay attention.

She had Nikki's full attention now.

"Nikki?" Jack asked. "What are you thinking?"

"If we can't find the evidence Mac was collecting, we need to find Saad Patil," she said. "He has to be the missing link in all of this."

"It adds up," Jack said. "We know Saad has experience with the wrong side of the law, and with his brother and King, he also has the connections to pull something like this off."

"But we still have no hard evidence he's involved," Gwen said. "So far no one we've questioned has mentioned him. We're still running on assumptions. We've gone through almost all of George's files, and if Saad did hire him, we've yet to find a shred of evidence behind it. Shoot, we're not even sure the man's in the country. And on top of that, we don't have proof that this antibiotic Mallory claimed is defective really is counterfeit."

"It's like we're chasing ghosts, except we've got a growing body count and a missing woman." Nikki sat down on one of the dining room chairs, knocking her handbag onto the floor in the process. She scooped up the scattered contents, then set the bag back down beside her. "The bottom line is that we have to find whatever evidence Mac was gathering. And we have to find Lucy. She's the closest link we have to Mac."

"If Saad is behind this, he has to be running scared," Jack said. "His brother has just been murdered. Part of his crew is either dead or being detained. He has to realize that at some point, one of them is going to break down and start talking."

"Something still doesn't add up," Gwen said, leaning back in her chair. "If George was playing both sides, you would think he would have to have some idea of who he was working for."

"Maybe," Jack said, "but King told us that George didn't know who he was working for."

Nikki gnawed the inside of her lip. "George could have easily lied to King. What if George knew exactly who he was working for? He finds a way to get Mac to hire him for surveillance work and in turn builds a trust between them. What better way to find out exactly what Mac knew? And when he called King Wednesday night, it was because he wanted King to see firsthand what happens if he doesn't keep his mouth shut."

"It's a stretch," Jack said, "but I suppose it makes sense. We know George had heavy gambling debts, so he's willing to do about anything to get his creditors off his back. So Saad is worried that Mac might have found incriminating evidence of what they were doing and hires George to find that evidence."

"I don't know." Tyler rubbed at his temples with his fingertips. The stress of the day was beginning to show. "As much as I didn't like some of my father-in-law's behavior, this all seems too low, even for him. You're saying that he willingly got involved with the distribution of a counterfeit drug and, on top of that, with murder and hit men."

"Either way," Gwen said, "how do we prove any of this? George is dead. And his files aren't giving us any of the answers we need."

"I don't know, but the one thing we can't forget," Nikki said, "is that our main priority right now is finding Lucy. If they get to her first, they will kill her."

"True," Jack said, "but if she is still on the run, we know she was prepared. Which means if she doesn't want to be found, we might never find her."

"Then what do we do now?" Tyler asked.

"We keep digging," Nikki said. "Because to save Lucy, we need to find the evidence Mac was killed for."

An hour later, Nikki stood in front of the kitchen counter debating whether or not to grab another dish of Virginia's peach cobbler and ice cream, or just settle for a cup of coffee. They were making progress through the rest of the files, but the work was tedious, making her wish she could snag a few minutes of downtime for a power nap. Instead she decided she'd have to settle for another cup of coffee to keep her going.

Liam wandered into the kitchen as she filled her coffee mug, a frown on his face.

"How are you doing, buddy?" she said. "You about ready for bed?"

"No." Arms crossed in front of him, Liam furrowed his brow as he leaned against the kitchen counter. "I wanna go home."

"Home? I heard you got to ride a horse this afternoon and go swimming."

"I did, but I don't even have my toothbrush."

"Your toothbrush?" Nikki set down her coffee. "I thought Miss Gwen brought you some goodies, including a new toothbrush."

"She did, but I like mine. It's a Spiderman toothbrush. With batteries."

"I remember." Nikki pressed her lips together, trying not to smile. "You'll only have to be here for a night or two."

At least she hoped it wouldn't be much longer than that.

"But in the meantime, this house has one of the best game rooms in all of Nashville. A pool table, foosball, a Wii—"

"I know, but what about Ollie?" Liam's lower lip quivered. "He's at home all by himself."

Nikki let out a soft sigh and knelt in front of him. So that was the problem. Ollie was the cream-colored teddy bear Katie had gotten him for his fourth birthday. Since her death, he never went to bed without it.

"You'd be surprised how brave bears can be," Nikki said, searching for the right words, when she wasn't sure there were any that could make this situation right. "In fact, I have it on good authority that Ollie is an exceptionally brave bear."

"As brave as you are?" Liam didn't look convinced.

"You think I'm brave?"

He nodded. "Maybe even as brave as Daddy. He has a medal, but you have a gun and chase down bad guys. You have to be really brave to do that."

"Did you know that even brave people sometimes get scared?"

Liam pondered her question. "You get scared?"

"Being scared is normal. Being brave isn't about not feeling scared at all. It's feeling scared inside, but not letting it stop you from doing what you need to do."

"Like chasing bad guys."

"Exactly. And I have a feeling Ollie is just as brave. I think he'll understand that you're helping to chase down bad guys by being here as well. And in the meantime, keeping your dad, your mamaw, and yourself safe is very important."

"But Ollie's at home all by himself. He's not going to be able to sleep without me."

Nikki breathed in slowly. Apparently her argument didn't apply to cute stuffed teddy bears named Ollie.

Nikki glanced up at the counter at the pile of groceries Gwen had bought, wondering what would distract him. "Would a glass of chocolate milk help?"

The appeal to his sweet tooth was a poor substitute for Ollie, but it was the best she could do at the moment.

Liam pondered her question. "I guess."

Nikki stood up and went to the fridge to pull out the half-gallon jug of milk. "Do you know what I do when I'm away from home and don't have my favorite things with me?"

Liam shook his head.

"I pretend I'm on an adventure." She pointed to one of the drawers before getting a plastic cup. "Why don't you grab a spoon for me."

Liam tugged open the drawer. "What kind of adventure?"

"You could choose whatever adventure you'd like best," she said. "Maybe an astronaut traveling to Mars, or a safari guide looking for lions—"

"Or Spiderman saving the city."

"Exactly." She spooned some of the chocolate powder into the milk. "If you imagine yourself on an adventure, it helps you forget you're homesick. And helps you feel braver when you really don't feel brave."

She handed him the glass and nodded at him to go ahead and stir in the chocolate.

"What kinds of places do you like visiting?" he asked as he grabbed the spoon and started stirring.

"Besides Mars?" Nikki chuckled, then pointed

to a lump of chocolate powder. "Last year I went to New York City with a friend."

"Is it a big city?"

"Very."

"Scary?"

"A little bit. I had to learn some new things." She took a sip of her coffee while he stirred. "Like how to take a cab and how to ride the subway."

"What did you do there?"

"Well, for starters, there's a huge park—Central Park—where we rode bikes. I also went up on the hundred and second floor of the Empire State Building so I could see all of New York City from the sky."

"Wow." Liam looked dutifully impressed.

"According to the man on the elevator, you can see up to eighty miles from up there."

"That's far."

"Very far. And you can't forget baseball."

"The Yankees." Liam's smile was back. If it had anything to do with baseball, the boy was on board. "I think I'd like to go to New York one day. Maybe we can go together and watch them play."

Nikki smiled as Liam took a sip of his milk. "I'd like that."

"Daddy could come too."

Nikki glanced up to see Tyler standing in the doorway and wondered how long he'd been standing there.

"So I am invited. Thanks, buddy." Tyler laughed as he caught Nikki's gaze. "Sorry, I caught the end of your conversation. So you're wanting to visit New York?"

"Do you think we could go one day?" Liam asked.

"Sounds like a lot of fun."

Nikki felt the tug on her heart and gave herself a brief moment to imagine what it would be like to be a family. The three of them. And in time, one or two more . . .

"I checked out our room, buddy, and I think we're all set." Tyler ruffled Liam's hair. "You've got everything you need on this end?"

"I don't have Ollie—or my Spiderman tooth-brush—but I think I'll be okay. At least for tonight."

"Good. Because do you know what time it is?" Tyler asked.

Liam glanced up at Nikki and rolled his eyes. "Whenever Daddy asks me that question, it means it's past my bedtime."

"Smart boy," Nikki said.

"And she's right, Liam. Listen, how would you like it if the two of us went horseback riding tomorrow?"

"Cool," Liam said, taking another sip.

"Why don't you finish up your chocolate milk, then brush your teeth," Tyler said. "Then we'll get you ready for bed."

Liam took the last swallow of his milk, then set the glass in the sink before scooting off toward the bathroom.

"You're good with him," Tyler said, grabbing a mug from the counter and filling it with coffee.

"That's not too hard." Nikki turned away to rinse out Liam's glass. "I love that kid."

"He feels the same about you. And you're good for him as well. He needs a mother figure in his life."

Just like you need someone to take care of you, Tyler Grant. I could be that person—

Nikki pushed away the thought. This was not the time for her to get all sentimental and emotional. She was already treading on thin ice with her role in this case. Besides, he'd said it to her more than once over the past few months. That he had no plans to start dating. That he still hadn't gotten past Katie's death.

"I'm sorry about all of this," she said, cradling her coffee mug between her hands. "I know it's tough on Liam when his routine is changed. And he's missing Ollie."

"That bear has been therapeutic." Tyler added two spoons of sugar and some cream to his coffee, splattered some onto the counter, then grabbed a paper towel to clean up the mess.

She took a sip of her own coffee, willing the caffeine to work overtime. "I'll try to get permission to go by your house tomorrow and pick up a few of his things."

"You think this is going to take more than a day or two?"

Nikki caught the concern in his eyes. She wanted to reassure him that all of this would be over soon but knew she couldn't do that. "I hope not, but I can't make any promises. I'm sorry. Until we find some answers . . ."

"It's not your fault." He leaned back against the cabinet. "I'm just worried about Liam and my mom. Plus, it's making me have second thoughts about taking this job. Just when things were finally settling down for Liam, I'm reminded again how hard it is for him to be out of his routine. I'm not sure he could handle me being gone."

"I think he's stronger than you think. You're stronger than you think."

"But just because he can handle it doesn't mean it's the right decision. I just . . . I just don't want to do something that will end up scarring him for life."

Nikki hesitated. Wanting to be supportive while realistic at the same time. But she could hear the conflict in Tyler's voice. See it in his eyes.

"What is it?" she asked.

"I keep thinking about George. How he was never there for his family. How the choices he made ended up hurting so many people. I don't want that to happen to me. But I know I can't keep going on in the direction I'm heading. I'm afraid I'll end up resenting my decision."

"Then go," she said. "Figure out what you need to do, then come back. Liam will be here. Your mother will be here."

And I'll be here as well. Waiting . . .

"I'm crazy for even considering it, aren't I?" he asked, staring at his untouched drink.

She shook her head. "George never made any changes in his life. He kept going down a path that didn't work, and in the end it cost him everything. But that's not you. You need to make a plan for your future. Which is exactly what you're doing."

Nikki's phone buzzed as a text message came in. Her brow furrowed as she read the caller ID. Aiden Lambert worked as a deputy commissioner for the Department of Corrections and had agreed to call in a few favors concerning her sister's case.

I could really use some good news here, God . . .

Aiden Lambert
Found the Coyote. Call me.

25

10:03 p.m.

Found the Coyote. Call me.

Nikki reread the message and felt her heart shudder. She took in a slow breath, trying to steady her nerves. The Coyote was the best lead she had to finding her sister. And if the deputy commissioner helping her had found him . . .

"Nikki?" Tyler set his drink on the counter. "Everything okay?"

"Yeah . . . I've just got to make a quick call."

She dialed the number, ignoring Tyler's concerned expression. A month of waiting for an answer had made her wonder if this latest lead wasn't simply another dead end. She'd been played by a man who was out to get her. The same man who'd given her the information about the Coyote. What if—once again—she'd been played?

"Aiden, it's Nikki," she said as soon as he answered. "You found him?"

"Yes and no."

"What do you mean?"

There was a long pause, which only managed to

add to the tension of her wound-up nerves. She'd hoped for this day. Prayed for this day. Answers to her sister's disappearance would mean closure for her family. Even if they never found her body, at least they'd have answers.

"I'd rather tell you what I found out in person," Aiden said finally. "I know it's late, but is there any way you can get away?"

"Yeah, of course."

"Where are you?" he asked.

"Southwest Nashville, at an undisclosed safe house, working on a case. But I can meet you."

"There's a coffee shop that stays open late not far from the I-840 and 65 interchange. The Roasted Bean. Can you meet me there? I'm due for a late dinner."

"Of course. I know the place." Nikki glanced at her watch, thankful traffic should be light at this hour. "I'll be there in twenty, twenty-five minutes at the most."

"What's going on, Nikki?" Tyler asked as soon as she'd hung up the phone.

She looked up at him, not ready to let any expectations of what Aiden might have found take over. "It's about Sarah."

"You've got some news?"

"Maybe. I don't know yet."

He stood there, hands clenched at his sides, waiting for her to continue.

"I told you that a couple weeks ago I contacted

a friend of mine who works with the state's Department of Corrections. He agreed to help me look for Sarah's abductor."

"The Coyote."

She nodded. "He found something. Wants to talk to me in person."

"Let me come with you—"

"No." She glanced toward the living room where Jack and Gwen were still working. "You need to be here where you're safe, Tyler."

"I know, but—"

She brushed her fingers down his arm, then quickly pulled away as a sliver of electricity shot through her. "I'll be back as soon as I can."

He reached out and grasped her fingertips, not looking convinced. "Promise me you'll be careful."

She nodded, pulling away from him again as she started for the dining room. "I'm not the one they're after. I'll be fine."

Grabbing her bag, Nikki quickly gave Gwen and Jack an update.

"Why don't you head home after you're done," Jack suggested. "You could use a good night's sleep."

"He's right," Gwen said. "On top of Aaron and his staff, there are officers outside guarding the house, so we'll probably leave within the next hour."

"Okay." Nikki swung her bag over her shoulder and nodded. "Gwen, if you could find out Dr.

Graham's hospital schedule, I want to pay him a visit first thing in the morning and see what more we can find out about Audrey Knight's case."

A minute later, Nikki slid into her car and started the engine. Night had fallen across the landscape, leaving eerie, moonlit shadows and an unsettled feeling in her gut, but she'd been right with what she'd said to Tyler. They weren't after her.

It was easy to believe something bad couldn't happen to you. Except sometimes it did. Katie had died. And Sarah was gone. She'd been sixteen when she disappeared, and ten years later the only lead Nikki had was a prison moniker given to her by a man who'd plotted to kill her. He hadn't exactly turned out to be a reliable witness.

The lead might not even be real.

She pushed away the doubts that continued to haunt her. She'd taken the word of a man who'd kidnapped her because of a vendetta. But he'd known things that only Sarah's abductor could have known. Which to her, meant he had to have been telling the truth when he'd told her he knew the man the media had dubbed the Angel Abductor.

But she didn't even have his real name. Just the Coyote. That name was the only solid lead she had on her sister's abductor after years of sifting through every piece of evidence and following every possible lead.

The Angel Abductor had terrorized East Tennessee in the early 2000s by kidnapping at least six girls over a period of four years. All his victims had been young girls with blond hair, and he'd left behind Polaroids of them at the crime scenes. Sarah had been one of his last victims.

Nikki had memorized the sketch that had been circulated after Sarah's disappearance of a man in his late twenties, with a reddish-blond beard and a small loop earring. And memorized the case files, spending months trying to track down the truth behind her sister's disappearance.

But no DNA or solid leads had ever been found. He'd been meticulous, planning every abduction after stalking his victims first, leaving nothing behind that had allowed the police to make a positive ID. He stalked them, grabbed them, then killed them and buried their bodies.

And the best lead she had was from another criminal.

Which was why part of her never expected what he'd told her to pan out. But neither did she plan to walk away from a possible lead.

The coffee shop where Nikki had agreed to meet Aiden was a bit off the beaten path, but presumably that's what he'd wanted. It was one of those cozy places sprinkled through Nashville where she would love getting her caffeine fix with a friend on her day off. Brick walls, tall ceilings, funky art, and plenty of comfy seating options.

But today she wasn't here to enjoy the barista's specialty.

Today she simply needed information. Information she hoped would be enough to help her find her sister.

Aiden was waiting for her in one of the cozy corners with a plate of waffles, bacon, scrambled eggs, and tea.

"Sorry," he said as she sat down across from him. "I missed dinner working on a case and decided not to wait."

"That's fine. I appreciate your calling me."

"Do you want anything? I can holler at the waitress and order you something."

She felt her stomach churn and shook her head. This moment held too much at stake for her to even be able to think about eating.

"Thanks, but I had pizza and peach cobbler earlier this evening." She pressed her hands against the table, ready to get straight to the point of their meeting. "What did you find out?"

"Turns out, your information was right," Aiden said, biting off the end of a piece of bacon, "though it wasn't easy finding him. I was finally able to cross-reference dates of when your source was in prison and find a connection to a prisoner known as the Coyote."

"What's his real name?"

"Robert—Bobby—Wilcox, but I'm not sure it's going to matter."

"What do you mean?" Nikki's stomach flinched. "He's dead?"

"No." Aiden took a sip of his tea. "As far as I know he's still alive, but he escaped during a prison transport seven months ago."

"Escaped?" Any lingering hope of finding him began to crumble around her. "You're kidding me."

"I wish I were."

They'd never found Sarah's body. It had been a cruel twist of fate, because until they found her—dead or alive—closure for her family would never come. Instead each one of them harbored fragments of hope that maybe she was still alive. It had become the constant question that refused to leave them alone. Could Sarah still be waiting somewhere, waiting to be rescued? It was a question that had brought with it enough motivation for her to leave her teaching job almost a decade ago and join the police force.

Aiden set down his fork and caught her gaze. "Listen, I know this isn't what you wanted to hear, but I pulled in every favor I could think of. I'm sorry. The guy's smart and, from what I've learned about him, has probably taken on a different identity by now. He could be living in Canada or Mexico for all I know. You know even more than I do that the Angel Abductor was like a chameleon when it comes to hiding his identity."

Nikki fiddled with the white cloth napkin in front of her. "Tell me everything you know about him."

"I managed to get a copy of his file for you, but it's pretty barebones."

He slid the file folder across the table.

Nikki felt her breath catch. If this was really him—the Angel Abductor—this was the closest she'd ever gotten to the man who'd allegedly abducted her sister.

Her hands trembled as she opened the file. His photo stared up at her, sucking the air out of her lungs. There was no doubt in her mind this was him. A decade older, but still fitting the description they had of the man. The only evidence they really had on him.

But it was all here—his criminal history, record of arrest, data from the local courts. He'd been arrested five years ago and had been serving a ten-year prison term when he escaped.

"Embezzlement?" she asked. "That doesn't make sense. He abducted and killed little girls, and he was in for embezzlement. He doesn't deserve to see the light of day."

"Unfortunately, there was never any reason to suspect that he was connected to any of those cases," Aiden said. "His defense attorney's number is in the file if you want to contact her."

Oh, Sarah, I'm so, so sorry.

She closed the file and pressed her hand against

it. If he'd been caught, maybe Sarah would still be with them today.

"The authorities are doing everything they can to find him," Aiden said, "but at this point, they don't even have a lead. And to the state, he's just someone who committed a white-collar crime. He's not a convicted or suspected serial killer."

She shook her head. "I need you to keep looking," she said, without even thinking. To stop looking meant giving up. "Please. He could be out there right now, hurting another girl. Causing another family to go through what ours did. I need answers."

Aiden took the last bite of his eggs, then pushed back his plate. "Can I give you some advice?"

Nikki glanced up from the file. "Okay."

"Nikki, I'm not talking to you now as someone who works for the Department of Corrections, but as a friend. I'm worried that you're just chasing ghosts. You know this case better than any of us, and yet in reality, you're no closer to finding the perpetrator now than you were the day your sister disappeared."

"That's not true. We have a name now. That's a huge leap forward."

"You need to stop."

"Stop what?" she asked. "Looking for my sister's abductor?"

"Not just that. The guilt and blame you put on yourself over Sarah's abduction."

"I don't blame myself," she said, then pressed her lips together. Because that wasn't true. If she'd been there to pick up Sarah on time the day she'd disappeared, Sarah would still be with them today.

"How long have we known each other?" Aiden asked.

Nikki shrugged. "I don't know. Five, six years."

"In that time period, I've worked with hundreds of families. I know how people react to a crime committed against them. Something happens that is completely out of their control, and they blame themselves."

Nikki squeezed her eyes shut. Some days, it still seemed like yesterday. She'd glanced at her watch as she threw the new box of shoes into the backseat of her car. She was going to be at least ten minutes late picking up Sarah. She'd scrambled into the driver's seat and cranked up the air conditioner to combat the warmer-than-normal temperatures.

Fifteen minutes later, she stepped out onto the curb in front of the school where she always met her sister, and breathed in the smell of fresh-cut grass. But Sarah wasn't there.

And she'd never seen her again.

"Nikki?"

Aiden's voice pulled her out of the past. The smell of fresh-cut grass vanished. She opened her eyes. "Sorry."

"Listen, I've heard your story. About how you

were late picking her up from school that day. You've got to forgive yourself and move on with your life."

"Deputy commissioner turned counselor?" she asked.

"I'm serious."

"I know." Nikki started fiddling with the napkin again. "But being on the victim side of a case isn't the same as trying to track down the bad guy. You can't just forget." She tapped on the file folder he'd given her. "And seeing this photo . . . it brings back everything."

Letting go would never be simple. Instead, it was a day-to-day struggle. And seeing the face of her sister's abductor for the first time was like a knife ripping through a wound that had never totally healed.

"Besides," she continued, "there's no way I can simply ignore this information. Even if we don't have a location, we have a name now. That's more than we had before. I have to find him. There has to be a contact person. Family . . . a girlfriend. Someone he's contacted in the past seven months."

"He did have a girlfriend," Aiden said. "Nancy something. I haven't been able to get ahold of her yet. They dated off and on in high school and later. I've left half a dozen messages on her phone."

"That's okay. I can run this lead down."

"I still think you should take my advice and let

this go. I know that's not what you want to hear, but Sarah's gone." He reached for his tea. "She'd want you to keep remembering her, but without letting it torment you.

"And even if the authorities find him," he continued, "from what I know about the case, there are no DNA samples. Nothing that would even tie Wilcox to the case. All you really have is a statement from a convicted criminal who's dead."

"Forensics has changed dramatically over the past decade. We can go through the evidence again and check for DNA. Because he's out there somewhere, Aiden. That means I have to keep looking. I need to know the truth so my family and I can put all of this behind us."

"I knew you'd say that." He signaled the waitress for his check. "But I've worked with so many people who can't accept the truth, and they only end up destroying themselves. Sometimes there's just nothing else you can do but let the past go."

That might be good advice, but not for her. She wasn't done searching for Sarah's abductor. Not by a long shot.

"I appreciate everything you've done," she said, reaching for her wallet in her purse to pay his dinner bill. "I hope you know that."

"If there's anything else I can do . . ."

"I was going to pay for your dinner," she said, digging through her purse. "Figure it's the least I can do, but I must have left my wallet back at the safe house."

"Forget it," he said, picking up the check the waitress set on the table. "I just don't want you to get hurt."

Nikki looked up and caught his gaze. "It's far too late for that."

She was going to find Robert Wilcox.

26

11:39 p.m.
Undisclosed location, southwest of Nashville

Nikki drove back to the safe house a different route than the way she'd left, making sure no one was tailing her. She flipped on the radio, searching for something peppy to cheer her up, then turned it off when she couldn't find anything. Aiden's news had left her feeling depressed, and had reminded her how much hope she'd placed in that one lead. She'd anticipated finding the Coyote, bringing him to justice, and then in turn finally bringing closure to her family.

And yet none of that had happened.

At the front door of the farmhouse, she punched in the security code and stepped inside. Tyler was watching the late news on CNN in the living room.

"Hey." She dropped her car keys into her jacket pocket and shot him a sleepy smile.

"I heard you were looking for this," he said, standing up and holding out her wallet. "It must have fallen under the table when you knocked your purse over."

"I was hoping it was here," she said, taking it from him and slipping it into her bag. "I didn't exactly relish the thought of having to cancel all my credit cards tonight on top of everything else."

He shot her a smile. "I don't blame you. It's been a long day."

She paused in the middle of the room. Knowing she needed to go, but at the same time longing for his company. "I thought you'd be asleep by now."

"I'm not sure I'm going to be getting much sleep tonight. Too much on my mind." He popped open a can of Coke that had been sitting on the coffee table and took a sip. "Can I get you something to drink?"

"I'm good. Thanks."

"When Aaron mentioned that you'd called because you forgot your wallet, I decided to stay up a bit longer and wait for you."

She noted the fatigue in his eyes as he sat back down on one of the cozy red-and-white wingback chairs. They both needed sleep, but first she wanted to make sure he was okay.

She sat down across from him on a matching

chair and caught his gaze. "How are you handling all of this?"

He held the drink between both hands and leaned forward. "It's funny in a sad way. George always said he'd go out with a bang. Just didn't expect it to affect my family like this."

"There's no way you could."

"I keep telling myself that. And while I know it sounds bad, part of me is glad Katie isn't here to see all of this. She would have had a hard time dealing with it."

"I've thought the same thing," she said. As much as George had hurt Katie, she'd still loved him and never stopped praying he'd find a way to get his life back on track. "Did Liam finally go to sleep?"

Tyler nodded. "Mom's still in there with him. I feel like I've spent the past year trying to find some sort of normality in our lives, and just when I feel like things are finally getting there, this is thrust upon us. He knows something's up, obviously, and doesn't understand any of it. I don't want him imagining things that aren't real, but I also don't want to tell him too much so he ends up worrying about things he shouldn't."

"Did you tell him about George?" she asked.

"Not yet." He took another sip of his drink. "I know it makes me sound like I'm a bit of a coward, but Mom agrees with me. While he's handling our being here better than I expected, I thought it wouldn't hurt to wait a day or two to tell him once we're home and settled down a bit. It's not like George was a big part of our lives, but Liam loved him, and Katie and I never spoke badly of him in front of Liam."

"I think that's a wise choice."

He glanced up at her. "I'm also finding that it's hard to tackle a problem when I don't know who the enemy is."

"We'll figure this out."

She glanced at the files stacked up neatly on the dining room table. Tyler was right. All they seemed to have discovered were more unanswered questions. And Lucy was still out there. Somewhere.

Liam walked into the room, eyes half closed, clearly trying to figure out where he was.

"Hey, buddy." Tyler scooped him up and gave him a bear hug, pressing him against his chest. "Did we wake you up?"

Liam snuggled against his father's shoulder, his eyes closed again, his long lashes fanned out against his cheeks.

"I don't think he's actually awake," Virginia said, just a few steps behind him. "I'll go get him back to sleep and stay with him in case he wakes up again."

Tyler nestled his chin against his son's hair, then kissed the back of his neck. "Are you sure?"

Virginia smiled up at her son and grandson. "You know I don't mind."

"I'll carry him back to his bed, then, and be right back."

Nikki grabbed her bag off the floor when Tyler returned a minute later and started for the front door. "I probably should go home and try to get some sleep. Between Aaron and the extra officers outside, you'll be safe."

"I know," Tyler said. "And I appreciate your setting this up for us. You'll have to thank your friend for me."

"I will. I just need to wind down a bit, then catch a few hours' sleep. Tomorrow is going to start early. We're planning to talk with the doctor—"

"What if I had the perfect way for you to wind down?" He looped his thumbs in his front pockets and waited for her response.

She had no idea what he had in mind, but a part of her didn't want to leave. Not yet. "Okay."

He grabbed her hand and led her outside to the open veranda that connected to the back of the house next to the pool. A comfy wicker couch and two chairs with colorful cushions and throw pillows sat facing a stone wall, fireplace, and hearth—all nestled beneath thick wooden beams and a plank roof.

Tyler clicked on a button and started the gas fireplace. "I discovered this room while you were out. It's probably not quite cold enough for a fire, but I thought you might like it."

"I do. This has always been my favorite part

of the house," she said, sitting down on the two-seater couch.

He sat down beside her and leaned back, their shoulders touching as the orange flames flickered and popped. A cricket sang in the darkness. She watched the fire dance and felt the muscles in her neck and shoulders begin to relax. It was a temporary reprieve from every-thing that had happened today. An unexpected chance to enjoy the quiet stillness of the night. And the calming presence of the man sitting next to her.

"You were right," she said. "This is perfect."

"If we're here another night, I might have to talk someone into picking up the ingredients for s'mores."

Nikki smiled. "Liam would love that."

"Yes, he would." He took her hand and laced their fingers together. "Do you want to tell me about your meeting?"

Nikki pulled her legs up beneath her, savoring the warmth of his presence next to her. They'd talked about her decision to continue looking for her sister, and he'd always supported her. But she knew he worried about how it affected her emotionally.

"His name's Robert Wilcox. The Angel Abductor. The Coyote."

Tyler rubbed the back of her hand with his thumb. "They found him?"

"I finally have a name, but he escaped from

prison seven months ago during a transfer. The authorities have no idea where he is, or if he's even alive for that matter."

A new wave of disappointment shot through her. Saying it out loud made the reality that she'd once again hit another dead end seem even more real.

"It's just a roadblock," he said. "Not the end of the road."

"I know. At least I have a name. But I don't know what to do. Wait until he kills again?"

He squeezed her fingertips. "You are Special Agent Nikki Boyd, who happens to work missing persons cases on a governor-appointed task force. If anyone can find him, I'd say you can."

She smiled, but her smile quickly faded. If they didn't find him, he would strike again. She was certain of that. Aiden had told her to stop looking. But was the right answer to simply walk away? Even after all these years, she knew she wasn't ready to simply give up. Maybe there would be a day when she decided it was time to leave the past behind. Because just like Tyler, there was nothing she could do to change that past.

"I'm sorry," he said, breaking the lingering silence between them. "I know how important this lead was to you."

"It just seems a bit . . . I don't know. Ironic, that I'd get this far only to find out that he's once again eluded the authorities. It's hard to swallow."

"Do your parents know about any of this?"

She shook her head. "I don't talk to them about the case. And I won't until I have something more concrete." She hesitated. "Aiden did give me one lead."

"What's that?" he asked.

"The number of a woman Robert used to date. He finally tracked her down but hadn't got ahold of her yet. I told him I'd call her."

"Then why don't you?"

"Right now?"

"You might end up sleeping better."

She wanted to, but she wasn't ready to have another door slammed in her face. Not today.

"It's late," she said. "I'll call tomorrow."

"Where does she live?"

"It was an Alaskan area code."

"They're what . . . three hours behind us?"

Nikki glanced at her watch and nodded.

"Which means while it's close to midnight here," he continued, "she's probably still up. Call her."

She hesitated, then pulled the number and her phone out of her purse and dialed.

A woman answered on the fourth ring.

"Hi . . . My name's Nikki Boyd." Tonight, she wasn't calling as a detective, but as the sister of the victim. "I'm not sure if I have the correct number, but I'm trying to track down a Nancy Martin?"

"Nancy?" A long pause followed.

"Hello . . . ," Nikki said, fearing the woman had hung up. "Are you still there?"

"Yes . . . I'm sorry. This is her sister, Jill. Nancy passed away two years ago, and your question . . . it took me by surprise. I haven't had anyone ask about her for so long."

"I'm so sorry to hear that."

Nikki felt a wave of melancholy settle over her. Another door closed. Another dead end. But surely Nancy's sister had to know something about Robert Wilcox.

"Were you friends with Nancy?" the woman asked.

"I . . . no . . . I never actually met her. But she had a friend. Robert Wilcox. Did you know him?"

"Robert . . . Oh, you must mean Bobby? Wow . . . I haven't thought about him for a long time. He was a nice guy. Always sweet on Nancy. They even thought about getting married at one point, but then he decided to stay in Tennessee when she took a job here in Alaska. The long-distance thing didn't work for them, so eventually they ended up going their separate ways."

"Did you know him very well?"

"Not really, and it's been years since I've seen him. He was quiet, but nice. Seemed to treat Nancy well. I was always sorry they broke things off, because he seemed to make her happy. In fact, I'm not really sure why they didn't try harder to make things work. She never gave me a reason, and I didn't push."

"So you haven't heard from him since she died."

"No. I think they kept in touch, but the last time I heard from him was Nancy's funeral. He sent flowers, but wasn't able to make it. I remember that the bouquet came with a card to tell me how sorry he was to miss it, but he was working somewhere in Europe at the time. London, if I remember correctly. I understood he didn't make it back to the States that often."

Two years ago Robert Wilcox would have still been in prison.

"What about family?" Nikki asked.

"I don't know. I remember his parents had died years ago, but he had a stepbrother. What was his name . . . Gregory, I think? Yes, I believe that's right. Gregory Jennings. I can't believe I remember after all this time."

Nikki grabbed a pen out of her bag and scribbled the name down on a piece of paper. "Do you know how I can get ahold of him? A phone number. An address. Anything."

"All I can give you is his name. I think he might have lived back East somewhere, but I'm sorry. That's really all I know."

"I appreciate your help. And again, I'm so sorry for the loss of your sister."

She hung up the call a moment later.

"One day, I'm going to have to come to the

realization that I might never find her," she said.

"But that day isn't today," Tyler said.

She nodded. If she couldn't find her sister's killer, she was going to find Lucy.

"Lucy's out there somewhere. Running scared. Not knowing who to trust." She let out a whoosh of air. "It's what has always scared me most about Sarah's disappearance. Knowing how terrified she had to have been when he took her. And she had to go through it alone."

She turned to him. He was close enough that she could see the reflection of the yellow-and-gold flames in his eyes. Close enough to make her heart race.

Tyler ran his thumb down her cheek before dropping his hands in his lap. "We're both driven by our past, aren't we?"

She nodded, her breath stilled. She'd learned to read his moods over the past few months and knew that there was something more to his statement.

"And George's death had to bring so much of the past back to the surface."

He nodded. "I've spent so much time the past few months searching my faith. Trying to figure out how to move forward. I've begun to realize that God wants more than me simply trying to survive. But that's exactly what I've been doing." He turned away from her and stared into the fire. "I'm hanging on to a raft that's sinking, and I'm tired of simply getting by. I'm tired of waking up every morning and feeling like every day is going to be an uphill battle. I'm ready for more."

She sat quietly beside him. They were alike in so many ways. He craved that adrenaline rush. The fight for justice. He was a soldier. A hero. Her hero.

"Then you're taking the right steps."

It had been their pain and loss that had bonded them together, but for her it had become far more than that. She loved him. But she also wanted what was best for him. And if that meant letting him go in order for him to step away from his past, then she had to encourage him to do just that.

"I think my biggest battle right now is learning how to fight the guilt. I sit here and worry about how Liam will get by without me for a couple months. How everything that has happened with his grandfather is going to affect him. How I might not be offering him the stability he needs."

She let out a low chuckle. "Aiden just told me the same thing a little while ago. He told me I should stop looking for Sarah. And to stop carrying the guilt I have over her abduction." She looked up at him again. "And while I'm not going to give up on looking for Sarah, he was right about the guilt."

Her heart beat faster at his nearness, her breath quickened as she fought the desire to lean forward and kiss him.

She swallowed hard. "I should probably go now."

He nodded. "Just promise me you'll call me when you get home."

"Okay."

Nikki stood up, told him goodbye, then slipped out of the house.

27

4:17 a.m., Saturday morning
Nikki's loft apartment

The message ringtone on Nikki's phone jolted her awake. She started to ignore it, then felt a wave of panic shoot through her. She glanced at the caller ID. Tyler. Her heart trembled. If something had happened . . .

She rolled over onto her back, held the phone above her head, and read the message.

Might have something. Headed to the marina. Meet me at the *Isabella*.

Nikki swung her legs off the side of the bed and sat up, trying to clear her mind. Why was Tyler going to the marina? It didn't make sense. He knew it wasn't safe for him to leave the farmhouse.

She pushed his number on speed dial and waited for him to answer.

Nothing.

She tried again. This time the call went directly to voice mail. She hung up, but the waves of panic refused to leave.

Quickly, she dialed Jack's number. He answered on the fifth ring.

"Jack?"

"Nikki?" He let out a low groan. "Do you have any idea what time it is?"

"Sorry, but I just got a message from Tyler. He said he was headed for the marina and wants me to meet him there."

"At the marina. Why?"

"I don't know. Something about the case. I tried to call back, but his phone keeps going to voice mail now. I can't get through."

"Okay." There were sounds of rustling in the background. "Call the safe house. See if they know anything. I'll meet you at the marina."

Nikki grabbed a pair of jeans from her dresser, tugged them on along with a white short-sleeved button-up shirt, then put in a call to Aaron.

"Aaron . . . it's Nikki," she said as soon as he answered. "I'm sorry to call you in the middle of the night, but I need to talk with Tyler and I can't get ahold of him."

"It's okay. Give me a second . . ."

While she waited, she tied her hair back and

pulled on a pair of low-heeled boots before grabbing her purse.

"I've checked the entire place," Aaron said once he got back on the phone. "He's not in the house."

"You're sure?" she asked.

"Positive. Do you want me to call backup to come out here and search the grounds—"

"No. I think I know where he is. Thanks, Aaron. I'll be in touch."

It was still dark outside when Nikki got to the marina just before five. A chilly wind blew off the water, quiet except for the gentle slapping of the waves against the pier. With no sign of Tyler or Jack, she tried calling Tyler again.

Still no answer.

Anger mixed with an uneasy feeling as she searched the shadows for anything that seemed out of place. There were dozens of boats bobbing in the water. Dozens of places someone could hide. Where was Tyler? He never should have left the safe house.

Unless this was some sort of trap . . .

She pulled her thigh-length cotton trench coat tighter around her waist, then slipped her fingers around her service weapon before stepping onto the *Isabella*. Something creaked behind her. She turned around to see a shadowy image and jumped.

"Jack?" She pressed her hand against her chest.

She was going to have to settle her nerves before she lost it.

"Sorry." He stifled a yawn and shoved his hands into his front pockets. "Have you ever noticed that there aren't any good coffee spots open this early in the morning? At least not where I live."

"Trust me, I noticed," she said.

"So where's Tyler?"

She shook her head. "I don't know. I expected him to already be here."

He stepped onto the boat beside her. "I'm guessing this boat holds a lot of memories for you."

"Mainly good ones." Her gaze shifted beyond the boat to where the sun had begun to peek above the horizon. "We used to go out on the water quite a bit before Katie died."

Nikki clicked on her flashlight. Her muscles tensed as she started down into the dark cabin. Whoever was behind this had been a step ahead of the police the entire time. They'd proven that they had both the money and the resources to kill anyone who stood in their way. If they'd managed to find a way to get to Tyler, she'd never forgive herself.

Her thoughts shifted as she stepped onto the varnished flooring of the cabin, with Jack right behind her. The beam of her flashlight caught evidence of where Mac Hudson had died. Tyler was going to have to hire someone to clean the bloodstains before selling the *Isabella*. He might very possibly have a hard time selling a boat where a murdered man had died.

She started toward the bathroom, then stopped. A man stepped out of the shadows with a weapon pointed at them.

Nikki turned and aimed her weapon back at him. "I'm Agent Boyd with the Tennessee Bureau of Investigation. I need you to put down your gun immediately."

She held hers steady. The last thing she wanted was another shooting on this boat.

"N-no . . . ," the man stammered. "What are you doing here?"

"We're the ones asking the questions. Who are you?" Jack asked.

Nikki studied the man's face in the white beam of the flashlight. "You're Saad Patil."

"Saad Patil?" Jack repeated.

But there was no mistake. The man standing in front of her was Adi's brother. The man they'd been searching for, who potentially was behind everything that had happened the past forty-eight hours.

"What are you doing on this boat?" she asked.

"My brother . . . he told me to meet him here. Where is he?"

"On the *Isabella*?" Nikki asked "Why this boat?"

"I don't know."

"He told you that this morning?" Nikki asked.

"Yes. He hasn't been answering my phone calls, then out of the blue I get a message telling me to come here."

Nikki glanced briefly at Jack, then back to Saad. "I'm sorry to have to be the one to tell you, but your brother's dead."

"Dead? No . . . You're lying. He told me to meet him here."

"Why would he ask you to meet him on a boat in the middle of the marina?"

The man's hands trembled. "I don't know."

"I need you to put down your gun, Saad. The last thing you want to deal with at this point is another murder charge."

"I have done nothing."

Nikki shook her head. Something wasn't right. None of them should be here. Unless someone wanted them here.

"Keep an eye on him," she said to Jack.

She moved her flashlight slowly around the inside of the cabin. A minute later, she found it. Lying on one of the seats, partially hidden, was a bomb covered in crisscrossed, colored wires.

"There's a bomb. Go! Now!" Nikki spun around and rushed up the stairs, running toward the dock. This was a trap. Someone wanted everyone involved dead. But even Saad?

There was no time to think through what was going on. She heard Jack stumble up the steps behind her, followed by Saad, not knowing if they had minutes or seconds until the bomb went off. She darted onto the deck of the *Isabella* toward the dock—

The force of the bomb slammed the boat into the dock. There was no way to check if the two men were behind her as the heat rippled up her legs and across her back.

Someone screamed her name, but all she could do was pray as the force from the blast propelled her into the water.

Nikki felt herself slam against the surface of the water, then plunge into the cold darkness. Lungs tight, she opened her eyes and fought to orient herself. The light of the explosion filtered through the water in an eerie glow above her.

At least she was still alive.

"Even though I walk through the valley of the shadow of death."

Her lungs began to burn and she kicked toward the light. Debris from the boat was all around her, but she had to get out. Had to breathe.

"I will fear no evil."

The surface was just out of reach. Her lungs begged for relief, but it was too far for her to reach. The murky water burned her eyes. Panic consumed her. She could see her friends and family as she pushed frantically toward the glistening light. Sarah . . . Katie . . . Tyler . . . her parents and brothers. They were there. Moving toward her in slow motion as the colors of light danced through the water.

Her eyes closed. She had no idea how much time had passed. Seconds . . . Minutes . . . But she did know she was on the verge of losing consciousness.

"I will fear no evil."

But I am afraid, God. I don't know which way to go.

"He makes me lie down in green pastures."

She needed to find Sarah. Needed to find Lucy.

But I don't know where they are, God. I don't know how to find them.

"He leads me beside the quiet waters, and refreshes my soul."

She could feel the intense heat from the orange flames on the dark surface. She forced her legs to kick. A few more seconds . . . A few more feet . . . That was all she needed.

And then she was suddenly there. Floating on the surface of the water. Taking in a lungful of smoky air. But the water was closing in on her again as she began to sink, and this time she couldn't fight it anymore.

Her mind shifted. Tyler was looking at her with those stark brown eyes of his. Mesmerizing her. Pulling her into his arms and telling her that he loved her.

Her mind shifted again. Lucy was running. She'd known secrets. Known what her husband was doing. Or maybe she'd simply vanish forever.

She closed her eyes. She was giving up. Being pulled back down into the dark waters. She could still see the orange glow of the fire. Pieces of scattered wood and metal. Maybe she was dead. Or maybe she was dying. She only knew she was so tired. So, so tired.

"Nikki . . . can you hear me?"

She tried to open her eyes. Someone was calling her, but her ears were ringing, and she couldn't hear what they were saying. She stared at the figure coming at her. On the boat, Saad had a gun. What if he wanted to kill her? What if it was him? Or the person who had planted the bomb?

Her lungs were burning again, but that voice. It was so . . . familiar. Her mind couldn't focus. Like when she searched for a memory she couldn't quite catch.

"Nikki?"

Tyler.

Her brain tried to reconcile what he was doing here. He shouldn't be here. It wasn't safe here. He was supposed to be at her friend's house. Wasn't he? She fought to remember. He'd told her to meet him here. She'd come. But so had Saad . . . Had he wanted to kill Tyler?

Suddenly it didn't matter anymore. He was wrapping his arms around her . . . drawing her against his chest . . . dragging her out of the water. She tried to wrap her arms around him, but she was too weak. She couldn't move. All she could do was lean against his broad chest.

Maybe she was just dreaming. Maybe she was dead.

But someone else was shouting. Sirens wailed in the distance. She needed to get out of the water and run. To warn Tyler that it wasn't safe. Because she had been right. His life was still in danger. Her life was in danger. But if that was true, why did she only want to nestle in his arms?

"Nikki? Can you hear me? I need you to answer me . . . please."

Water spewed from her mouth. Then she was coughing, lying on her side on the hard dock. Her insides felt as if they were being ripped out of her. Ears still ringing.

"Nikki? Please tell me you're okay."

She nodded, then felt the tears well up in her eyes. "I just need . . . I need to breathe."

"Good. It's okay now. You're okay now." He was holding her as she lay on the dock. Protecting her from the fire. She could see a row of boats bobbing sideways in the water. "Take slow, deep breaths. You're going to be okay."

"The *Isabella* . . ."

The boat was burning. She could feel the heat. Orange and yellow flames licked at the hull, crackling and popping in the morning air.

And Jack. Where was Jack?

She forced herself to sit up, while trying to stuff

down another wave of panic. "Jack was with me. I don't know where he is—"

"Hey . . . slow down," Tyler said. "Just keep breathing. Someone else pulled him out. We'll go check on him in a minute. But for right now, I just want you to lie still and catch your breath until we can get you checked out by one of the paramedics."

"I'm okay." She looked up at Tyler, head throbbing as the marina spun around her. She tried to focus. "Why did you leave the safe house?"

"I got a text from you," he said.

"No." She shook her head. Everything might be fuzzy, but not this. "I didn't send you a text, Tyler."

"Someone did." His voice broke. "And I would have been here when the bomb went off except there was a wreck on the freeway."

"I would never ask you to come here."

Which meant they *were* trying to kill him. They'd missed him this time, but if they tried again . . .

"We need to get you out of here," she said. "Someone thinks you know something. That George told you something, or you have access to Mac's evidence. I don't know what."

"I don't know either," he said, pulling her into his arms. "I don't even know who the bomb was meant for. All I do know is that you're safe. We're both safe. And that's really all that matters to me right now."

· · ·

An hour and a half later, Gwen entered the curtained-off section of the emergency room where Nikki sat perched on the edge of a bed. "Hey, how are you?"

"I'm okay. A few superficial burns."

"You were lucky," Gwen said. "We found Saad's body."

"We needed him alive." Nikki frowned. "What about Jack? I've been waiting for an update."

"He's going to be fine," she said. "He should be released in the next few minutes."

"And Tyler? Where is he?"

"He and his family are being moved to another location, just in case the farmhouse was compromised," Gwen said. "But here's what I need to know. You told me you received a message from Tyler to meet him at the marina."

"Yes."

"Tyler says he never sent a message. But he received one from you."

"And Saad said he received one from his brother," Nikki said, still trying to understand how it all fit together. "Or at least that's what he said."

"Since your phone is pretty waterlogged, I've requested your phone records from your service provider so we can detect any unauthorized use, but we believe that your phone was hacked."

"Hacked? How is that possible?"

"An experienced hacker can take control of your phone."

"Meaning?"

"They can send texts, make calls, even access the internet. And while this shouldn't alter your call history, it's possible for them to cover their tracks."

"So someone else sent Tyler and me—along with Saad—to the marina."

"Exactly. I've already looked at Tyler's phone, and it was definitely hacked. It's why you received a message from him. Someone wanted both of you to be on the *Isabella* when the bomb went off."

But why her?

"The doctor gave me a clean bill of health," Nikki said. "All I need is a clean set of clothes, and I'm ready to get back out there. We need to know who's behind this."

Gwen held up the large canvas bag she'd been carrying. "Your sister-in-law got you some clothes from your apartment, but you know if Carter was here, he'd make both of you take some personal time after what you've been through."

"Carter isn't here, and we still need answers. We need to find out who was behind this bomb, and find out if it can lead us to Lucy—"

"Stop," Gwen said. "You don't have to convince me. But there is something you're going to need to see. We just discovered evidence of who was behind the bomb."

28

Nikki stood in the middle of Saad Patil's million-dollar condo and held her breath. The incredible view from the living and dining room overlooked Music City from the twentieth floor. But that wasn't what had her attention.

It was her photo—and the photos of four others—that had her struggling to breathe.

The black-and-white photos had been laid out along the kitchen counter. George, Lucy, Tyler, King . . . and hers.

She stood between Jack and Gwen on the hardwood floor in the middle of the upscale kitchen with its dark oak cabinets, silver state-of-the-art appliances, and creamy, tiled backsplash. Hers was a photo her brother had taken at a family get-together a few months ago to celebrate her new job with the task force. And while she tended to avoid photos, this time she'd smiled up at the camera.

She turned to the sergeant who was in charge of investigating the bombing. "What else have you found in the house?"

"In the bathroom, we found traces of bomb residue. We're having samples sent to the lab, but I'm expecting it to be a match with the bomb that exploded at the marina."

"And his motive for the bombing?" she asked.

"A suicide mission's the most obvious explanation I've been able to come up with."

She pointed to her photo. "But why am I on his list?"

"I'm sorry, but I can't answer that yet, ma'am. And to be honest, with Saad dead, I'm not sure we'll ever find all the answers to this case. Though there are a couple other interesting things we found."

Nikki's fingers pressed against the polished granite. "What's that?"

"We found a written confession in his bedroom. I can get you a copy of it, but it's already been sent to the lab to be analyzed. In it Saad confesses to finding a way to infiltrate the US market with a substandard prescription drug with the potential earning power of millions."

"Did he mention what the drug was?" Jack asked.

"No," the sergeant said. "He just admitted that he couldn't take the guilt any longer of knowing people might die because of what he'd done."

"And you think the letter's authentic?"

"At this point, I couldn't say one way or the other."

Nikki's mind spun with the implications. "And then what . . . he tries to kill everyone involved in the investigation, including himself? Why would he do that? When we were on that boat with him, he seemed scared. And shocked that his brother was dead."

"Again, I don't know, but this might answer some of your questions. We also found a prescription for anticonvulsants in his medicine cabinet," the sergeant said. "They're used to treat a number of psychological conditions and mood swings."

"So we simply blame all of this on a psychotic disorder and move on?" Nikki let out a huff of air, then turned to Gwen. "And why are we just now finding the location of Saad's residence?"

"The owner of this condo is recorded as a corporation. Not in his name. Like he was trying to hide his assets."

Nikki's gaze swept across the meticulously kept living area. White couches with gray and orange throw pillows. A few pieces of expensive art hung on the wall. Well organized. Well planned. But something clearly had gone wrong with Saad's plan. Mac's probe into the drug. George's investigation. Perhaps even his brother's death? Whatever it was had been profound enough to cause him to take his life.

And now the man was dead and couldn't answer their questions.

"Were there any other properties you were able to trace back to Saad or his brother?" Nikki asked. "If he did find Lucy—and she's alive—she might be at one of them."

"I'm looking into it," Gwen said. "But so far, no."

"I still think we should speak with Audrey Masters's doctor. If Lucy's out there trying to find Mac's evidence, maybe her search will somehow lead us to her."

"I've already spoken with someone at the hospital," Gwen said, pulling out her phone. "I'll call again and make sure he's in."

Nikki and Jack stepped into Dr. Ryan Graham's office in the medical center west of downtown. The room was neat and efficient, and more than likely a reflection of the doctor's personality. In his late fifties with a receding hairline, the doctor looked up from behind a wide mahogany desk, pulled off a pair of thick-framed glasses, and stood up to greet them.

Nikki reached out her hand. "Thank you for taking the time to see us, Dr. Graham."

"Of course." He shook both of their hands, offered them two padded arm chairs across the desk from him, then sat back down. "I understand you're here regarding the journalist, Mallory Philips."

"That's one of the reasons," Jack said.

"One of my nurses told me what happened to her," the doctor said. "She'd been here—I don't know—half a dozen times over the past few days, talking to several of my patients about counterfeit drugs. I knew the minute I met her that she was going to be trouble. Even did a bit of digging on my own, and quite frankly, I came to the conclusion that she just wanted to make a name for herself."

"While that might be true," Nikki said, "Mallory did have a personal motivation behind her behavior. Her sister had diabetes, and Mallory believed her sister died while using a counterfeit drug."

"I'm sorry. I really am, but that doesn't change the fact that she spent her time throwing out accusations and upsetting my patients. I ended up having to call in hospital security to escort her out of the building." Dr. Graham leaned forward, a heavy scowl on his face. "Do you know what it does to our practice when something like this happens? When someone comes into the hospital and convinces the mother of my patient that one of the drugs I prescribed to her daughter was counterfeit, and that it killed her daughter? The Knights are currently looking into suing both me and the hospital."

Nikki gripped the chair's armrest. "Mallory might have been right."

"What?"

"She had the antibiotic you prescribed to Audrey tested by a third party. According to these results, it didn't meet the FDA's specifications."

The doctor shook his head. "I don't believe that. Not unless I saw the results from a lab I trusted."

"We're in the process of having the antibiotic retested right now," Jack said.

Dr. Graham rubbed his temples, clearly upset by the news. "In the end, I lost a patient. And I'm the one who's going to have to go to bed every night wondering if there's anything I could have done to save her. Sometimes things go wrong. Things doctors can't account for. But believe me, the hardest part of my job is telling parents like the Knights that they've just lost their daughter.

"Here's the bottom line, and what Mallory didn't understand." Dr. Graham rested his elbows on his desk and steepled his hands in front of him. "While antibiotics—for example—save thousands of lives every year, they've also been linked to sudden heart deaths. And while we won't know if any of the medications she was taking had a role in Audrey's death until the autopsy results are published, it is possible this is what happened in this case."

"Can you explain?" Nikki asked.

"There can be an increased risk—while very rare—for irregular heart rhythms and even sudden cardiac death with certain antibiotics."

"So even with the possible evidence that there

was a problem with the antibiotics, you don't believe she could have died because of counterfeit drugs?"

The doctor frowned. "Like I said, it would take a lot to convince me. There simply are risks with every medication you take, and the bottom line is that any medication can potentially trigger anaphylaxis. Thankfully, in almost a hundred percent of cases, the benefits far outweigh any risks. Especially if you consider we're talking maybe twenty deaths out of a million courses of the drug taken." Dr. Graham slipped his glasses back on, then rolled his chair away from his desk. "Of course, I realize that doesn't justify a loss when you're the mother or father of a child. Or when you've lost a spouse. As a father and husband, I understand that. But as a physician, I can't stop using something that I know saves lives."

Nikki stood up to leave, understanding the doctor's position, but knowing that nothing he had said was going to even begin to ease the Knights' loss.

Five minutes later, Nikki's phone rang as she slid into Jack's car outside the busy medical center.

"Gwen? What have you got?" she asked as she put the phone on speaker.

"I found out something interesting about your Dr. Graham," Gwen said. "Now this might simply be a coincidence, but last year he received close to two hundred thousand dollars . . . all from Byrne Laboratories."

"Is that legal?" Jack asked, pulling out of the parking space.

"It is, actually. Doctors are paid to test products in clinical trials, provide advice, lecturing, consulting . . . They are working for the fee, and there's nothing illegal about receiving compensation for that kind of work. And while there are instances of the pharmaceutical companies taking advantage of the system, the majority are simply working hard to get better products into the marketplace in order to save more lives."

"Thanks, Gwen. We'll be in touch," she said, then hung up, only to have it go off again.

"Hello," she said, answering the call.

There was a long pause on the phone before anyone spoke. "I need to speak to . . . Agent Boyd?"

"This is she," Nikki said. "Who is this?"

There was another long pause before the frantic voice responded. "This is Lucy Hudson."

29

Nikki's breath caught at the sound of Lucy's voice. After days of searching, had they actually found her?

"Lucy?" She put the call on speakerphone and held it out so Jack could hear the conversation. "Lucy, are you all right? We've been trying to find you."

"I know. I . . . I've just been so scared." Lucy's breath came in ragged bursts as if she was running.

A high-pitched static buzzed on the line.

"Lucy?" Nikki felt her own heart race; the call sounded as if it were cutting out. They couldn't lose her now. "Lucy? Are you still there?"

"Yes . . . I'm here. George . . . George told me I could trust you." She was still breathing hard. "I don't know how to do this on my own anymore. I don't know where else to go. And now . . . they're here and they're about to find me."

"They're not going to find you," Nikki said, hearing the panic in her own voice. "I won't let them. Just tell me where you are."

"You don't understand. They're close."

"I understand. But tell me where you are. We won't let them find you."

"You can't promise me that. Mac tried to protect us, and now he's dead."

"All you have to do is tell me where you are, and I'll come get you. I'll do everything I can to ensure you're safe until we find out who's behind this."

"I'm close to where you are," Lucy said. "I saw you outside Saad's building. And then I saw you go into the medical center. You were there to see Dr. Graham, weren't you?"

"Yes." Nikki tried to mask the surprise in her voice. Had she really been that close? "I thought he might have answers to what your husband had found. And I thought that might help lead me to finding you."

"Mac tried to find out what they were doing, but by the time he discovered the truth, it was too late." She was sobbing now. "We were planning to run together so they couldn't find us."

Nikki's heart pounded as she searched for a way to convince Lucy to come out of hiding. "I know you're scared—"

"They're here." She was breathing hard again. Running. "Close. Looking for me."

"Do you know who they are?"

"The men who were behind the death of my husband. Men who will kill me if they find me."

"Where are you, Lucy?"

"I'm at Centennial Park. I needed a place to lose them. There are so many people here. I thought I could get lost in the crowd."

"That was a good idea."

"I'm on it," Jack said.

Nikki held on to the dashboard as he whipped the car in a U-turn on Patterson Street. She glanced out the window as they drove back past the medical center. They were only a few minutes away, but finding Lucy in the park that was a hundred and thirty–plus acres wasn't going to be easy. They were going to need an exact location.

"We're headed toward the park from the medical center, Lucy, but I need you to tell me exactly where you are."

"I don't know. I think I lost them, but I'm so scared. I saw on the news what they did to Mac. They shot him—"

"Lucy, I want you to take a deep breath. What you've been through is horrible, but you can do this. For Mac's memory. And for your baby."

"You know about the baby?"

The line crackled again. Nikki drew in a quick breath.

"Lucy?"

"I'm still here."

"Good. Listen, I know you're scared, but I need you to help me so I can find you. Are there any landmarks around you?"

Her breath was still coming in spurts. "I . . . don't know."

"I hear music in the background," Nikki said. "Can you see what's going on?"

Jack turned again and was now driving along the edge of the park.

"There's a stage set up," she said. "A band's playing."

"That's great. There's usually a concert in the park on Saturdays. Lucy, I want you to go to where the crowd is the heaviest and try to blend in."

"Okay."

"Just stay on the phone until we find you. We're almost there."

"I'm calling in backup," Jack said, pulling out his phone.

Nikki grasped the armrest. Saad—who had claimed to be behind this—might be dead, but if Lucy was right and someone was still after her, then either Saad hadn't been working alone or the confession was a forgery. This was far from over.

"Tell me what you're wearing," Nikki said as they got closer to the entrance.

"What? . . . The crowd—I can't hear you."

"What are you wearing?"

"Jeans and a gray T-shirt. Sunglasses and a baseball cap."

"Do you see any security guards or maybe a policeman?"

"No."

"Okay. Give us five minutes, Lucy. All you have to do is wait there for us. We're coming."

The connection crackled again, but this time the line went dead.

"Lucy?" Nikki tried to call her back. "Jack . . . If they've got her . . ."

"Don't jump to conclusions," Jack said. "Not yet. Her phone might have gone dead. She's on the run with no time to charge the battery."

"Maybe." But Nikki wasn't convinced.

"Send Gwen her number and see if she can trace the phone's GPS. We might be able to find her that way."

Nikki exited the vehicle, then ran with Jack in the direction of the concert. Seconds ticked by. Jack's assurances—that there was nothing more sinister at work in losing the connection with Lucy than a dead battery—were plausible, but it was just as plausible that the killer or killers had found Lucy. She was another loose end in the scenario, with millions of dollars at stake. And they—whoever they were—weren't going to stop until they found her.

Nikki and Jack pushed through the trickle of pedestrians toward the afternoon concert. If Lucy was really being followed, they were going to have to be very careful. The last thing they needed was another hostage situation.

Nikki called Gwen as they approached the crowd. "How long before backup gets here?"

"Three . . . four minutes at most," Gwen said.

"I sent you her number," Nikki said, maneuvering past a couple pushing a double stroller. "Were you able to trace her phone?"

"I'm trying, but it looks as if she was using another burn phone with no GPS."

"Great," Nikki said.

"She's smart."

"Which is why she's still alive," Nikki said. "But that doesn't help us find her."

"Maybe not, but if anyone can find her," Gwen said, "you can."

Please, God . . . Please help us find her . . .

The music was getting louder. Saturday afternoons were always busy with weekly concerts by local and nationally known musicians, and today was no exception. Nikki stood on the edge of the growing crowd for a moment in order to catch her breath and tried dialing Lucy's number again.

"I can't get her back on the phone," she said to Jack, who stood beside her. "How in the world are we going to find her?"

The afternoon temperatures had warmed up quickly. A group Nikki recognized from a concert she'd attended last year performed on the stage. The audience was filled with families with young children, older couples, and everything in between, including a few dogs. The smell of barbeque came from one of the food trucks, reminding her she hadn't had lunch. But she wasn't hungry. All she wanted to do was find Lucy and take her somewhere safe. She wasn't going to be able to relax until they had Lucy out of here and in a secure place.

Nikki scanned the crowd, searching for the young woman's face she'd memorized. Families sat on blankets or in lawn chairs, listening to the thigh-tapping music, while venders sold copies of CDs by local artists. No one had any idea that the life of a young woman was at stake.

"I think we're going to have to split up to find her," Jack said. "Plus, I just spotted a uniformed officer to the right. I'll make sure he knows what's going on."

Nikki nodded, then started left around the perimeter of the spectators. Thirty seconds later, her phone rang. "Gwen?"

"It's Lucy. I'm sorry. We got cut off."

Nikki's heart pounded as she searched the crowd. She was here. But where? "Just tell me where you are."

"Up near the left of the stage."

"I'm almost there," Nikki said.

A woman sang on stage to the twang of her guitar and backup band. Soulful. Moving . . .

Nikki spotted her a dozen feet from the stage. Gray shirt. Jeans. This was all going to be over soon. It had to be.

She quickened her steps.

"Lucy?" Lucy jumped when Nikki put her hand

on her shoulder. "It's okay. I'm Nikki Boyd."

Dark eyes caught hers. She'd been crying and looked exhausted. "They're here. One is behind us. The other one is on the other side of the stage. I lost the third one. All three are wearing dark pants and shirts, and they have guns."

Nikki nodded, grabbing Lucy's elbow. "Just stay close. I'm going to get you out of here. Safe."

She looked for Jack. He was on the other side of the stage, scoping out the crowd.

She got him back on the line. "Jack . . . I've got Lucy, but there are at least three men following her. All armed and wearing dark pants and shirts. One on my side of the stage. The other on your side. I don't know where the third one is, but I need to move her out of here safely. Now."

"I'll take care of the one near me. You head toward the entrance with Lucy. Backup should be coming any second. Just get her out of here. Now!"

Nikki rushed with Lucy toward the parking lot and called Gwen. "Gwen . . . where's our backup?"

"Another minute out."

"We don't have a minute. Have a squad car waiting for me at the closest entrance to the stage."

"You've got it."

Nikki pressed through the crowd beside Lucy as they rushed toward the parking lot. A man, his weapon visible, came toward them, blocking their way. She looked behind them. A second man was making his way toward them, his weapon exposed as well.

They were surrounded.

A little boy let go of his father's hand and ran between them, chasing after his balloon into the grass.

"I need you to take your son and get out of the way. Now," Nikki told the father.

She grabbed Lucy's elbow and started running across the grass toward the parking lot, trying to remember the layout of the park from when she'd been here before. Lucy was her responsibility, and now that they'd found her, she wasn't going to lose her again. There was too much at stake.

A black van roared up beside them out of nowhere. Nikki pulled out her weapon, but she was outnumbered and couldn't fire without fear of hitting an innocent bystander. The two men grabbed her and Lucy and shoved them toward the vehicle. Her shoulder rammed into the side of the van as they disarmed her. She could still hear the roar of the music from the park as they pushed them into the van and the door slammed shut. Someone had to have seen something. Someone would see them being abducted, call 911, and her team would find her.

One of the men shoved a sweet-smelling rag into her face and then everything went blank.

30

Nikki opened her eyes, then immediately closed them again at the bright overhead lightbulb. She tried to move. A stab of pain shot through her. She sat in a chair, her hands tied behind her, head and left shoulder throbbing. But at least she was alive.

For now.

She waited a few seconds for her eyes to adjust to the light, then tried to assess her situation. The warehouse-type room was large and empty except for a few cans of paint, some wooden crates, and the eerie shadows hanging in the corners.

She searched her memory, trying to remember how she'd gotten here. She'd been at the park to meet Lucy. They'd started running. The men had been following them, and then—

"Agent Boyd?"

She turned her head toward the left to the sound of the small voice beside her. Lucy sat on another chair. Hands tied behind her back. Fatigue clearly marking her expression. "Lucy . . . are you okay?"

"I'm so sorry." Silent tears fell down her face. "This is all my fault—"

"No. None of this is your fault," Nikki said. She tried to loosen the zip ties around her wrists, but the hard plastic cut into her skin. She turned back to Lucy. She'd told her she'd get her out of this situation safely, and she had no plans to go back on her word. There had to be a way. They had to find a way out before their captors returned. "Do you have any idea where we are?"

"I don't know. Some sort of warehouse is all I can tell."

Nikki frowned. They could be anywhere. She had no idea how much time had passed. No idea where they were.

"Mac really is dead, isn't he?" Lucy asked.

Nikki continued working to loosen her hands. "Yes. I'm sorry."

"I guess I kept hoping that the news got it wrong. That there'd been some mistake . . ." Lucy breathed in a ragged breath. "Now I've had my entire life ripped out from under me. Mac . . . I just . . . I don't know what I'm going to do without him. I'm not sure I'll ever be okay again."

Nikki caught Lucy's gaze. "It won't ever be the same. It never is when you lose someone. But you've proven these past few days that you're a survivor. You're strong enough to get through this. And we *are* going to get through this."

Lucy pressed her lips together as if trying to

wrap her mind around her new reality. Life wouldn't ever be the same for her or her unborn baby. "They're after what Mac had."

"Do you know where it is?"

Lucy shook her head. "That's what I've been trying to find. Mac would never tell me the details of what was going on. I think he was trying to protect me." She drew in another long, slow breath. "I do know he was collecting piles of evidence. Paperwork, voice recordings, photographs . . . everything he thought he might need to put them behind bars. He even made a backup plan in case we needed to escape in a hurry, but now . . ."

Nikki caught the pain in her eyes. "I know things didn't work out like the two of you planned, but we're going to find a way out of here."

"How? They don't care who they hurt. They killed my husband."

"Tell me more about Mac," Nikki said.

A faint smile crossed her lips. "Mac was . . . brilliant. All he wanted to do was make a difference in the lives of others. He was working on this new medicine for cancer. It would have been a huge breakthrough. The only other thing he really wanted was a son. I was planning to go home that night and take a pregnancy test."

Nikki looked around the large room, searching for a way out. There was a good possibility that there was a guard outside the one door, and the frosted windows were all at least eighteen feet off the ground. The men she'd seen were all armed.

So where did that leave them?

Jack . . . her team . . . even Tyler. No one knew where they were.

But she had to find a way out. And this time she was on her own.

The bottom of the metal door grated across the floor as it opened. Dwight King stepped into the room with two of his armed goons.

"Well, well . . . ladies. This is a surprise, isn't it?"

"Dwight King," Nikki said, frowning as he stepped in front of them, arms folded across his ample midsection. "It's good to see you again as well."

"Why is it that everywhere I go lately, you seem to show up, making my life more difficult?" The friendly smile he'd given her when they first met was missing. "You really have managed to become a thorn in my flesh, Detective."

"I'm sorry," she said, not trying to hide the sarcasm in her voice.

"I'm sure you are, though I'll be honest, these idiots working for me weren't supposed to bring you here. But now that you are here, I think I might be able to use you to my advantage."

"I'm assuming you hoped that I'd be dead by now."

"It only proves—once again—that when you

want something done correctly, you do it yourself. Which is why I'm here." He shifted his attention to Lucy. "And you, Lucy Hudson . . . you've caused me almost as much grief as your husband did. He just couldn't look the other way. I even tried to cut him in on the deal. Promised him half a million dollars. Half a million dollars. He could have even given it away for all I cared, if that would have eased his conscience. Can you imagine how many people that would feed in a third-world country? But he was apparently too good for that."

"My husband didn't want your blood money."

"Which is a shame. Because he'd be alive now if he'd simply looked the other way. And you wouldn't be here, tied up in the middle of an old abandoned warehouse. Unfortunately, it's going to cost both of you your lives. I'm tired of playing games and tying up loose ends."

Nikki glanced at Lucy. She looked scared, but determined. But they were out of options. They needed to keep King talking. And in the meantime, pray that Gwen and Jack would somehow find them.

"I guess I'm correct, then, when I say that your sob story wasn't exactly true?" Nikki said. "You're clearly not the victim in this situation."

"Oh, the blackmail was real." King shifted his weight, seemingly enjoying his moment of triumph. "I didn't get to be the CEO of a Fortune

500 company by sitting around and letting people walk over me. I found an opportunity and decided to take advantage of it. And let's just say that the rewards from Aryox proved to be far greater than I ever expected. It might not have lasted as long as I'd hoped, but I think in the end the return is going to prove quite . . . adequate."

She studied his smug expression. He was gloating. And she still had questions. She needed to keep him talking.

"You're the one who set off the bomb?" she asked, holding his gaze. "Then planted evidence to blame Saad?"

"I'll admit it was a risk. Cleaning up other people's messes has turned out to be quite . . . messy. I have an associate who thought a bomb was a perfect option, considering Saad's experience with firearms and explosives. Turned out he was wrong, but that's okay. It's not over yet."

"Why kill Saad?" she asked.

"Saad didn't trust me. Thought I was going to double-cross him, though I suppose he had reason to think that. He was the one who broke into Mac's office looking for whatever evidence Mac had found. When I found out about the break-in, I'd hoped to keep the situation in-house, but my ever-efficient secretary had already called you in to get involved. Playing the victim to you as well became my only option."

"Not your only one," she said.

His smile made her stomach turn as he continued. "Say what you like, but even with a few hiccups along the way, I'd say my plan worked. I'm still a free man and you're . . . well . . . you're not."

"You're wrong if you think you're going to get away with this," Nikki said.

"Don't be so quick to judge. I only have one last problem to take care of—besides you, of course, Detective—and that is you, Mrs. Hudson."

"I don't have what you're looking for, and even if I did, I wouldn't give it to you."

"Well, that would be a pity for you," King said. "Because that makes both of you quite disposable."

"What do you want?" Nikki asked.

"Just one last thing. Turns out Mac was smarter than I thought. Until the end, at least. I need access to Adi's bank accounts. His untimely death has put me in a precarious position. The man paid me for my help—quite generously, I might add, but it still wasn't near enough. Turns out Mac wasn't just a whiz with science and formulas, but with computers as well. He found a way to freeze Adi's assets as the leverage he needed. I need the codes to unfreeze them and get into the account."

"Like I said," Lucy said, "I can't help you."

"And I don't believe you. Now, we can do this the easy way or the hard way. It's your choice."

"She said she doesn't have the code," Nikki said.

King snapped his fingers and the two men dragged over a tub of water that had been sitting behind them. They put it in front of Nikki.

"It's simple, really, Lucy. I believe you have information I want. And I'm prepared to do anything to get it. Which means, you give me what I need, Lucy . . . or your detective friend here dies."

"No . . ."

One of King's men grabbed Nikki by the back of the neck and shoved her entire head into the water. Ice-cold liquid plunged up her nose. Seconds passed. Her lungs began to burn. She was back at the marina. Under the water. The *Isabella* smoldered above her. Flickers of orange fire fell onto the water. She was going to drown. And this time, Tyler wasn't here to save her.

She struggled against the man holding her down, but she couldn't move. Another few seconds passed. Thirty . . . a minute . . . she had no idea. Except that she was going to pass out . . .

The man jerked her out of the water.

"Leave her alone!" Lucy shouted.

Nikki sucked up air, filling her lungs with the precious gas, only to be pushed under again. She could hear Lucy shouting and, just as her lungs were about to burst, they sat her up again, hands still tied behind her, cold water dripping down her face.

King grabbed a chair and sat down beside Nikki, but his gaze was on Lucy. "How this ends is up to you."

"I swear I don't know where Mac's information is."

"And I still don't believe you." King pulled a gun out of its holster and cocked the hammer. "But enough of the games. I'm sorry, but since Lucy isn't cooperating, it looks as if I won't need you anymore, Detective. I'll have to find another way of getting what I want, which I will."

Nikki heard the sound of screeching metal and turned to see a dozen men in black burst into the warehouse. They shouted at King's men to put their weapons down. Shouted at King to stand back. He stood up, jerking Nikki in front of him, but she swung away from him as hard as she could. King lost his balance. Someone fired a shot, and the CEO fell to the ground beside her.

Nikki stared at the trickle of blood snaking away from the man's still body. She was shaking, as much from fear as from the wet cold.

Jack rushed up to her. "Nikki . . . it's over now.

She nodded, unable to look away from King's body. Someone untied her wrists. They were handcuffing the other men and escorting them out of the room.

"Nikki? Are you okay?" Gwen slid someone's jacket across her shoulders.

She nodded. "How did you find us?"

"They dumped your cell phone near the park, so I couldn't trace you, but one of the men who broke into Tyler's house decided he wanted a deal," Gwen said. "He knew about this warehouse. It was the best lead we had. Actually it was the only lead we had."

"He was going to shoot me." She pulled the jacket tighter around her shoulders, her teeth chattering, as she glanced around the warehouse. "Where's Lucy?"

"They're taking her out now as well. She's going to be fine. And so are you." Gwen put her arm around Nikki and led her toward the exit. "Because Jack was right. It's all over now. King can't hurt anyone else. He's dead, Nikki. Dead."

Two hours later, Nikki stood in the back of a darkened room at the precinct, with a fresh set of clothes and a hot mug of coffee. It might be warm outside, but she was still freezing. Lucy sat in a chair in front of a computer screen, watching her husband's video testimony.

Nikki watched Mac sit down in front of the camera, adjust the angle, then start talking. "My name is Mac Hudson. If you're watching this video, it probably means that I'm dead. I only hope that everything I did to save my family was enough. Even if I didn't make it. Three months ago, I was just another researcher in a lab, doing my job."

Mac's gaze shifted to a point beyond the camera and he hesitated as if trying to compose his thoughts. "I'd heard the statistic that as much as seventy-five percent of counterfeit drugs come from overseas, but none of that affected me. Not until I realized it was happening right here . . ."

Nikki turned to Gwen. "You've already watched this?"

"Yes. It gives us everything we need. Between this video and the packet of Mac's evidence we now have, the pieces of the past few days are finally coming together," she said.

"Where did you find the evidence?" Nikki asked. "Lucy told me she wasn't able to find it."

"George sent it to you, actually, here at the station. We figure Mac had the envelope with him when he was attacked at his house, then gave it to George, who mailed it on the way to the marina the night he had Mac in the car with him."

"George?" Nikki asked.

"I guess, in the end, George did something right. He could have kept that information and turned around and blackmailed King, but he didn't."

Mac stared at the camera as he continued speaking. "Lucy . . . If I am dead as you watch this, please know that I prayed this day wouldn't come. All I can really do is hope I did enough to keep you safe. Never forget how much I love you. How meeting you completely changed my life for the better and made me the man I am today . . ."

"What all's on the video?" Nikki asked, stepping out into the adjoining room with Gwen in order to give Lucy some privacy. She'd watch the video later. When all the events of today didn't feel quite as raw.

"It's a sad story of two brothers," Gwen said. "One a computer hacker and the other a brilliant scientist working, as we know, for Byrne Laboratories. And how they found a way to make some big money."

"Adi and Saad Patil."

"Mac started getting suspicious about four months ago and began gathering evidence of their dirty deeds," Gwen continued. "Adi must have become suspicious and went to tell his brother. There were hundreds of thousands of dollars at stake with a counterfeit medicine they'd managed to slip into the market."

"Aryox," Nikki said.

Gwen nodded. "Mac found a chance to hack into Adi's computer, where he got most of the information. The formula and hidden bank account details. Sad thing is, it looks like they got to him right before he went to the police with what he had."

"And King was in on it as well," Nikki said, leaning against the edge of her desk.

"We're still trying to figure out some of the details. King was probably the one who gave the order to get rid of Mac and any evidence he might have. But things didn't turn out the way they'd thought. Mac had worried that they might try to stop him, so he was ready to run. And when they showed up at his house, he was ready for them too."

"He shot them," Nikki said.

"Lucy confirmed that Mac called George and her, terrified that they'd find her as well. The plan was for Mac and Lucy to meet up and then disappear, but with Mac shot, the plan quickly went south. And in the meantime," Gwen said, "George had to be panicked. He knew that the men behind the hit were powerful and determined to do everything they could to stop the leak of information. They managed to take out George, but obviously, by this point, there were too many questions being asked and too many people involved."

"And when they still couldn't find the evidence, they deduced that George must have given the packet to Tyler," Nikki said.

"That's what it looks like."

Nikki glanced back to the room where Lucy sat in front of the television screen. "She still has to be in shock from everything that's happened to her the past couple of days."

"Yes, and this isn't going to be easy for her going forward," Gwen said. "Mac might not have been able to save his life, but he was able to save hers. And her baby's life. Shows how much he loved her."

"I learned a lot about her these past few days," Nikki said, turning back to Gwen. "She's been in tough situations before, and I really believe she's stronger than she thinks."

"And what about you?" Gwen said. "You've been through a lot yourself."

"I think I'd like a couple days off," she said, reaching for her jacket, still feeling cold.

"I'd say some time off is definitely in order. We'll make sure Lucy's taken care of as well. And in the meantime, my advice for you is to go sleep for the next forty-eight hours."

"Sounds like heaven." Nikki grabbed her bag, then turned around as someone entered the room. Luke stood in the doorway, wearing dark jeans and a suit jacket.

"Luke? I've been trying to get ahold of you. You ducked out on me the other night."

"I know, and I'm sorry." He shot her an apologetic grin from the doorway. "That's why I was hoping I might run into you today. Though you . . . you look like a mess. Everything okay?"

Nikki glanced at Gwen, then let out a low chuckle. "It's been a rough day, but thankfully, it's over now. What about you? Honestly, a police precinct is the last place I would expect to find you."

"Believe it or not, the other night ended up being a sort of wake-up call." Luke leaned against the doorframe, hesitating with his answer. "I might be clean, but there need to be a few changes in my life. I spent all of yesterday just walking around downtown. I realized that my life isn't going in the direction I want it to. And that I keep blaming everyone else for my problems. Pretty profound, isn't it?"

"You could say that."

"I keep thinking I'm going to regret my decision, but I took your advice and turned myself in."

Nikki's brow rose. "You turned yourself in?"

"Don't look so shocked. They actually believed my story."

"Wow. I'm proud of you."

"I'm not so sure Mom and Dad will be, but at least it's a start. And before you jump to conclusions, I'm not giving up on my Nashville singing career, but I actually have a job interview this afternoon. It would be something I enjoy and would bring in a bit of income to supplement my music gigs."

Nikki crossed the room and gave her brother a bear hug. "I love you, Luke. And I'm always here for you. Just remember that."

"I know." He smiled down at her. "I'm heading out now, but I'll see you tomorrow night for dinner with the family?"

"Sunday night at Boyd's BBQ. I'll be there."

"Bit of a family reunion?" Jack said, entering the room as Luke left.

"Yeah," Nikki said. "My little brother might finally be growing up."

Jack stood in the middle of the room, scratching his wrists.

Nikki tossed him his phone off his desk.

"What's this for?"

"I think it's time you made another appointment with your allergist. That scratching's driving me crazy."

"We actually have a date planned for tonight," he said, shooting her a frown. "I made reservations at the Bluebird Café."

"Sounds like fun," Gwen said.

"And if she's really interested in you—like she seems to be," Nikki said, "she'll find a way to get used to your odd hours. And hopefully that will also mean toning down the number of times she calls you every day."

"I hope so. Because I do like her—"

"And especially the fact that she brought you cake," Nikki added.

"Funny."

"You need to leave," Gwen said. "Both of you. I'll make sure Lucy's taken care of."

"I'm going home now," Nikki said, grabbing her bag. "I've just got one more thing to take care of on my way."

31

5:14 p.m.
Tyler's house

Nikki pulled up in front of Tyler's house, then shut off the engine as the sun dipped toward the horizon. She gripped the steering wheel before getting out of the car. Even knowing that he was home now and safe, the emotion of the past few days still rushed through her. This case had affected people she loved. Now all she had to do was convince herself that it was really over. They'd found Lucy. King was dead. Saad was dead. And their crew was behind bars.

Which meant Tyler and Liam were safe.

But in spite of all that, her heart was still reeling.

She exited her car and made her way up the sidewalk past the For Sale sign, wondering if life was about to take another unexpected twist.

Nikki sat down beside Tyler on the front porch swing where he was engrossed in his iPad. "What are you working on?"

He set the tablet in his lap and smiled up at her. "Hey. Sorry. I guess I was a million miles away. Didn't even hear you pull up."

He was preoccupied. Distracted. Which wasn't like Tyler at all.

"Thought I'd come by and check on the two of you," she said.

He shook his head. "Liam and I are fine, but what about you? I was told that the case was closed, but didn't get any details."

"I'll fill you in later, but we found Lucy. It will take time, and it's not going to be easy, especially with the baby coming, but I think she's going to be okay. She has more support than she realized. Her foster mother . . . her friend Gage . . . They've all promised to be there for her."

"That's good. The past couple days have been rough for you too."

"For all of us. But thankfully it's over, which is why I'd rather not talk about work right now." She shot him a smile, then picked up the bag she'd brought with her. Right now she'd like to put the past forty-eight hours as far away from her as possible. "How about dinner instead? Mom sent you some barbeque."

A grin spread across Tyler's face. "Is there any of your mom's jalapeño cornbread?"

"You bet."

"You know I appreciate this, but you didn't have to check up on me. You've just wrapped up a huge case. I know you must be exhausted."

"Don't worry. I was told I needed to go sleep the next couple days, and believe it or not, I don't think it's going to be very hard."

"Good." He glanced back down at the tablet.

"Tyler?"

"Sorry." He rubbed his chin. "I'm just feeling a bit preoccupied."

"I noticed."

"Like you, I'm still trying to shake off the past few days. George's death, worrying about my family, the loss of the *Isabella* and all the memories it held . . ."

But it was more than that.

Her stomach sank as the inevitable seemed to swallow her. "You've made a decision about the job, haven't you?"

He nodded. "Yeah. I was just reading through a bunch of the preliminary stuff they gave me."

"How long will you be gone?"

"Three months. I just have to keep telling myself that it's just temporary. One job and I'll be back." He shut off his iPad, then looked back up at her.

"And after that?"

"I don't know. I'm looking into a few options, including the FBI."

She knew his situation wasn't unique. Thousands of men and women who left the military struggled to find jobs in the civilian world. And it wasn't as if he wasn't qualified. But he needed the challenge. The adrenaline rush that he was never going to find sitting behind a desk in a regular nine-to-five job.

But still.

She stared off across the street, past the For Sale sign. Her hands trembled. She knew if Tyler left, he might end up never coming back to Nashville. The house would sell. And life would go on for him, just like it should. But not with her. After all, what right did she have to make him stay?

Her lungs constricted. If only he'd given her a clue that he might see their relationship move to a place where they might be more than friends one day. If only he'd shown her that he'd wanted more than just what they had right now. But he never had. And she wasn't going to take advantage of their friendship by trying to make a move when he was vulnerable.

"What does Liam think about all of this?" she asked.

"I sat down with him last night. Tried my best to explain to him what I was going to be doing."

"And . . ."

"I don't know. I keep being reminded that he's wiser than your ordinary six-year-old. He knows what it's like to lose and feel pain. So I was honest with him. Told him I felt lost too. That I needed time to figure out what I was going to do with my life. That in order to be the best father I could be, I had to find my way again, and that I didn't think I could do it here."

Nikki nodded. She might not agree with his decision, but that was the thing. It was his decision. Not hers.

"He's been through a lot, but you're right. He is wise for his age. And you'll be able to keep in touch."

Tyler's gaze dropped. "He's not the only one I need to understand." He turned and looked up at her for a long moment. "I need you to understand as well."

Her breath caught at the intensity of his gaze. "Why? Why do you need me to understand?"

"Because you're an important part of my life. And no matter what happens, I don't want that to change."

"You know you don't have to convince me you're making the right decision. We'll all miss you, but I want you to be whole again. If you need that in order to move forward with your life, and to be the best father you can to Liam, then this is what you need to do."

He caught her gaze, but she didn't know how to read his expression. Pain and loss still lingered in his eyes, but she also caught a new determination. Sometimes it took time to figure out what you wanted in life.

"Thank you for understanding . . . and for coming by."

Nikki bit the inside of her lip, fighting to keep back the emotions, as he reached out to squeeze her hand.

She pulled her hand away slowly, hoping he didn't notice her hesitancy. What she'd said was true. No matter what, she'd always be there for him. "I'll check on your mom and Liam while you're gone. Take him out for Happy Meals. Make sure he works on his baseball skills."

"He'll love having you around. He always does."

She couldn't help but smile. "Liam isn't the only one who will enjoy hanging out."

"You're right, but when I get back, you and I need to plan to go rock climbing. There are still a couple climbs I want to tackle that we didn't get to try the last time we were there."

"I'd like that."

"You want to come in for some coffee? Liam's watching a movie."

"Thanks, but I think I'll head on home." She blinked back the tears, hoping he didn't see them. "I've still got some paperwork to finish filling out, and then I think I really will sleep for the next day or two."

Tyler nodded. "You deserve it."

"When's your flight out?" she asked, not ready to go.

"Three days."

Three days. It was sooner than she'd expected.

"Need a ride to the airport?" she asked.

"Yeah. If it's not too much trouble. I think taking Liam to the airport with me will be too hard. I'd rather say my goodbyes at home."

"Of course. I'd be happy to." She swallowed

hard. "I'd better go. If there's anything you need between now and then, let me know."

"I will."

Nikki said goodbye, then hurried down the porch steps before he could catch the tears in her eyes. She should just tell him how she felt. It couldn't make her feel any worse than she did right now. She slid into her car and started the engine. He needed to get on with his life. No distractions. No complications. Which was why she'd said nothing. And why she wouldn't say anything.

Three days later Nikki drove in silence down the freeway toward the Nashville airport with Tyler beside her in the passenger seat. A jumble of emotions simmered beneath the surface as they had the past three days. She'd tried to find a way to justify what she wanted to say, even to the point of rehearsing. In the end, she'd stuck with her resolve that he didn't need her to complicate things. That it wasn't fair to Tyler. He had enough to deal with, without her.

Tyler pressed his hands against his thighs as she pulled into short-term parking. "Do you have time to come in with me?"

"Of course. That's one reason I took the day off."

Nikki pulled into an empty parking spot, wondering how she was supposed to say goodbye.

She had no idea what he was going to encounter overseas, but more than likely he'd come back a different, stronger person. And hopefully he'd return with whatever it was he was looking for.

But where did that leave her?

"How was Liam this morning?" she asked as she headed toward the terminal beside him, matching his pace.

Tyler nodded at his backpack as they entered the building. "He gave me Ollie. Told me it would help me to not get homesick. And that if I imagined I was on some grand adventure, it would help me not be homesick. I wonder who gave him that advice."

Nikki laughed. "He's going to be okay. It's just temporary."

"That's what I keep telling myself."

"You're not doubting your decision, are you?" she asked.

"It's a little too late for that." He let out a soft chuckle as they approached the ticket counter. "And honestly, it depends on the moment, but I confess that my stomach's churning. It feels worse than if I were heading into a combat zone."

She fiddled with the strap of her bag as he checked his bag through, then slowed down as they approached security.

"I guess this is it. I can't go any farther."

Tyler slung his backpack across his shoulder and stopped in front of her, taking her hands.

"Thank you. For everything. You've once again gone above and beyond the duties of a friend. I don't know what I'd do without you, Nikki. I mean that."

Her heart sank. A friend. That's all she'd ever be in his eyes. She was simply Katie's best friend. Liam's godmother. The girl who made chocolate tarts and brought over Chinese takeout.

"And as much as I didn't like him most of the time, you were even able to prove that George had some good in him as well. I think that will help Liam one day."

"I hope so," she said.

He wrapped his arms around her and let her nuzzle her face into his chest, fighting to hold back the tears. How could he have no idea how much his touch affected her? How much she craved being with him? And now he was leaving . . .

"Goodbye, Nikki." He stepped back and lifted her chin with his thumb. "I'll let you know once I get settled."

She blinked back the tears and watched him walk away, knowing he wasn't the only one who needed to move on. So did she.

Noise from the other passengers surrounded her. An overhead announcement blared, reminding passengers not to leave their bags unattended. She stood there in the middle of the bustling airport, her heart feeling as if it were going to explode.

She'd never be able to move on without knowing. "Tyler, wait."

She started walking toward him, but he didn't hear her. He was making his way through the line snaking its way to security. A lady with two large bags walked in front of her. Nikki tried to maneuver her way around the woman.

Tyler was almost to the front of the line when he stopped, then turned around and wound his way back through the line toward her.

"Did you forget something?" she asked. Her voice was barely above a whisper.

Tell him.

"No . . . ," he said, then frowned as he caught her gaze. "Are you okay?"

She had to tell him or it would be too late, but still she hesitated, realizing it was fear stopping her. Fear that he didn't love her in return. Fear of losing him before she even really had him. Fear that all of the crazy daydreams she'd collected of them were about to shatter into a thousand pieces.

How could she find the courage to put her life at risk and go one-on-one with a sniper and yet when it came to her heart, she was a mess?

She sucked in a breath. "Tyler, I—"

"Wait." He took her hand and pulled her away from the busy traffic. "I need you to know something before I get on that plane. Something I don't know how I missed, because somehow it's been right in front of me this whole time."

"What?" She looked up at him, trying not to read anything into his words that weren't there. Trying not to read anything into his eyes as they searched her face.

"My leaving isn't just about Katie anymore. I thought it was, but now . . ."

Nikki felt her breath catch. There were so many things she wanted to say. So many questions she wanted to ask. "But what?"

Her heart pounded as his gaze searched hers. "Liam's not the only one I'm going to miss. And I know this is crazy," he rushed on, "but walking away from you just now, it all suddenly became clear. I don't want to lose you, Nikki, and I don't mean just as a friend. I don't even know when things changed for me, but . . . but all of a sudden everything has. I think I'm in love with you, Special Agent Nikki Boyd."

People rushed past them, but all she saw was Tyler, gazing at her in a way that left no doubts about his feelings toward her.

"You're smiling," he said, looking confused. "I thought you might want to slug me."

"Slug you? Stop trying to explain yourself and just kiss me."

Tyler pulled her back into his arms, but this time it wasn't just to say goodbye. She felt her body tremor as he leaned down and kissed her with a passion she'd never felt before. Because kissing Tyler was everything she'd ever dreamed of. A sweet mixture of eagerness and delight she knew she'd never tire of.

He pulled back after a few seconds and pressed their foreheads together while she tried to catch her breath.

"I'm sorry. Maybe I shouldn't have done that, but I didn't know what to say. I realized I couldn't just walk away without telling you how I feel, but if you don't feel the same way—"

"No . . ." She shot him a smile. "I've wanted you to do that for a long, long time."

His eyes widened. "I guess I always thought . . . I don't know. That you saw me as Katie's husband. A good friend. Nothing more."

"I used to," she said. "But then everything changed a few weeks ago, and I didn't want to complicate our friendship. I didn't want to say or do anything that would make me lose you."

"You and me . . ." Tyler smiled down at her. "This doesn't have to be complicated. Somehow this feels like the most natural thing in the world."

She smiled up at him, feeling a completeness from his nearness. And a gut-wrenching ache in her heart because he was leaving.

"I will come back," he said, running his thumb down her cheek. "Just wait for me, Nikki. Promise you'll wait for me."

He kissed her once more, a slow, lingering kiss that left her breathless, before turning around and slipping back into the crowd.

About the Author

Lisa Harris is a bestselling author, a Christy Award finalist for *Blood Ransom*, Christy Award winner for *Dangerous Passage*, and the winner of the Best Inspirational Suspense Novel for 2011 from *Romantic Times*. *Vendetta* won Best Inspirational Suspense Novel for 2015 from *Romantic Times*. She has sold over thirty novels and novella collections. Along with her husband, she and her three children have spent over twelve years living as missionaries in Africa, where she homeschools, leads a women's group, and runs a nonprofit organization that works alongside their church-planting ministry. The ECHO Project works in southern Africa promoting Education, Compassion, Health, and Opportunity and is a way for her to "speak up for those who cannot speak for themselves . . . the poor and helpless, and see that they get justice" (Prov. 31:8–9).

When she's not working, she loves hanging out with her family, cooking different ethnic dishes, photography, and heading into the African bush on safari. For more information about her books and life in Africa, visit her website at:

www.lisaharriswrites.com
or her blog at
http://myblogintheheartofafrica.blogspot.com.
For more information about The ECHO Project,
please visit www.theECHOproject.org.

Center Point Large Print
600 Brooks Road / PO Box 1
Thorndike, ME 04986-0001 USA

(207) 568-3717

US & Canada:
1 800 929-9108
www.centerpointlargeprint.com

Brunswick County Library
109 W. Moore Street
Southport NC 28461